PIRATE TRAP

— A Clay Wolfe / Port Essex Mystery —

Novels by Matt Cost
aka Matthew Langdon Cost

Velma Gone Awry, A Brooklyn 8 Ballo Mystery

The Clay Wolfe / Port Essex Mysteries
Wolfe Trap

Mind Trap

Mouse Trap

Cosmic Trap

Pirate Trap

The Goff Langdon Mainely Mysteries
Mainely Power

Mainely Fear

Mainely Money

Mainely Angst

Mainely Wicked

Historical Fiction
At Every Hazard

Love in a Time of Hate

I Am Cuba: Fidel Castro and the Cuban Revolution

PIRATE TRAP

— A Clay Wolfe / Port Essex Mystery —

MATT COST

Bob & Diane,
Enjoy the Pirates !

Matt Cost

Encircle Publications
Farmington, Maine, U.S.A.

Paperback ISBN-13: 978-1-64599-508-1
Hardcover ISBN-13: 978-1-64599-509-8
E-book ISBN-13: 978-1-64599-510-4

Library of Congress Control Number: 2024931804

Encircle editor: Cynthia Brackett-Vincent

Book design: Deirdre Wait

Published by:

Encircle Publications
PO Box 187
Farmington, ME 04938

info@encirclepub.com
http://encirclepub.com

*This book is dedicated
to the wonderful community
of writers and readers.*

Chapter 1

"Well, Mr. Wolfe, to get straight to the point, we want you to help us find a lost pirate treasure." The man was of medium height, had a brown bushy mustache that matched equally abundant hair and eyebrows, all framing a slightly rounded face. He'd introduced himself as Andy Kozak.

Clay Wolfe had been slouched in the desk chair of his P.I. office, but now he straightened up and sat forward. His normally natty attire was ruffled, stubble dotted his face, and his eyes were red. "In Port Essex?"

The third person in the room, a woman who'd said her name was Dannie Cox, was looking at Clay disdainfully from narrowed blue eyes. Her hair was slightly more blonde than brown and was tied snugly into a bun at the back of her head. She wore a black tank top, revealing well-toned arms and shoulders.

"We have reason to believe that there exists in Port Essex a buried treasure from over 300 years ago." she said, her tone low and cryptic.

"I don't recollect that Maine was much of a hotbed of pirates," Clay said, spreading his hands wide. "Too damn cold."

"We have documentation that says otherwise," Andy said. His face resembled a bulldog, round eyes and a heavy jaw. "And we'd like to retain your services to help us find it."

Clay shrugged. "That's your prerogative. I charge $150 an hour, plus expenses."

Dannie looked sideways at Andy. "We don't have very much money. Certainly not that much."

"How do you propose engaging my services with no money?" Clay asked, settling back, again bored. It'd been another long struggle of trying to drink enough brown liquor to sleep through the night without the nightmares.

Andy cleared his throat. "We thought that you might do it for a percentage of the profits once the treasure was found. It promises to be quite lucrative."

Clay chuckled. The sound was hoarse in his ears. "What is ten percent of nothing?" He stood up, indicating the meeting was over.

The office was not only spacious and well-appointed, but its main feature was a stunning picture window overlooking Essex Harbor. There was a torn and ragged leather couch on which Clay had grabbed many a nap, and where he'd even slept the night through a few times. His desk was made of cherry wood that was now dull and scuffed. On the left was another desk for his partner, Baylee Baker. There were two armchairs of rich brown leather like the couch, but much less worn, in which Andy and Dannie currently sat, not following the hint to stand and leave.

"Please, Mr. Wolfe," Dannie said. "Sit and hear us out."

Clay cocked his head. It wasn't like he'd anything else going on. He figured it might be entertaining at the least. He sighed, sat down, and steepled his fingers under his chin. "Do tell me about this buried pirate treasure."

Andy looked at the closed door behind them. He licked his lips. "We'll tell you the story as we know it. If you agree to go further with this search, we'll provide the more tangible and concrete proof of what we're about to share with you. After, of course, absolute confidentiality is assured."

"Go on."

"It started as a love story," Dannie said. "A poor British man, the son of a tenant farmer, who'd joined the Royal Navy, and, for whatever reason, ended up in Eastham, Massachusetts, in 1715, where he fell in love. Her name was Maria "Goody" Hallett. She was sixteen years old, stunningly beautiful, the daughter of a well-off merchant in town, and promised to another. It was love at first sight. Samuel Bellamy and Maria Hallett met up for trysts in local barns, promised their undying love, and made plans to run off together. Unfortunately, they were discovered, and Maria was put under lock and key. Her parents deemed a poor sailor not to be a proper match for the young lass."

"A tale as old as time," Clay said. There might've been a hint of bitterness to his voice.

"So, Samuel Bellamy decided to go seek out his fame and fortune," Andy continued. "He went down to Florida to look for treasure lost from a sunken Spanish Armada, but when that didn't pan out for him, he turned to the glorious life of a pirate. He earned his stripes sailing under Benjamin Hornigold and Edward Teach, otherwise known as Blackbeard. After he struck out on his own, he had huge successes over the next year, becoming potentially the wealthiest pirate in the world."

"I've never even heard of him," Clay said. His interest was again piqued, even though his fatigue and cynicism pushed him to deride the story.

"His reign didn't last long," Andy said. "With his coffers full and loaded into the hull of his new state-of-the-art galleon, the *Whydah*—which he'd recently captured from its English owners—Black Sam Bellamy, so nicknamed for his long black hair, headed north to reclaim his love, the exquisite Goody Hallett. He thought it best not to sail into Eastham, not sure of the reception he'd receive, so he went up the coast and found a calm port to pull into, where he went ashore to bury his treasure, or at least the most valuable parts of it."

"Port Essex?" Clay asked.

"There was a village of Abenakis living in the area," Andy said, ignoring the interruption.

"He hid the treasure, meaning to come back for it once he'd recovered his love, and set sail back down the coast," Dannie said.

"But, alas, it was not to be. As he approached Cape Cod, Black Sam was caught in a violent nor'easter and shipwrecked, leaving only two survivors behind, neither of which was him."

"Taking with him any knowledge of the whereabouts of the treasure," Clay said. "What of the two survivors?"

"It was readily believed that the treasure went down with the *Whydah*," Andy said. "Of the two survivors, one took any knowledge he had with him to the gallows, as he was hung for piracy."

"And the other?" Clay asked.

"The other was a sixteen-year-old Miskito Indian from Central America," Andy said. "John Julian was his English name. He was sold into slavery to John Quincy, the great-grandfather of U.S. President John Quincy Adams."

"He carried with him a letter and a map," Dannie said. "The letter he was unable to read, and the map wasn't helpful as he hadn't even known where they were when they buried the treasure."

"How was it that a pirate, sold into slavery, was able to keep these documents?" Clay asked.

"They were in a King James Bible," Andy said. "The authorities, and then John Quincy, took mercy upon him and allowed him to retain possession of it. He passed the Bible on to his son, who was given his freedom at the time of the American Revolution. The map and letter were forgotten until I came upon the Bible at an estate auction last year. I discovered the King James Bible in a box of books, and realizing that it was worth about $20,000, I bought the box. It wasn't until later that I found the documents hidden within its pages."

"And the map was of Port Essex?"

Andy shrugged. His brush-like mustache quivered. "Somewhere in the vicinity. It is fairly rough."

"And the letter?"

"The letter was a key for the map and detailed the contents of the treasure."

Clay looked at them. They appeared to be ordinary people, not hustlers. And what could the hustle be? They only wanted his time, not his money. Of course, Clay had recently received a substantial inheritance on the sudden and violent death of his Grandpops. They could indeed be treasure seekers of another sort.

"What are you?" Clay asked.

"What do you mean, what are we?" Andy asked.

"The two of you," Clay said. "Business partners? Marital partners?"

"We are engaged to be married," Dannie said. "After we find the treasure."

So, both, Clay thought. Business partners as well as lovers. That was a tough row to hoe, he knew from personal experience, having been in love with his business partner for some years now. Somehow, both had been too afraid to take that step into the uncertainty of an intimate relationship that might jeopardize the firm foundation of friendship and trust they shared. What might the discovery of a vast treasure do to the relationship that these two shared?

"How much are we talking here?" Clay asked.

Andy looked at Dannie and shrugged.

"In 1715, there was a Spanish Armada disaster when a treasure fleet carrying silver, gold, and other gems ran into a violent storm," Dannie said. "Of the twelve ships, eleven went down off the coast of Florida, between modern day Vero Beach and Sebastian. One other ship, a French ship sailing under their protection, may have made it back to Europe. The letter left in the King James Bible in the care of John Julian said there was actually a thirteenth ship. The *Nuestra Señora del Carmen.*"

"A thirteenth ship nobody knew of?" Clay asked. "That seems far-fetched. There must have been records."

"It was kept secret because of its cargo," Dannie said. "Rare fire opals from a mine in Mexico. Very unusual at the time, actually, unique. Conquistadores stumbled upon a cache in, well, the details don't matter. Just understand that they were very rare, very valuable, and disappeared from the face of the earth without anybody knowing they existed. Until Black Sam Bellamy put into port in *Cayo Hueso*, now known as Key West, for some rest and relaxation, and realized that the local *Calusa* people were sporting these gemstones."

"The thirteenth ship, this *Carmen*, shipwrecked south of the rest of the fleet," Clay said. "A ship that nobody knew anything about, and which, therefore, was not missing."

"Exactly," Andy said. "Until Black Sam came upon them. He traded trinkets and silver and gold for them, loaded them up, and took them straight to…" he looked out the large window behind Clay, "somewhere around here, so as to hide the treasure before going to reclaim his love, Goody Hallett, down in Eastham."

"But then he got caught in a storm and sunk," Clay said. "And everybody thought whatever treasure he had was on board at the time and went down with him."

"Some gold, silver, and trinkets have indeed been found," Andy said. "But not the Mexican fire opals."

"It's a pretty good yarn," Clay said, leaning back. "What is it that you want from me, exactly?"

Chapter 2

The man had money. That was the only reasonable explanation. His wife, Gina, who'd hired Baylee the previous day, was drop-dead gorgeous. And he was not. Now, Baylee knew of many a wonderful marriage between people of disparate attractiveness, often the women being the better looking of the couple, but that usually included the husband adoring the ground his wife walked on. And that did *not* include cheating on her with another woman.

Which was what Gina Yates had hired Baylee to find proof of—his infidelity, that is. Adultery seemed very likely, as, in the first hours of tailing the man, he'd not driven to the airport as he was supposed to, but rather, had pulled into the Port in a Storm Inn. Baylee was always disappointed that they hadn't called it the Port Inn a Storm instead.

Tobias Yates was about sixty with a wide, florid face. His thinning, gray hair left an exposed forehead filled with wrinkles. His face, at best, could be called paunchy. His lips were mere slits over a weak chin. Yet, his suit was expensive, and his persona screamed money.

Gina Yates had come into the office around five the previous night, just before Baylee went home for the day. About twenty-five years younger than her husband, she had a body that screamed of hours at the health club, personal trainer at hand, which made Baylee envious. Her skin glowed from the pampering of expensive products and was matched by her shining hair. And if her boobs were natural, Baylee was an orangutan.

Gina had fumbled around the story, teared up several times, and managed to reveal that she thought her husband was cheating on her. There was a prenuptial agreement that would be void if this were true, meaning a divorce under those circumstances would leave things very much in her favor. And Tobias had a very rich bank account. Baylee had almost believed that the woman was upset about the philandering. Almost.

The long and short was that Gina had told Baylee that Tobias claimed he was flying out to a conference in Arizona the next morning. That is, this morning. Gina didn't believe that he was attending a conference, as she'd overheard him on the phone making plans for this weekend in Port Essex.

Gina had asked Baylee to tail Tobias, gain proof of his infidelity, and share this with her. An open-and-shut case of a cheating spouse. Which was why Baylee had been parked in a small pull-off for a hiking trail just across the road this morning when the gate of the estate opened, and the Bentley Bentayga pulled out onto the road. The Yates lived on Townsend Island, in the town of Essex, a land mass between the Dunbar River to the east, and the larger Sibosek River to the west.

Baylee could imagine that it was quite the mansion back in there. She'd scouted the perimeter of the fence and the estate was no small place. It ran right up on what Google Maps told her was the Winnegance Nature Preserve to the south, the road ending soon afterward to the north. Google showed just a green area with some ponds and streams for several miles. The Yates certainly had privacy, even just a couple of miles outside of downtown Port Essex.

True enough, once crossing the bridge from the island, Yates had stayed to the right, traveling toward Port Essex, and not taking a left to Route 29, which led down the peninsula and toward Portland Jetport. Baylee hadn't asked, but she supposed that Tobias could possibly have his own private jet at the Brunswick Executive Airport, also down south and not towards town.

Baylee had followed him on the meandering road that merged

onto Commercial Way, the main drag of Port Essex. She'd passed the turn-off to Spruce Island where she lived by herself... well, with her basset hound, Flash, and one-eyed orange cat, Ollie. A bit further on was the Pelican Perch, a favorite for drinks and food. The next block held the P.I. business that she was one-quarter owner of, Clay Wolfe being the majority shareholder. She'd noticed a car that looked like a rental that didn't belong to Clay or Crystal in the small parking area. Perhaps a new client.

Up the hill to the left was where Clay lived in an apartment above the garage of his Grandpops' house—well, no longer his Grandpop's house, but Crystal's. Baylee smiled wickedly at the thought that Clay now lived above the garage of Crystal Landry's house, his receptionist. *Their* receptionist. She followed Tobias on past the Seal Bar—where Joe Murphy had most likely already taken up his spot at the bar this morning—and onto the toe of the harbor.

And that brought things up to the present, Baylee thought, a wry grin creasing her tan face. Tobias Yates got out of the car, and he was one ugly motherfucker. She'd seen a picture, of course, but that had been taken in better days and chosen to cast him in a good light. The man who climbed out of the fancy sports car was a chode, for sure. Baylee mentally kicked herself for typecasting the man just for his looks, but sometimes the face, the eyes, the pallor, the physique—told a story of personal neglect combined with a contempt for others.

Baylee slid out of the car and followed the man into the Port in the Storm Inn. This certainly had all the makings of an open-and-shut case, no more than a few hours' work. Tobias went to the counter, spoke for a few minutes, and then strode off, not toward the guest rooms but down the wing labeled 'conference rooms'. He went through a door, closing it behind him. Baylee settled onto a couch positioned at the end of the hallway with a view of the door. In her purse was a book, a necessity when on stakeout—*Off Island* by Lara Tupper.

After an hour, she texted Clay where she was. He replied that he'd picked up an interesting new case this morning that he'd share with her when she made it to the office. Or, if not, maybe over drinks at the Pelican Perch later.

Baylee tapped out her reply. **Sounds good.**

Clay had been in a dark place since his Grandpops had died, Baylee mused. Her heart still picked up a beat whenever she was near him, but he'd gone to a place she knew all too well. It was the same black hole she'd inhabited for some time after she'd killed her husband. The man had been an abusive creep, it was true, but still, it wasn't easy to shoot somebody you thought you'd loved. Been intimate with. That had taken some coming back from.

She couldn't even imagine what it was like for Clay, having lost his parents and grandmother back when he was just eight years old. Mack Wolfe, seemingly golden boy of Port Essex, had driven his wife and mother over a cliff while high on cocaine, orphaning Clay and widowing Clay's grandfather, Gene Wolfe, at the same time.

Baylee had been happy when her own asshole of an alcoholic father had died of liver complications when she was twelve. Less happy when she was eighteen and walked in on her mother having sex with Baylee's boyfriend of the time. In a way, Baylee, too, had become an orphan that day. And neither one of them had any siblings.

She knew she truly loved Clay. At the same time, they'd twirled around each other for the years since she'd known him, and she didn't know if it was still possible to transform the yearning into something more. It was as if they'd both become comfortable with the steps to this particular tango, teasing, tantalizing, tickling—but neither one of them ever quite taking that dare after the dance ended to push it into anything more than just a polite good night at the end.

She also knew that she couldn't pull him out of the desolation that he'd been thrust into by the murder of his Grandpops. That was something that only he could achieve, when he was ready. All she hoped was that she could be there to catch him when he was flung from that netherworld as no longer welcome.

Baylee thought about that first day, a few years back, entering the office to fill out an application to be a receptionist in a P.I. firm. How she'd stepped through the door, and her heart had fluttered, and she'd known. He was smartly dressed, roguishly charming, and had a sarcastic humor that she absolutely loved. Her knees weakened just thinking about his rare combination of blue-green eyes, and that dirty-blond hair, always slightly tousled, but styled to be so, Baylee thought with a smirk. On the surface, he was a bit of a dandy, but at the same time, he was one of the toughest men she'd ever known.

The door down the hall opened, and Baylee made sure to bury her nose in the book. Tobias came down the hallway flanked on either side by bespectacled men in expensive suits. "My wife is to know nothing of this," he said as he passed by Baylee.

"Of course, sir, there won't be any…" The voice trailed off as they crossed the lobby and went out the front door.

Baylee stood and followed them. The three men conferred briefly, and then went to three separate cars. She hurried to her own beat-up Subaru that was oddly out of place in the lot. This being Maine, there were plenty of Subarus, but none nearly as old as hers.

Tobias continued down to a marina in Knox Cove. He went into the office and spoke for about twenty minutes with a barrel-shaped man with a rough beard. Then he came out and went out on the dock where a dingy moored just long enough for him to board for a trip out to a much larger boat in the harbor. It looked to be a working boat, not a pleasure yacht where a wealthy man might meet a mistress for a rendezvous.

Baylee stood behind a stack of lobster traps and snapped pictures of the vessel, making sure to get the name, *Coronado*, in several shots from her cell phone camera. Westy, who fished out of this harbor, was sure to know more about this boat. Maybe it was taking Tobias out to meet a yacht in the ocean, but Baylee didn't think it was a transport vessel.

Baylee watched as the *Coronado* chugged out of the harbor, past her own home on Spruce Island, and around the point of land out of sight.

*   *   *

Clay was at his desk researching Black Sam Bellamy, also known as the Prince of Pirates, when Baylee came sailing into the room. As ever, he took a moment to appreciate the grace and beauty that was his business partner, friend, and heart's desire.

She was seven inches over five feet with legs that went on forever, a face graced with caramel eyes that matched her hair. Baylee's hair was complemented by rich skin, tinted golden from her Native American heritage, her father's side tracing back to the Abenaki tribe who had inhabited these very shores. Her eyes flashed between bewitching, provocative, mischievous, caring, and intelligent, depending on the situation. Clay was still undecided if he had a preference. On the inside of her left forearm the words *Real People*, a modest tattoo, a nod to her Native American ancestry.

Today, Baylee wore a white jumpsuit that left her shoulders bare and clung to the rest of her a little too closely for Clay's comfort, sending a tremor through his body. She had a navy-blue sweater in tow which she put on before sitting down at the desk next to his. Clay liked to keep the office cool in the summer, and she dressed accordingly.

She swung her chair toward him as he did the same, their knees catching the other and locking themselves in place looking at each other. Neither one moved, the contact, comfortable, excruciating. Just her presence, her fragrance, her soul, lifted him slightly above the morose state he'd all too often found himself in since the death of his Grandpops.

"What's going on with Tobias Yates?" Clay asked. "You get pictures of him already with his pants down in the company of some young lady titillated by the size of his wallet?"

"Well, he didn't go to the airport like he told his wife," Baylee said. "Went down to the Port in a Storm and met with a couple of fellows in a conference room for about an hour, then went down to the marina at Knox Cove, talked to a guy in the office for twenty minutes, and went out on a boat, which is where I lost him."

"You didn't sneak yourself on board and hide under a sail to see where they might be going?"

"Thought crossed my mind but there were no sails to hide under." Clay smirked. "Pleasure yacht?"

"No," Baylee said slowly. "Looked to be a fishing boat of some sort. Not what I expected Tobias to be boarding in his thousand-dollar suit."

"You think he was catching a ride to a secret rendezvous with Miss Right?"

"Miss Right Now, you mean?"

Clay chuckled. Waited.

"No. He seemed all business. Not a man going off on a booty call, if you ask me."

"Mrs. Yates thinks that he is having an affair?"

"My gut tells me that Gina is hoping that Tobias is having an affair so that she can void their prenup."

"How long they been married?"

"Two years."

"She's young and beautiful and he's older, uglier, and richer?"

"You got it."

"Him keeping secret business dealings from her isn't going to get her what she wants."

Baylee shifted, extending her foot out so that her left leg was between his. "No, but today was just the first day. Plenty of time to catch him fucking around."

Clay chuckled. "Hard to understand why men go out to eat when they have steak at home."

Baylee pulled her leg back and slapped his knee. "That's rude."

"Sorry." Clay had pushed that particular button on purpose. The heat in the room had become torturous, and he was afraid of the next move if he didn't slam the door. He didn't want to screw up what he had with Baylee. He wasn't ready to feel happiness, still reeling from the death of his grandfather. This he knew. He just didn't know how to properly navigate those waters just yet. "Had an interesting new client this morning, or rather, clients."

"Do tell."

"Yo, Crystal, you wanna come on back?" Clay said. He knew she was most likely eavesdropping out front where her receptionist/administrative assistant desk was.

"Thought you'd never ask, boss," Crystal said, flittering through the door.

She had on a short skirt under an orange tube top she'd most likely bought at Goodwill, even though she lived in a two-million-dollar house and had a trust fund that she'd inherited from Clay's Grandpops, Gene Wolfe. It seems that money wasn't enough to take the trailer park out of the woman. She walked like a sandpiper, one of those shore birds that skittered along the tides at the beach, and was just as rail thin.

"I'm sure you can hear just as well out there if you're more comfortable," Clay said. "Noticed you turned the country music off when Baylee came in."

"Yeah, well that fuckin' 'Things a Man Oughta Know' tears me up some. It ain't always about you, boss."

Clay wasn't quite sure if Crystal was bantering with him or sharing some emotional weakness, which was unlikely. He decided to play it safe and move along as she sat down in one of the leather armchairs. "We've been hired to find pirate treasure." He was tempted to throw in an "Aaargh, lassies!" but then thought that might be a little over the top.

Crystal clapped her hands. "By them two this morning? They didn't much look like pirates."

"They've come into possession of a treasure map and a letter they believe to be authentic." Clay filled them in on how they'd acquired the map in an estate auction and how the research showed that Black

Sam Bellamy very possibly had been in the area in 1716-1717. "The two of them followed the lineage of John Julian and came up empty. It seems that perhaps the map and letter came into the possession of John Quincy, the man who bought John Julian, because Andy found them in a Bible that he bought at an estate sale when a descendant of Quincy recently died. Passed down through the generations, the Quincy and Adams family must never have known what they had in their possession, hidden away in a King James Bible."

"You believe it's authentic?" Baylee asked.

"In 1982, the remains of the *Whydah*, Bellamy's ship, was found off the coast of Cape Cod near the town of Wellfleet." Clay pushed his chair back, hands behind his head. "Over the years, artifacts and treasures have been brought up, suggesting that there was plenty of indigo, ivory, gold, silver, and precious stones."

"So, the suggestion that fucking treasure was buried here in Port Essex is bogus?" Crystal slipped at least one swear word into every comment she made. Not the best demeanor for a receptionist trying to garner business, but Clay figured it helped weed out those not so seriously in need of P.I. work.

"The letter states that Bellamy secretly transported a chest of gemstones onto land and hid them, keeping this secret from even his own men. He planned to retire from the pirate business, turning the ship over to his crew along with the treasure aboard, once they'd rescued his love, a young lady from Eastham, Mass., and returned the two of them to the village of Port Essex, then known as Winnegance."

"You gonna share the fucking letter, or we gotta keep playing these guessing games?" Crystal said.

Clay smiled. Nodded. "It's right there on the desk. Or photocopies of it, anyway. I'm sure they've got the original tucked safely away somewhere."

Crystal grabbed the paper, and Baylee went around to sit next to her.

My sweet Maria,

If this finds you, know that I Love
you. Will always Love you. I have spent
the past two years trying to make a future
for us. When I left You my plan was
to find the Lost Treasure of the Armada.
That was not possible. So I became a
Pirate to acquire the Wealth that You so
Deserve and for your family to accept me.
Then I found the Lost 13th Ship of the
Armada. The Nuestra Señora del Carmen. A
Ship Nobody knew of. Because of what it
carried. A Cargo of Gemstones known as
Fire Opals taken from the Earth in Mexico.

And it was All by Chance. We put into
a key called Cayo Hueso to clean the Hull
of the Whydah. It is Located All the
way to the bottom tip of the Land called
Florida. The native people are a Peaceful
People called the Calusa.

When we landed in Cayo Hueso we
noticed the Calusa wearing these beautiful
Gemstones in their hair, on their scant
clothes, and littering their huts. We traded
Gold, Silver, Knives, and trinkets for all the
Gemstones we could find. It came to be
Eight Treasure Chests. All for Us, my
Love. All for You.

My Men will take with them the Bounty aboard the Whydah, but I have Hidden the Fire Opals, in the village of the Abenaki at the settlement known as Winnegance. Their Village is situated on the Sibosek River. Just past Their dwellings is a rock outcropping in the formation of a Church Bell. There is a place just around that to go ashore. Climb to the top. You will see a Pine Tree taller than the rest back toward the Village a hundred steps. At the base of the Tree, face the River, and walk twenty steps. There will be a granite Boulder shaped like a Heart. Underneath that will be the entrance to Catacombs, within which lay Fire Opals, Gift from me to my love, from Sam to Maria, from Black Bellamy to Goody Hallett.

Know that I will always love you. Every Time You look at One of the Fire Opals, Think of me. Think of my Love for You.

Yours forever,
Samuel

"Ain't that fucking sweet," Crystal said.

"Our new clients spent some time researching the claims, most notably about the ship, the *Nuestra Señora del Carmen*," Clay said. "They have found credible evidence suggesting that it did indeed exist, had been in Mexico, and then disappeared."

"But nothing about fire opals?" Baylee asked.

"Nope. But it is possible. The stones have historically been found in Mexico, and they still mine them today."

"And there is a map as well?" Baylee said, looking up.

Clay opened his desk drawer, pulled out a photocopied paper, and pushed it across the desk to her.

Chapter 3

Clay and Crystal closed shop at five on the dot and set out on the short walk to the Pelican Perch. They'd also leisurely strolled to the diner for breakfast this morning, and then down the hill to the office. Crystal had grabbed them subs from Kurt's Deli for lunch and they'd eaten at a bench behind the office overlooking the harbor, enjoying the sunshine of the day.

It was almost like they were an old married couple, Clay mused as they walked down the sidewalk. Maybe that had been Grandpops' intention, leaving her the house, him the money, giving each of them a companion. Crystal Landry had come into his P.I. firm a few years back, wanting him to find out who was dealing heroin in town—the person responsible for pushing the drug that killed her granddaughter. Although only in her early forties, Crystal had looked old then, perhaps from her own previous heroin use; life had been rough on her exterior.

Her interior was another thing entirely, Clay thought with a wry inward smile. Her skin might be lined and her mouth foul, but her heart was pure and loyal. And that was the Crystal that Grandpops had seen, the woman he'd taken into his house, ate, conversed, and watched television with. The silver fox lawyer and the former heroin junkie. Clay chuckled. What a pair they'd been. That is, before some psychopath had killed the only family Clay had left.

The Pelican was a restaurant on the first floor, an event room on the second, and an outdoor deck bar on the top, hence, the Pelican

Perch, even though it'd have to be a wayward Pelican to find its way to Mid-Coast Maine. It was just far enough out of downtown that it wasn't mobbed with tourists, even though this time of year, just after the July holiday, Clay knew that half the crowd would be from away. Better than down in the heart of things where you wouldn't even be able to get in, much less find a seat.

Westy was at the bar when they reached the top floor, his broad back taking up three spaces, tourists and locals alike wise enough to leave the stool on either side of him free.

Weston Beck had been Clay's best friend since third grade. They'd played, studied, and fought together. They'd shared their first drunk and ensuing puking session. Clay's house had been in-town and easier to sneak out of at night and thus had been the more regular choice for weekend sleepovers. Clay had been the quarterback and Westy the running back on the Port Essex state championship football team their senior year. When Clay went off to Boston University to pursue a career as a policeman, Westy had enrolled in the Navy's SEAL program and eventually gone to the Middle East.

He had gray eyes, was only six inches over five feet, but his shoulders were wider than most doorways and his chest resembled a barrel. His left arm was fully tatted up—a Viking warrior, then patterns of knots leading up to the bone frog and finally the trident ink adopted by the SEALs. The images took on a life of their own in the rippling muscles of his arms. His hair was short and tight on top, but a powerful beard sprouted from his face, somehow wild and groomed at the same time.

Crystal squeezed in on one side and Clay on the other. Westy had a Budweiser in a bottle in front of him.

"Ahoy, matey," Clay said.

Westy looked at him with his blank stare. "What the fuck is an ahoy matey?"

"I'll start with a Stowaway," Clay said to the bartender before turning back to Westy. "Just trying to talk your lingo, you being the Navy SEAL and all."

"Well, don't." Westy turned to look at Crystal. "Might I buy you a cocktail?"

"Oh, I'll get my own. But thank you, Westy." Crystal raised her hand. "Margarita. Rocks. Salt."

The bartender brought Clay his beer just as a hi-top table by the railing opened up. "Baylee's coming, too. Gonna grab us a table."

Clay wended his way through the crowd, his full beer spilling slightly as he went. He set the beer on the tabletop and sat down just as a deeply tanned man in a business suit grabbed the stool on the other side.

"Sorry," Clay said. "There's four of us."

"I was here first." The man was wearing expensive sunglasses and had a gold stud in his ear.

Clay looked at his beer, raised his hands. "Don't think so, pal. I'm sitting here with a beer on the table, and you're standing there with a chair in your hand."

The man stepped around the table. "I said that this is my table."

Clay smiled lazily. The man was about to have an awakening. "I'm sitting here waiting for my friends to join me. Skedaddle while you still can."

The man stepped forward menacingly. He had that look of somebody who spent a fair amount of time in the gym. "Move," he said.

"Is there a problem here?"

The man turned around angrily. His eyes took in Westy's own flat stare and broad head, his gaze moving down, realizing that Westy was about four feet wide, then his eyes went to the tattoos rippling on the muscles of his arm, seemingly with a life of their own.

"No. No problem." The man stepped carefully around the former SEAL-turned-fisherman, his muscles earned on the water, and not in the gym.

"New York City," Westy said, sitting down. "Bet you a sawbuck that fellow came up from New York City. Boston don't even make them that fake."

Clay smiled. If there was anything Westy disliked more than out-of-staters, it was city folk. "They're the one buying your fish, if not directly, out to the fancy restaurants."

Westy snorted. "I get a nickel and the restaurant charges forty bucks for it."

"Somebody get up on the wrong side of bed this morning?"

"Faith's been talking about wanting to go to one of those all-inclusive beach resorts down to the Caribbean this winter. The two of us go down and sit on the beach and sip drinks all day long while little Joe makes sandcastles."

"Sounds pretty fucking good," Crystal said from across the table.

"Yes, it does," Clay said.

Westy glared at them. "A waste is what it is."

"Money?" Clay asked.

"Time," Westy said. "And money. You know how many Budweisers you gotta drink to get your money's worth at one of those places? And what do you do? Just sit there and stare at the waves? I'd rather do Hell Week again than sit on my ass on a beach staring at the ocean."

"What are we talking about?" Baylee asked, sliding into the fourth seat.

"Westy was comparing an all-inclusive week at Turks and Caicos to SEAL Hell Week," Clay said, "and opting for the latter."

"Mm. I'm all in," Baylee said. "For the beach, not Hell Week. Faith said something about that to me. You tell her I'll go, and we'll leave you boys behind. Maybe find us some men."

"Might take you up on that."

The waitress, having recognized them as regulars, appeared with a rum punch for Baylee and refills for the other three without having to be asked, knowing them probably better than they knew themselves.

"Speaking of the Caribbean to Port Essex shipping line," Clay said, "we picked up an interesting case today involving pirates and buried treasure."

"Somebody filling your head with that nonsense about William Kidd burying a pot of gold up the river at Foley's Island in Edgecomb?" Westy asked. "I can tell you that whole island has been dug up twice and there ain't nothin' there."

"William Kidd?" Clay said. "No, this is Black Sam Bellamy. He had a run of just under two years as the wealthiest pirate in the Caribbean and had ties up this way."

Westy nodded. "Ah, the Prince of Pirates. Captain of a crew who called themselves Robin Hood's Men. He gave a famous speech denouncing wealthy men as worse than pirates, exploiting the working man as they do."

"Yeah, that's the one," Clay said. "Seems he was all about inclusion long before that became a thing. His crew was a mix of freed slaves, Native Americans, and Europeans, all with an equal say in what they did and did not do. A true democracy aboard ship."

"As I recall," Westy said, "the legend has it that Bellamy buried his treasure up to Machiasport. That he was building some sort of pirate retirement community up that way."

"That seems to have happened," Clay said. "But the love of his life was down in Eastham on Cape Cod, and he wanted to break away from the pirate life and live happily ever after with his bride to be, Maria 'Goody' Hallett. He had a secret cache of gems—fire opals from Mexico—that he buried in Port Essex, before he went to fetch Goody. He intended to marry her and find a safe place to hide out. He even left the rest of the treasure to his crew. Unfortunately for him, and her, on his way to gather the love of his life, his ship, the *Whydah*, sunk off the coast of Cape Cod in a terrible storm."

"Hadn't heard that before," Westy said. "Probably just another pirate treasure myth out there like all the others. Why the hell would anybody with a bunch of treasure leave the Caribbean for the freezing cold coast of Maine?"

"Weren't you just saying you had no desire to leave the freezing coast of Maine for the beaches of the Caribbean?" Baylee asked.

"That's me. Pirates are another breed. Lazy sons-of-bitches."

"I wouldn't mind being a pirate," Baylee said. "Drinking grog and ogling men. I'd get myself a couple of swains to wait upon my every desire."

"Amen, sister, whatever a *swain* is," Crystal said. "A-fucking-men."

"The British crown was concentrating on running the pirates to ground down that way," Clay said. "Who'd think of looking for them in Maine? Technically, of course, it was still Massachusetts then."

"Good point," Westy said. "What proof of any of this do you got? A story some joker heard from some drunk in a bar?"

"A letter and a treasure map," Clay said. "My clients shared a photocopy with me but assure me that the original has been authenticated to the time period." He looked over at the bar and saw the man he'd had an altercation with staring at their table. It looked like his attention was focused on Baylee.

"Great," Westy said. "Go dig it up and get rich."

Clay chuckled. "The map is pretty rough. The letter gives more details and tells you how to use the map but is dated. You know where the Abenakis lived in this area 300 years ago?"

Westy shook his head. "My family came across to Boston in 1718, moved to the Merrymeeting Bay area outside of Brunswick, and then soon afterward, to Port Essex. There was no official settlement here as King William's War had driven all the English out in 1689, but they were the forerunners to a new settlement in 1730 called Townsend. My people lived in harmony with the Abenaki prior to that happening. Do I know exactly where? No. But I might be able to find out."

"My people might've known your people," Baylee said. "But us Abenaki weren't real good on keeping written records. Any oral history has been long since lost, far as I know."

"Spent the day trying to locate the Native American village of Winnegance, but it's all a bit murky," Clay said. "Seems that it was right about here, where we are, but that doesn't jibe with the map."

"I got some family records in the basement," Westy said, standing up. "I'll see what I can find. Got to get home for dinner now." He threw a twenty on the table and walked off.

"Didn't know his family went back so far in Port Essex," Crystal said.

"Presbyterian Ulstermen," Clay said. "Migrated from Scotland to Ireland and then to the New World looking for freedom of belief. The Becks have been here in town for nine generations, longer than anybody else."

"Except us Abenaki," Baylee said, holding out her arm. The tattoo on her left forearm read *Real People*, the loose translation of 'Abenaki' in English and her tribute to her Abenaki blood.

"Your people go back that far in this area?" Crystal asked.

Baylee shook her head. "No idea. That was the asshole side of my family. Barely knew my grandparents, not that they were worth knowing."

The waitress came over.

"Anybody want to get food?" Clay asked. "Or do you have to get home to feed Flash and Ollie?" he looked at Baylee.

"Stopped home before coming over," Baylee said. "Fed and walked down to the water with both of them." Ollie, the one-eyed orange cat, liked to walk as much as the basset hound. "I could eat."

"Give us a moment," Clay said to the waitress.

Crystal looked at the two of them, started to speak, stopped, cleared her throat. "I got some mac and cheese with hot dogs in it left over at home and a date with *The Bachelor* at seven, so I guess I'll mosey on out of here." She sucked up the last of her margarita, stood and picked up her purse to get her wallet, but when Clay waved her away, shrugged and left with a wave of the hand. She might've muttered, "Bye, bitches," as she walked off.

"What're you thinking of getting?" Clay asked Baylee.

"Haddock sandwich with side salad."

Clay nodded. "Think I'll do the pasta with scallops."

"How are you doing?" Baylee asked.

"Fantastic," Clay said. "Peachy keen."

"I mean, really?"

Clay shrugged.

The waitress came over and they ordered, Clay suggesting a bottle of white wine, to which Baylee agreed.

"You find out anything more on that lady's philandering husband?" Clay asked.

"Went in and spoke with the man at the marina who he was chatting with," Baylee said. "He kept his mouth pretty tight."

"A Mainer custom," Clay said.

"Ah-yup."

"How about the boat he went out on?"

"The *Coronado*? It was still gone when I left. Got the owners name. You know an Adam Dube? Didn't get a chance to research him, yet."

"Adam Dube?" Clay pursed his lips. "Don't think so. You should've run it by Westy. He knows everybody in town who owns a boat."

"I'll give him a jingle tomorrow."

They sat in silence for a minute, activity buzzing around them, a chill within.

"You wanna talk about Gene?" Baylee asked. "Grandpops. We haven't spoke of him since the funeral and that was some time ago."

"What's there to talk about?" Clay asked.

Grandpops had died over a year ago, thanks to an arrow that had pinned him to his own home like some halibut at the end of a speargun's shaft. In this case, it'd been a crossbow, Clay thought, his mind slipping into the black vacuum inside which he'd spent so much of the past year. The death had been hard, especially it being murder, but the true pain came from knowing it was his fault. He was the reason that Grandpops was dead. Plain and simple. His killing had been meant as a message for Clay.

The waitress brought them a bottle of wine, and a busboy appeared with the food before she had it open.

"Maybe some stories about him?" Baylee said gently. "Going to your high school football games? Threatening that other school with a lawsuit when they intentionally walked you three times in a row? Anything that will help you heal."

"I'm not the one that got hurt."

Baylee started to say something, took a sip of wine. "What else is going on in the life of Clay Wolfe?"

They spent the next half hour eating and just chatting about inconsequential things until Baylee picked up her purse. "I should be getting home to Flash and Ollie."

Clay had moved on to whiskey by this point. "I might stay for a nightcap."

Baylee gave him a long look. "Okay."

"I walked down the hill this morning," Clay said. "I'm not driving."

"What are you doing?" she asked.

"I got dinner," Clay said, ignoring the question. What he could've said was that he was drinking the ache into submission and thinking about asking some fellow from away what his major fucking problem was. "We'll write it off as a business expense."

"Goodnight, Clay." Baylee walked off.

Clay watched her go and sat staring at the top of the stairs for some time. He paid the waitress and took his drink with him back to the bar.

"You need another one, buddy?" the bartender asked. He was about average height with brown hair and normal features.

Clay looked at his glass, shrugged. "Sure. You new here?"

"Yessir. Just got hired last month for the summer season. What are you drinking?"

"Gentlemen Jack. Neat. Double."

The bartender sloshed the brown liquor into a glass and handed it over. "Silas Laskin. Good to meet you."

Chapter 4

Clay woke with a throbbing head and a mouthful of sandpaper. There'd been many of these mornings over the past year. It wasn't that he was sad. Or depressed. Or perhaps he was too sad and depressed to even know how bad he was feeling. It just felt so good when the brown liquor embraced him with its fuzzy mellowness. No more thinking. No more worries. No more pain. Shut the entire mechanism down.

This morning was a bit different as there appeared to be crusted blood on his face. He was in his boxers, so at least he'd undressed. He was in his own bed. Above the garage next to Grandpops' house that Crystal now owned. His pants, shirt, one sock, and his waistcoat were piled next to him. The shirt and waistcoat were spattered with blood.

He rose creakily to his feet, wondering if men in their mid-thirties were supposed to creak when they stood and walked. Only if they dissipated the lubrication of their joints with liquor, he supposed, as he worked his way to the bathroom. He relieved himself first. Then he studied his face in the mirror. A crust of blood was clotted under his nose, dark-red streaks across his lips, and again crusted on his chin, mixed in with the sparse goatee that he sported there.

If he had to guess, he'd say he'd been punched. Not fallen. Not bumped into a doorway. Struck in the face by another. That conclusion was supported by raw knuckles. He'd been in some sort of brawl.

He stripped his boxers off and climbed into the shower. What were the details of the night? Drinks with the gang. Dinner with Baylee.

She'd left. He'd moved to the bar. Ordered a double. Let the brown tendrils slip into his being. Ordered another. He'd been chatting with the bartender. What was his name? Silas. Silas something or other. The man was interesting. A nomad of sorts with no roots who wandered from place to place, his license as a bartender paving the way.

Silas had been asking if Clay was sure he wanted another. He'd been sure. Then a shadow moved in next to him. It'd been that fellow who tried to steal his table. And then been staring at them. Sitting next to him. Pretending to be friendly but making disparaging remarks. Arrogant. Dismissive. Entitled. That was the last that his mind could dredge up, the hot water massaging his head, clearing the cobwebs, leaving just a taste of unease. He carefully cleaned the blood away. Stepped from the shower as there was a knock on the door.

That disquiet that came from blacking out the night before and not knowing what to expect surged through his body like broken glass. The police? A spurned woman? The owner of the Pelican Perch with a bill for damages? No sense hiding. Clay tied a towel around his waist and went and opened the door.

Crystal.

"Good morning," she said.

"Need something?" he asked.

"Yeah, as a matter of fact, I hit a fucking water buffalo just now and was wondering if I could borrow your towel?" She ran her eyes up and down his body.

Clay chuckled. It hurt to laugh.

"Is it sexual harassment to ogle your boss?" Crystal asked. "Even if it is with intent?"

"Good morning, Crystal. Did you need a tablespoon of sugar or something like that?"

"Thought we might hit the diner for breakfast, but you look to be running a tad bit behind schedule. Maybe some clothes and a gallon of Visine for your eyes, and then you'll be right as rain."

"Maybe some coffee first," Clay said.

"Tough night? You seemed all good when I left you in the care of Baylee."

"Yeah, she went home, and I thought I might have one nightcap."

"Your face is bruised."

"You mind bringing me a bacon and egg sandwich to the office? And I'll work on putting myself together."

"No problem, boss. Take your time. I can handle things down there until you come in. I'll check and see what Baylee's schedule is. Let me know if you need anything." Crystal turned and went down the wooden steps.

Clay turned the Keurig on and brewed a cup of coffee while he shaved. He dressed, brushed his teeth, and poured the coffee into a to-go cup. He wasn't going to let Crystal beat him to work. There was no way that he'd admit that his drinking was interfering with his work. Maybe his personal life, but not his work. Clay hadn't been on a date since Grandpops died. The last woman he'd slept with had tried to kill him. That seemed to be a pattern, this desire of women to murder him after sleeping with him for a bit. A pattern that he meant to break.

He knew that he had hang-ups where women were concerned. Most likely the untimely death of his mother and grandmother when he was eight, or so the therapist had told him, the one time in his adult life he'd visited a mind doctor. It'd cost him a bundle to be told what he already knew.

It was a beautiful July morning. The sun had risen from the sea and hung suspended over the harbor as he started down the hill. The water was sparkling like so many diamonds as boats trundled back and forth. It was a good place he lived in. But he was considering moving. Grandpops had been the reason he'd returned. Now, his anchor was gone.

Clay had a business in town. Knew people. Had friends. Westy was like a brother to him. Baylee. She was a powerful tug for him to stay but also the reason he had to leave. Where would he go? Maybe he'd become a nomad like Silas the bartender. Or Jack Reacher. He could wander the country setting things right everywhere he went, even if with a healthy dose of death and destruction.

Baylee's car was in their small lot next to the office. Clay looked at his phone to check the time. It was just before eight o'clock. She wasn't usually in until nine. Probably had something to do with the guy she was trying to find proof of his cheating, Clay figured. He climbed the outdoor stairs to the second floor where his office resided above a gallery. The door was unlocked. As he entered, there was a yip from his and Baylee's inner office.

Clay paused, squinching his face, wondering what the sound was, and then it repeated. He crossed to the open door and found Baylee on the floor. She was on all fours facing away from him and his face reddened as he realized he was staring at her bottom.

"Morning," he said.

Baylee turned to look over her shoulder at him. "Morning."

She was dressed casually, yoga pants that left little to the imagination, and a T-shirt that said 'Straight Outta Port Essex' with a V-neck that plunged dangerously low between her breasts. Her straight golden honey hair was tied back with a purple scrunchie, and her smile was infectious. But it was her caramel eyes that made his knees wobble.

"What are you doing?" he asked in a husky voice.

"Playing."

Clay tore his eyes from Baylee and realized that she was faced off against a tiny puppy. A yellow Lab whose collar matched the color of her scrunchie. "Who's this?" he asked.

"Don't know yet," Baylee said.

Clay stepped past her and knelt, his hand scratching the floor. "Hey, there, fellow."

"You're right on that. He's a boy."

"What's his name?"

"That's what I don't know yet."

"What do Flash and Ollie think of him?"

"They haven't met as of yet."

The puppy took two steps and pounced on his hand with a yip, his impish minuscule dog body all jerky and awkward. His teeth were sharp, but Clay took the nip as part of the game, flipping the puppy onto his back and rubbing his belly.

"I didn't know you were getting a new dog," Clay said.

"Been planning it for about six weeks," Baylee said.

"Have any ideas on what to call him?"

"Not up to me." Baylee moved forward so she could rub the puppy as well, her body pressing against Clay's, tiny little tremors leaping between them, neither one drawing away. "The owner gets that chore."

"The owner?" Clay's hand rubbed not only the puppy but managed to caress Baylee's forearm as well. "He's not yours?"

Baylee turned her head so that her face was scant inches from his, her eyes dancing devilishly. "Nope."

Clay's head twitched, his eyes leaving hers to stare at the ripeness of her lips. "Who's dog is he?"

"Yours."

"Mine?"

"Happy birthday," Baylee said. She leaned the last iota of distance between them and kissed him on the cheek and then stood up in one fluid motion.

Chapter 5

Clay spent the day researching the Abenaki village of Winnegance, but he couldn't make today's geography align with the rough map that Andy and Dannie had shared. He thought the village might have been roughly where Port Essex was, not somewhere up the Sibosek River; without the village as a starting point, however, the directions would be almost impossible to use. It could be anywhere between Port Essex and Alna, up past Wiscasset, and far too many miles or tangled shoreline to comb through.

Andy and Dannie had gone back to Brooklyn to tie up some loose ends but planned on being back in Port Essex Monday. Hopefully, he'd have something for them. They'd settled on a thousand dollars and five percent of whatever treasure was found. Clay didn't hold out much hope that anything would turn up, but he had nothing else going on now, and this gave him purpose. Sort of like being the owner of a new puppy.

Of course, he had to take Frank outside every hour, trying to teach the pup potty training skills. Yes, he'd decided to go with Frank as a name, much to Baylee's chagrin, but after all, she did have a cat named Ollie. Crystal thought it a terrific name. Her exact words were *'that's a fucking awesome name for a pooch'*. Clay was a bit ambivalent at receiving a puppy for his birthday, a date that he wasn't sure anybody had remembered, not since Grandpops had died, but Baylee obviously had.

He wasn't quite sure what to do with a puppy. He imagined that he could bring it to work with him every day. He was the boss, after all. People brought their dogs to the Pelican Perch on occasion, so he figured that would be fine. Clay touched his bruised face and hoped that he hadn't been banned from the Pelican Perch. He was fairly certain that there'd been an altercation with that smug out-of-towner. He certainly hoped that he'd wiped the arrogance from the bastard's face, but couldn't remember, and had doubts as to his fighting ability when that drunk. His knuckles were scraped and tender, so he must have gotten at least a few punches in.

His phone buzzed with a text from Westy. You want to get a birthday beer at the Perch?

Maybe more people remembered his birthday than he thought. He looked at the time. Five o'clock. On a Friday. Crystal had vamoosed about half an hour ago. Baylee was out looking for Mr. Unfaithful. Might as well go find out if he'd been kicked out of his favorite haunt. He doubted it. A couple of years back he'd done some work for the owner, and he was owed.

He texted back. Sure. 15 minutes. Okay if I bring a friend?

Thought I was the only friend you had but fine with me. Are you paying them?

Ha. Frank has the potential to replace you as my best bud.

Leaving the house now. See you there.

"They can't kick me out if I bring a puppy as cute as you," Clay said to Frank. He'd gone out earlier and bought a bag of puppy food, and now he encouraged the yellow Lab to eat, which he did ferociously. He was a lab, even if only a puppy, after all.

Clay closed up the office, picked Frank up, locked the door, and went down the stairs. Tomorrow he'd have to get the pup a dog license, likely some shots, and a leash. Baylee had provided a purple collar. He went to the grassy area by the harbor to see if Frank had any business he needed to attend to. The pup was prancing around full of energy after having slept the last couple of hours in the office.

A sightseeing schooner was coming back in, loaded to the gills with tourists, and Clay waved to the captain, a woman who he knew slightly. It was a good town, he thought. It'd be a hard place to leave.

Frank peed and pooped, and Clay congratulated him heartily. He'd always heard that this potty training of puppies was a difficult thing, but maybe it wasn't so bad after all. Only one beer tonight, he told himself, maybe two. The trick would be to take Frank outside a couple of times throughout the night, and that wasn't going to work out if he got into the brown liquor.

It was only a few hundred yards to the Pelican Perch, and Clay carried Frank there and up the stairs, not trusting him to not veer into the street with no leash to restrain him. As he rounded the top of the steps, he was met with a rousing 'Happy Birthday!'

The first person he focused on was Baylee wearing a cone-shaped hat strapped to her head. Westy. Crystal. Murphy. Cloutier. His people. There were others as well, outside of his core group. Westy's wife, Faith. Baylee's friend, Tammy. A few former clients. Other regulars at the Perch who he knew by name if not much else. Everybody wanted to buy him a drink.

Frank was a fan favorite. Clay worried that it'd all be overwhelming for the puppy, but the canine embraced the attention and even reveled in it.

Several large pizzas were bought. Crystal had brought a cake from the bakery around the corner, a peanut-butter mocha delicacy that melted in the mouth.

Presents included two bottles of brown liquor and many a gift for Frank. It seemed that the word had gotten out that Baylee was getting him a dog, and, surprisingly, people had kept their mouths shut.

Silas the bartender was there working. When things subsided slightly, Clay worked his way to the bar and ordered a cranberry and ginger ale.

"Wise choice," Silas said.

"What happened last night?" Clay asked.

"You remember any of it?"

"Not so much." This was a gentle way of saying not at all.

"You were feeling pretty good." Silas moved down the bar and opened two beers and placed them in front of a couple of locals. "When you got up to leave, you stumbled into the gent next to you. He took offense. You told him to fuck off. He punched you in the nose."

Clay touched his nose gingerly. "Yeah. I got that part."

"It took me and two others to pull you off him," Silas said. "You knocked him down, straddled him, and were raining punches on his face like a Chinese monsoon."

"Sorry about that."

"Glad to see you taking it easy tonight," Silas said. "Oh, and happy birthday."

"Yeah, thanks."

Clay went back to the corner his friends had secured. Westy came over, gave him a hug, and said that he and Faith had to get home and let the babysitter go.

Baylee was sitting by the railing with Frank in her lap, who was sound asleep. Clay wasn't sure which of them was the more adorable.

"I best be getting Frank home to bed," Clay said as he sat down next to her.

"I'll walk you home."

"I should be able to find my way up the hill."

"You got all those presents to carry. Who's going to carry Frank?"

Clay chuckled. "Flash is going to be jealous when you get home smelling like another mutt."

"Cover your ears, Frank." Baylee put her hands over the puppy's ears. "You are not a mutt. You are a perfect little tail-wagger of the highest pedigree."

"I'd love the company," Clay said. "And Frank does look pretty happy." He couldn't quite keep the jealous tinge from his voice as he looked at Frank nestled on Baylee's lap.

Clay gathered the presents, two bottles of liquor, and eleven assorted dog toys, and put them all into a bag. Marie Cloutier, the editor of the daily newspaper in Port Essex, and Joe Murphy, the retired clamdigger and current barfly, were in deep conversation. They were two of his closest friends and fabulous sources of information for his business when needed.

"Thanks for coming out," Clay said.

"You leaving?" Cloutier asked.

"Got a puppy to take care of."

Murphy looked at Baylee and Frank. "He seems to be doing just fine, but you're probably right, it'd be a good time to crack on." He stood up. "I'll walk out with you."

"I need to pick both your brains sometime soon," Clay said. "For a new case."

"I'm around tomorrow," Cloutier said. "You want to give a teaser what it's about?"

"Buried treasure and pirates," Clay said as he walked off.

At the bottom of the stairs, Murphy took a left, assuring Clay that he'd be in the Seal Bar the next morning until eleven and then on to Lucky Linda's for the rest of the day. He liked to vary his drinking spots, if not his schedule.

Clay and Baylee walked the other way in comfortable silence before turning left onto Oak Street to go up the hill to Clay's place. He was wondering if he should invite her in for a nightcap, a game of cribbage, or something else entirely. There was a hustle and bustle and low hum of noise emitting from Port Essex on this Friday evening just past eight o'clock.

It took a moment for Clay to notice the rumble, deeper, thicker, than a car or truck exhaust. He looked back over his shoulder as four motorcycles turned off Commercial Way onto Oak Street and started up the hill behind them. Harleys, he guessed, from the resonant growl of the bikes. Frank roused his head in Baylee's arm and yipped, not sure if the noise was a threat or not, his puppy eyes gone from sleep to alert in a split-second. Clay reached over to pat Frank's head, his hand brushing Baylee's shoulder.

"Clay," she said. "What the...?"

He looked back to the bikers who were starting to pass and realized they all had masks on. Skull masks. The white material glowing softly in the reflection of the streetlamp. The eyes were ragged rips in the fabric. They all had black hoods up over their heads.

Two bikes pulled over blocking their path while the other two stopped behind them. They got off their bikes.

"What the hell?" Clay said.

All four of them reached over their heads, as if orchestrated, and pulled gleaming cutlasses from scabbards hung from their backs. Slightly longer than a machete, shorter than a sword—the thick and curved blades flashed in the night air.

Clay looked at Baylee holding Frank. Confrontation seemed to be a poor option. What did these apparitions of the night want?

"The circus was in town last week," Clay said. "Did you fellows get left behind?" Why hadn't a car come by, he wondered? Or people. The hum of activity could be heard just down on Commercial Way, but here, halfway up the hill, all was quiet.

"You take Frank and go get help," he whispered to Baylee. He stepped forward toward the two masked figures closest to him who were holding their blades menacingly, but not quite threateningly. "Why don't you be good little trick-or-treaters and scoot out of the way?"

Clay sensed movement from behind and half-turned as the broad side of a cutlass blade whacked him upside the head. He stumbled, but remained standing, his head ringing from the blow.

A skeleton stepped up beside Baylee with an old wooden pistol in his hand, flared at the muzzle. A blunderbuss, Clay thought through the ringing of his ears. Cutlasses and blunderbusses?

The skeleton placed the muzzle against the side of her head and cocked the ancient pistol with one thumb. Frank was snarling and yipping in his tiny voice. Baylee licked her lips and looked at Clay.

"Wait. Stop." Clay shook his head to clear the cobwebs. "What do you want?"

The one who'd struck Clay with the cutlass stepped forward and placed the tip of his blade to Clay's throat. "Do not look for Black Sam Bellamy's treasure. You have been warned."

The skeleton with the blunderbuss pulled the trigger.

Click.

He cackled, stepped back, shoved the pistol into the sash at his waist. The four of them sheathed their cutlasses, climbed aboard their hogs, and roared off up the street.

Chapter 6

Clay woke at 6:00 a.m. not hungover. That was strange. Oddly disconcerting. He'd cordoned off an area in his room with newspapers on the floor for Frank, who'd whined a bit through the night, but had not been too bad, all things considered. The young fellow had, after all, been accosted by a group of bikers with skull masks and cutlasses the night before, a terrifying proposition for anybody, much less a young pup.

He took Frank down and into the backyard of the main house and let him tumble his awkward self here and there, sniffing, growling at butterflies, and entertaining himself with some game he was the only one privy to. Clay sat on a bench drinking a cup of coffee, and occasionally throwing a pine cone at Frank, who thought that was great fun.

Clay and Baylee had stood on the side of the street last night for a full minute after the pirate bikers, as Baylee called them, had ridden off. They'd decided not to call the police. The chief was already not much of a fan of their P.I. business in his town, and often felt they were stepping on his toes. To report that they'd been braced by four pirate bikers with cutlasses and a blunderbuss seemed to be just asking for ridicule.

He had insisted on getting his Jeep and driving Baylee back to her car and then following her home. Clay had walked her into the house, checking all the rooms, and suggested that perhaps he should stay in the spare room. Baylee, to his disappointment, had said that she was fine, seeing as she had a fierce guard dog to protect her. They'd both looked at Flash, who was on his back doing an upside-down doggie paddle in the air as Frank climbed all over him. It certainly appeared that they'd hit it off.

Baylee had agreed to getting her Smith & Wesson MP Shield from the lockbox and loading it. At the door, Clay had enfolded Baylee in his arms, asking if she was sure she was fine. There'd been just a moment there when that embrace may've led to more, and then Frank had yipped up at them and the moment was broken.

As if on cue, Frank yipped at his feet, bringing him from his reverie to the present, biting the toe of his boat shoe. "You probably could use a bite to eat," he said, swooping the puppy up into his arms.

They went back up the stairs to his apartment and poured a cup of puppy food into a cereal bowl. Clay mentally put it on his list that dog dishes were also needed. For now, though, he had little ambition to do anything. Before Grandpops had died, Clay was up with the sun and ready to start cracking. Now he was lucky to drag himself to the office just to scroll through social media for a large chunk of the day before walking down to one bar or another for the rest of the evening.

Weekends? Well, there didn't seem to be much purpose in getting up and going too early, because that just meant the drinking would begin sooner. Not that there was anything wrong with that, as it made the time pass like a breeze on a hot summer day.

Clay lay down on the floor and rolled a ball for Frank, played some tug, wrestled a bit—chuckling at the antics of the puppy.

After about an hour of play, Frank grew tired, so Clay lay down on the sofa with the puppy on his chest and the two napped.

Clay drifted in and out of slumber, the perfect recipe for dreaming and remembering one's dreams. At first, he and Baylee were being pursued by pirate skeletons riding choppers that turned into horses and then fire-breathing dragons. No matter what they did, they couldn't elude these bogeymen from hell intent on killing them.

He woke from the nightmare with a start, but that didn't affect the dozing dog on his chest. He shifted Frank so the canine was nestled on Clay's left shoulder against the back of the sofa, safe from being inadvertently tossed to the floor. This time, his dreams were better, if not just as torturous. He and Baylee were on a beach, the sand white as snow and the water aqua and inviting. They had frozen drinks in coconut shells and reclined in beach chairs. Baylee had on a tiny bikini, a floppy straw hat, and dark glasses.

There was no talk of work nor of the past. They did not worry about the future. The two of them were cemented firmly in the present, living life, enjoying the moment, oblivious to carried baggage or the unknown morrow. He was not in the dream but was watching from above. Clay said something, he couldn't quite tell what, and Baylee snickered. She reached out a hand to his shoulder, her nails green, her thumb stroking his bicep as she replied to him. With that touch, he dropped from the sky and into his own body next to Baylee.

Clay looked around and realized they were the only two on the entire beach. Behind them was a cabana, the top pointed and covered with thatch, the sides enclosed with sheets rustling gently in the breeze. He looked up, realizing that Baylee had stood, her hand grasping his. Her white bikini showcased the darkness of her tan, of her ancestry, of her beauty. His eyes dragged up her legs, her stomach, past her breasts, to the white smile of her teeth and her caramel eyes and honey hair.

"Come," she said.

He allowed himself to be pulled to his feet and trailed Baylee, hand in hers, as she led him to the cabana. She pushed aside the light canvas flaps and pulled him inside. A bed filled most of the space, a faint mist sifted down from above, and soft jazz music was piped in, just audible, mixing with the lap of waves onto the shore. Baylee reached down and pulled back the cotton comforter and creamy sheet. She turned back to him and stepped into him, her lips pressed to his, her tongue flickering in and out, her teeth nibbling on his lips.

Clay felt the desire building within him to a bursting point, and at that moment she stepped back, breaking from his body, from his lips, as if splitting one whole into two. Baylee reached up behind her back and her bikini top fell to the floor. With a coy smile, she stepped out of her bottoms, and then lay back on the bed in a beguiling sprawl that left him standing agape in astonishment and amazement at her raw enticement.

For just an instant, a tiny fraction of time, Clay took a moment to appreciate the stunning vision of all that he desired, inviting him, lusting for him—and then the sirens went off. The howling, low, long, and ever-growing in intensity vibrated through the fleshy tropical air. Clay looked over his shoulder, wondering where they were, what danger existed outside their paradise. It didn't matter. If he was to die today, he'd die happy. He turned back to Baylee, only she was gone, replaced by Crystal. She stood up to kiss him, no less naked than Baylee had been.

The howls shortened and became shriller. Clay opened his eyes. Frank was licking his face. His cell was ringing on the floor next to him. He picked it up.

"Hello." The words were husky in his throat as he tried desperately to banish the image of a naked Crystal kissing him and go back in his mind to the splendor that was Baylee.

"You feel like buying me lunch?"

"What?" He shook his head. Crystal. Baylee. Sirens.

"Am I waking Prince Valiant up from his morning slumber?"

It was Cloutier. Marie Cloutier. "No," he lied. "I was just in the middle of something."

"Yeah, I can tell." She laughed. "Like sleeping. Hey, you said you wanted to pick my brain about something. Buried treasure and pirate booty, I think it was. Well, my day got busy, but I can squeeze you in for lunch at Kurt's, if you want. On you, of course."

"That'd be great. When?" Kurt's was a deli, but they had some pretty damn good draft beer. The twenty-two-ounce kind of IPA that made him happy.

"Fifteen minutes."

"Got it."

"And Clay?" Cloutier said. "Bring Frank. I already miss that adorable little whelp."

Clay took a quick, very cold, shower. He dressed casually in shorts and a Green Day T-shirt, grabbed Frank, and was out the door. Kurt's was only a few minutes' walk down the road, as most of Port Essex was. He was still trying to banish the disturbing image of Crystal and the lascivious thoughts of Baylee as he walked into the deli, noting that he'd beaten Cloutier there. He got a beer and downed half of it as he sat down.

Tony, the owner, who'd bought the place from Kurt, came over to say hi and rub Frank's head. "Who is this fellow?"

"Frank. Frank, this is Tony. You be nice to him, and he might bring you a snack next time he comes by."

Frank licked Tony's hand. The pup was proving he could turn on the charm when needed.

Cloutier came rushing in the door. She had mousy brown hair cut in a bob, glasses perched on her daintily upturned nose, and a few freckles on her rotund cheeks.

"Got a big story going down at the Botanical Gardens," she said. "I got twenty minutes."

"Reuben?" Tony asked.

"Yes, and whatever beer he's drinking. I'll come get that."

"I'll get a steak and cheese," Clay said. "And grab me another of these," he called to Cloutier, raising his glass.

Tony went back behind the counter to get the sandwiches going. It wasn't normally table service at the deli, but they were regulars and in a hurry. Or at least Cloutier was.

Clay finished his first beer as Cloutier returned with a fresh one for him. "What's going on at the Botanical Gardens?" he asked.

Twenty-eight years ago, when he was eight, Clay had thrown a fit that he didn't want to go see the Christmas Lights at the Botanical Gardens. As a result, Grandpops had stayed home with him, confiding that he didn't really want to go either, and his mother, father, and grandmother had gone off without them. They would never make it home again as Mack Wolfe, high on cocaine, had driven their car straight off a cliff on the return journey.

"Somebody graffitied one of the Trolls." The gardens were hosting an exhibit of five giant trolls made of recycled wood woven into the fabric of their rolling grounds. "You can read about it Monday. Let's get to what you got going on. Pirate booty?"

Clay chuckled. "Couple of New Yorkers came in the office the other day to retain my services in the search for a supposed buried treasure of an early 18th-century pirate named Samuel Bellamy. Black Sam Bellamy."

Cloutier nodded. "I wondered about that. I wrote a story about him ten, maybe twelve years back."

Clay took a gulp of beer. He knew that Cloutier was waiting for him to admit he hadn't read her article. "I think I was walking a beat in Boston at the time. Didn't have much time for reading the *Port Essex Register*." That would've been before he'd risen to the rank of homicide detective.

Tony came over with their sandwiches. He also had a piece of cheese and a meatball for Frank, who stood on the table to eat his lunch. Clay wasn't sure if puppies should be eating a breadless meatball sub, but Frank seemed happy, so he let it go.

"Thought you might have come across it, researching the case, is all," Cloutier said. She took a huge bite of her Reuben but that didn't stop her from talking. "According to this guy, Charles Johnson, who was a journalist and writer who hung out with retired pirates, Bellamy went up the Machias River to do ship repairs in 1717. There, they dug trenches, erected fortifications, built huts—all with the idea of laying the foundation of a new kingdom. This would be based on a more democratic ideal, mind you, as Black Sam was ahead of his time. Every man had an equal say, or vote, in what they did, whether it was attacking a ship or where to put in to port."

"A kingdom?" Clay asked.

"More a utopia based on the egalitarian principles that ruled the ship. A retirement home for pirates. Well out of the reach of the crown and others that might be chasing them."

"But what's that got to do with Port Essex?" Clay asked. "Machiasport has to be 150 miles up the coast."

"Here's the rub," Cloutier said. She shoved the last of the Reuben into her mouth and finished her beer in two huge swallows.

"What's the rub?" Clay asked a tad impatiently. He realized he was about to lose her.

"Well, the thing is, history becomes a bit fuzzy starting in 1675 when the Abenaki Sachem, King Phillip, rose up in rebellion against the Europeans who'd come to claim his land. It came to be known as King Phillip's War."

"Didn't that take place down around Plymouth in Massachusetts?"

"Yeah, Chief Metacom, later known as King Phillip was there, but the rebellion spread all the way up to Maine. Especially when a bounty was offered on anybody who brought Native American scalps in. Redskins, they were called." Cloutier leaned forward across the table. "Nor did it help when some English settlers down toward the Saco River came across Chief Squando's wife in a canoe with her baby. They decided to test the theory that Native American babies can swim as naturally as animals. Needless to say, the infant drowned, and this kind of pissed off the chief."

"Okay, okay, I'll read your damn article. Get to the rub."

"A woman came to me from town. Her ancestors in the area date back to before the Abenakis. The Etchemin People, they were called. She had a diary from her great-great-grandmother who'd written down a story that had been previously passed down orally through their people for generations. It was a time after King William's War and then Queen Anne's War had between them driven all but a few hearty Europeans from the area. The legend spoke of a god who came sailing up their river to the home of 'Chbo So Clan' who brought them food, guns, ammunition, and a way out of the starving time. Black Sam he was called. He settled next to them and built a fort and treated them like real people."

"He didn't go to Machiasport at all," Clay said. "But came here to Port Essex."

"Or, he went up there, changed his mind, and came back down the coast." Cloutier shrugged. "According to this woman, Niben Glenn, Black Sam spent some time in this area."

"When?"

Cloutier stood up. "I got to go," she said. "Read my article."

"Where was their village?" Clay asked. "Was that Winnegance?"

Cloutier shook her head. "That, I don't know, my friend." She walked out.

Chapter 7

Baylee walked into the Knox Cove Marina wearing a yellow sundress, high heels, and a green scarf over her head, tied under her chin. She had on large, round sunglasses and imagined that she looked a bit like Jackie Kennedy Onassis. Rich. Famous. Beautiful.

The same barrel-shaped man with a rough beard who Tobias Yates had spoken to a couple of days earlier was in the office. As she stepped through the door, a chime went off, and she pretended not to notice the man's eyes slithering across her body.

"Can I help you?" he asked.

There was fishing and boating equipment for sale in jumbled shelves and signs with cheesy sayings adorned the walls.

Warning:
Fishing Tales Will Be Told.

Jerk It Till She Swallows.

It's A Fishing Thing.
You Wouldn't Understand.

Nice, Baylee thought. *Classy. Real classy.*

"Yes, well I certainly hope so," Baylee said. "I wanted to go out on a boat."

"We got two tour boats going out of here twice a day," the man said. "Were you wanting a yacht or a sloop experience?" He fished around on the desk and lay two brochures in front of her.

"Well, I don't know." Baylee leaned forward to look at the pamphlets. Her breasts felt the man's eyes, and it was all she could do to keep herself from slapping him. "My friend has recommended the *Coronado*. Is that one of these?"

The man guffawed. "Who is your friend?"

"A friend of a friend, actually."

The man's eyes finally rose to hers. "The *Coronado* is a fishing vessel, sometimes used for salvage. Not a tourist boat."

"My friend said that if I wanted the true Maine boating excursion that I should go out on the *Coronado*." Baylee slid her sunglasses down her nose and met the man's gaze. "Perhaps you could point me to the owner so that I might make my own inquiries?"

"Adam Dube does not take tourists out for day cruises."

"My friend said that he took Tobias Yates out for a cruise the other day, and they had a fabulous time," Baylee said. It was a bit of a lie, but enough truth to cover her tracks.

The man grinned. "So, you know Mr. Yates? He's a grand fellow. One of a kind, he is. He's been going out with Dube on the *Coronado* a couple of times a week for the past few months. I think it has to do with something more than just sightseeing."

"Yes?" Baylee cast a smile at the man like a fishing line, baited, and enticing. "What could Tobias be looking for?"

"Don't know. They go out for three, four hours at a stretch. Matter of fact, they went out this morning. Only got back a bit ago. Mr. Yates is gone, but Dube's still onboard out there, cleaning up, I reckon."

Baylee followed his stubby finger pointing out into the cove. She could see a man puttering about on the *Coronado*. "How do I get out there?" she asked. "You got a dingy I can use?"

"I'll get Jared to take you out." The man stepped out from behind the desk, went to the door, stuck his fingers into the corners of his mouth, and gave a piercing whistle. "Jare. Take this lady out to the *Coronado*, would you? And stick around to bring her back. Don't imagine she'll be there long."

Baylee followed the direction of the command down to the pier where a young teenage boy, scrawny and dirty, waited for her. "Ma'am," he said.

"Hello, Jared."

The boy ducked his head and motioned her into a dingy, not offering her a hand to steady, pulled the rope free, and followed her in. It had a small outboard motor, and he gunned it as the boat swung away from the dock, almost throwing her clear, and sped off across the harbor like it was a race.

The man on board stopped what he was doing and watched the dingy approach. He wore jeans and a blue-plaid shirt that hung loosely on his large frame. He was one of those men whose physique at first glance was confusing, hard to tell whether he was overweight or just built big. Chest. Shoulders. Waist. Arms. Legs. The only thing not immense about Adam Dube were his ears, two little nubbins on either side of his broad head, a red baseball cap pulled down low over his eyes.

Jared swung up next to the boat and stood, grabbing the railing.

"Mr. Dube? Do you think I might have a word with you?" Baylee asked as she rose to board the *Coronado*.

"What's it you want?"

Baylee stepped carefully up onto the boat, regretting her choice of kitten heels, but at least they were better than her stilettos. A wave caught her with one foot on and one in the air and she tumbled forward. Adam Dube stepped toward her with an agility surprising for a man of his bulk and caught her with strong hands.

"Careful, there, miss," he said. "Don't want to be explaining to the wife what you were doing on my boat in the cove when you hurt yourself, no ma'am, I don't."

Baylee extricated herself from his grip in irritation. She doubted that Jackie Kennedy Onassis would've fallen overboard or been anything but the picture of grace. The truth was, heels, even kitten heels, were not something she was used to, or comfortable in. She was more of a Chuck Taylor, high-top sneaker, kind of gal.

"Thank you, Mr. Dube," she said.

"Adam will do just fine," he said. "What is it I can do for you?" He was clean-shaven, his face smooth like a young boy, even though he was probably close to forty.

"I was looking to hire you to take me out on the *Coronado*, Adam."

Adam laughed nervously. "Why would I do that?"

Baylee looked around. There was a hydraulic pump and winch, the cable still glistening slightly with wetness. Her arrival appeared to have interrupted Adam from deflating a large balloon with a basket on the bottom.

"This is a salvage boat, isn't it?" Baylee looked around. There was a crane on the back of the boat attached to a winch. Various large hooks hung from one wall and Dube was busy stowing scuba gear in a box.

Adam shifted his feet. "Some of the time. Thing is, I'm booked pretty full for the next few months."

"What is it that a salvage boat does?"

"I mostly go out and pull up sunken boats. Sometimes they've been deserted, and I unload them to a fellow out to East Essex who reclaims them and then sells them. Sometimes people pay me to get their vessel back for them."

"I'd like go out with you sometime and see that process," Baylee said. "I'm not a woman who likes to sit on the deck of a ferry and sip white wine and look at seals."

"Sorry, miss, but I'm really booked full right now."

"My friend Gina said you might be able to fit me in. I'm onto something big."

"Gina?" A slow blush crept across his already florid cheeks. "Don't know who that is."

"Gina Yates? You've been doing some work for her husband?"

"Yates?" Adam drew the name out slowly. "The redhead? He calls her something different. Rose is her name. Who's this Gina?"

So, there was another woman, Baylee thought. "I, uh, am friends with Gina Rose from back in college, when she still went by her first name." Baylee laughed softly. "I haven't been able to wrap my head around calling her by her middle name. Don't know why she ever..." Baylee waved her hand in the air. "Never mind all that blathering. Yes, Gina Rose told me that you might have some time to fit me in. It's... connected to what they're searching for."

"Funny, Tobias hasn't told me anything about any of that. I best give him a call." Adam pulled a cell phone from his pocket.

"Oh, please, don't get Rose in trouble," Baylee said. "She was most likely speaking out of turn when she told me that you had time. The thing is, a few years back, more like twenty, my uncle sunk his boat out off the coast here, and some family heirlooms went down with the *Luisa*. I was hoping to maybe retrieve them. You know... what's the word... salvage."

Adam slowly put his phone away. "There's a boat you wish to salvage?"

"I best check in with Rose," Baylee said, stepping toward the stern, the teenage boy, and the waiting dingy. "Before I go any further. I don't want to get her in trouble with Tobias."

"I'd be interested in speaking more about this, miss. What'd you say your name was?"

Baylee stepped into the dingy. "Once I get back to my hotel room, I'll check in with Rose and get this cleared up, make sure Tobias knows about it, and then I'll come back out tomorrow or the next day."

Adam nodded, "You must be staying at that fancy Port in a Storm place same as them, I reckon."

* * *

Baylee sat in a corner of the lobby of the Port in a Storm Inn in an armchair. She had a cup of coffee next to her and her laptop up and running. She'd called the front desk and asked to be put through to Tobias Yates' room. The phone had rang and rang. Either he was not there, or he was in there enjoying the pleasures of his mistress, the redheaded Rose.

After calling, she thought to check the parking lot for his car. The bright-red Bentley Bentayga would've been easy enough to spot, but wasn't there. Baylee called Gina Yates, ostensibly to give her an update, but really to find out if she'd heard from him. Gina had gotten a text message the night before telling her that he was swamped with the conference, and he'd call when he got a chance.

Baylee had told her that first day that Tobias had not gone to the airport but asked that she refrain from calling him out on it, as that would tip him off and lessen the chance of Baylee catching him in a compromising situation with another woman. At that point, she didn't actually believe that he was having an affair but that he had something else going on. She'd kept mum about that.

Baylee leaned back in the chair and half-closed her eyes. What was going on, she wondered? Tobias had lied about going to a conference in Arizona. Instead, he was staying right in town at the inn. Port Essex wasn't so big that he didn't risk running into his wife, so, why? The man was going out on a salvage boat on a regular basis, suggesting he was looking for something, a shipwreck, or a lost treasure. For the first time, Baylee allowed herself to wonder if this was somehow connected with Clay being hired to find the gems cached by Black Sam Bellamy.

Of course, now there was the suggestion of another woman. Somebody named Rose with red hair. A regular on the salvage boat with Tobias Yates.

And was this all connected with the bikers in skull masks and wielding cutlasses who had threatened her and Clay the night before? The one had put the pistol with the wide muzzle to her head and pulled the trigger, and the truth was, she'd been too confused by the entire spectacle to even be scared. Thinking about it, the threat had been real, and she could've been killed. At the time, it'd seemed too darned bizarre to take seriously.

Tobias Yates came through the front door of the inn. Baylee got up casually and followed him down the hallway. He stopped at the elevator, and she continued on past to the stairwell. The place was only three floors. She was betting that he was on the top floor and hurried up the steps. There were vending machines in an alcove by the elevator there, along with an ice maker, and Baylee busied herself in there waiting. She'd almost given up, thinking she'd guessed wrong, when the elevator doors opened, and Tobias emerged.

Baylee watched out of the corner of her eye as he went down the hall, stopped, and entered a room. She did a walk-by. It was room 37.

Was Rose the redhead in there? Would she have answered the phone when Baylee had called? It was quite possible that she wouldn't have done so, if she was in the midst of an illicit affair with a married man. Baylee stopped at the door on the way back past and listened for a few seconds but could hear nothing.

Should she knock? No, it was too early to blow her cover, Baylee thought, and went back down the hall and the stairs to the lobby. If Rose showed up, or if Tobias left with Rose, she could snap a picture. Tobias not in Arizona, but rather in Port Essex, in the company of another woman would be a decent start to prove his cheating. Not enough to hold up against the array of lawyers Baylee was certain would be hired to tear the accusations of infidelity to shreds.

Her thoughts turned to Clay. Buying a puppy for him had been a spontaneous decision, though it had been six weeks ago when she put money down for the fellow. He had been the last one in the litter, available because he was not fit to be a duck dog, or so Tammy, her friend, claimed. She'd told Baylee why, but the reason had whooshed over her head much like algebra had back in school. Baylee smiled. And then Clay had named the pup Frank. What a name. She'd caught him grinning at the tiny dog with a pure happiness that she hadn't seen since his Grandpops had been killed.

A woman came through the front door carrying a shopping bag. She was pixie-thin and wearing a white tank top that covered only a small portion of her delicate frame and shorts so tiny Baylee figured she must shop at the Barbie doll store. Her hair was short and very red.

Tobias got off the elevator and came down the hallway as the woman went to the front desk of the lobby. They might've briefly made eye contact, possibly, but fleeting at best, and then he walked past her and out the door.

Baylee was at a dilemma. Follow Tobias? Or stick with the woman who might be Rose based solely on her hair color? She stood and sauntered past the woman who'd finished her business at the counter and went toward the elevators with bouncy yet jerky steps.

The redhead didn't look at Baylee as they passed each other. Looked everywhere but, as a matter of fact, her neck turning left, tilting up, careening sideways to look over her shoulder, with eyes flickering this way and that.

Baylee went out the front door to see Tobias climbing into his Bentley. She hurried to her Subaru and pulled out onto the road five cars back from the man in stop-and-go traffic that was a constant affliction of Port Essex in the summer, most certainly on a weekend. They crawled their way down Commercial Way. The pedestrians were starting to make the shift from shoppers to party goers, the bands of walking people more boisterous, more likely to veer into the street without looking.

As they passed the P.I. office, the congestion eased slightly, and they picked up to a steady twenty miles an hour. Baylee figured he was on his way back to the Knox Marina and the *Coronado*, but he went on past, not turning left until he came to the short bridge over to Spruce Island.

Where Baylee lived. The road was a loop, the distance around the small island just four miles. Tobias took the slightly longer route, passing by Westy's house as he cruised along, but in the end, pulled into Baylee's driveway.

Baylee pulled in beside him. She opened the glove compartment and took out the pepper spray, sliding it into the yellow clutch along with her phone and wallet. Her MP Shield was in a holster under her dress at her side. With a deep breath, she opened the door and got out.

Chapter 8

Clay stopped home to drop Frank off after his lunch with Cloutier. He figured the pup was due for a nap and the Seal Bar was no place for a youngster. Certainly not Lucky Linda's, if he ended up going there.

He had a faint glow from the two large IPA's. Enough of a warmth to think it a good idea to get a scotch, neat, as he slid into the only seat available at the Seal Bar. There was a line out the door for the restaurant but not many solo people looking for bar seating on this weekend summer day. Those locals had migrated to less-touristy destinations.

"Murphy come in this morning?" he asked as the bartender slid the healthy pour of brown liquor in front of him. The people from away got the strict 1.5 ounces. His was almost double that.

"Yeah, he was here, 'til bout eleven, then he split to go up the hill." The bartender, a woman with brown hair, intelligent eyes, and ample cheeks moved off to fill an order.

This Clay had known, but he wanted to have a few drinks without judgment. He'd seen Cloutier eye him as he ordered his second lunch beer. At least she had a perch from which to look down upon his habits, but there was nothing worse than being lectured by an Irishman who was belly up to the bar by nine every morning and then spent the next eight hours there. It was Joe Murphy's form of a nine-to-five job. Clock in. Clock out.

Of course, Clay had never seen the man drunk. Or maybe he'd just never seen him sober to know what drunk looked like. Either way, the wizened clam digger who had a fair resemblance to Dobbie from the Harry Potter movies was sure to call Clay out on his consumption, or at least, the rate at which he was putting them back. Best to have a few here on his own, contemplate life a bit, before going up the hill to dig into what Murphy knew about pirate treasure in Port Essex.

As Clay got his second round, the chair next to him opened up, and a man sat down. Out of the corner of his eye, Clay thought it very well might be the man from the Pelican Perch who he'd had an altercation with. Dark hair and features. His face was long and sported a mustache and a couple days growth of beard. The corner of his eye was discolored, turning a deep shade of purple.

"What do you want?" Clay asked, swinging his stool to face the man.

The man looked at him. "To apologize."

"What?"

"I was very drunk. I shouldn't have hit you."

Clay stared the man in the eye. There was a scrape on his forehead and his lip had been recently split. "I might've been overserved myself," he said.

The man stuck out his hand. "Roderick Guerrero. My friends call me Rod."

Clay took the hand. It was strong. Firm. "Clay Wolfe."

Rod looked around the room. "I believe I prefer the Pelican Perch but I'm not sure I'm allowed back," he said.

Clay chuckled. "Not many fights up there. Lot more here. What brings you to town?" The man had outsider written all over him. Clay wasn't sure quite how he knew, but figured it was most likely the speech, eyes, and overall mannerisms that didn't fit the local profile.

"Mixing business with pleasure. You live here?"

"Born and raised," Clay said.

"Ah, a native. Know any good-looking broads?"

"Where you from?" Clay asked, ignoring the question.

"Manhattan."

Score one for Westy, Clay thought, who'd guessed that was where the dude was from the first time they'd laid eyes on him. "What business brings you to a coastal Maine fishing village all the way from New York?" Clay had figured the guy either had a summer house here or was a tourist, but business?

"Nothing exciting. You know much about the history of Port Essex?"

"Such as what?" Clay asked.

"Ever hear any stories about the natives who inhabited the land before the Europeans arrived?"

Two things struck Clay as off-putting. The first was he didn't like how the man said 'natives'. And the second was this sudden interest in the old history of Port Essex. Everything seemed to be circling back to the past, more specifically, 300 years ago. "Got a historical society down to Essex," he said. "If you wanted to look into them."

"Might just do that," Rod said. "If I get some time free of work."

"What's it you do?"

"I'm a businessman." Rod knocked back the shot he'd ordered. "Investments, generally. Got to get going. Nice meeting you."

* * *

"Can I help you with something?" Baylee asked.

"Why are you following me?" Tobias asked.

Baylee mentally kicked herself. He'd probably caught wind of her tailing him due to the fact that she'd dressed the part of a wealthy tourist to gather information at the marina. Her loud yellow dress and floppy hat were not conducive to being discreet.

"I don't know what you're talking about," she said.

They stood in the driveway of Baylee's home, faced off against each other, just outside their cars.

Tobias laughed coarsely. His face was red, either from sun or drink, it was hard to tell, and his jowls quivered with the exertion of the grating cackle. "You were in the lobby of the inn. Then you followed me here."

Baylee shrugged her shoulders. "I live here. This is my house."

"What were you doing at the inn?"

"Don't suppose that's any of your damn business." Baylee stepped around him. "And I have no idea who you are. So, if you wouldn't mind leaving, I'm going to go inside my house. Where I live."

"Adam called me to say some lady in a yellow dress was down at the boat asking questions and throwing my name around." Tobias sidled up to block her path.

Baylee paused, just a scant foot from the man. She could smell his sour breath. "I don't know any Adam. Or who you are, for that matter. As a matter of fact, I didn't see you at the inn while I was there being stood up for an appointment. Are you a guest there?"

"I recognized you, of course," Tobias said. "Your picture being in the *Daily Register* a couple years back about that whole mouse thing. You and that pop singer. What was her name? Kalinda, that's it. You're a private investigator. While you sat in the lobby I Googled you, Miss Baker, of Wolfe & Baker. Quite a history you have. Shot and killed your husband?"

Baylee watched in wonder as one of his bushy white eyebrows crawled up his forehead like a caterpillar. "You're starting to creep me out." Baylee pulled her phone from her clutch, adjusting the pepper spray for easy access. "If you don't leave, I'm going to call the police."

"Go right ahead," Tobias said, sidling forward so that his face was mere inches from her own. "Chief Roberts is a good friend of mine."

Baylee gagged from his breath. She stepped back. "Just what is it that you think I've done?"

"You're following me. Why?"

"I have no idea who Adam is or what boat you're talking about," Baylee said. "I was supposed to meet a client at The Port in a Storm this afternoon. They called to say they'd been held up, and I waited, and then they never showed and didn't answer their phone, so I left.

The fact that you have been stalking me, have come to my house, and are throwing around crazy accusations is deeply disturbing to me."

Baylee moved around him, taking a step, but no more, as Tobias grabbed her elbow. "You're lying to me," he said.

Baylee spun on her heel, jerking her arm free, and drove her fist into his neck.

"Don't fucking touch me," she said.

Tobias stepped back, gasping for air.

Baylee took another step toward him. She was only aware of her actions as if from the perspective of a bird floating above. "Don't you ever put your hands on me again, do you understand?"

Tobias, his face gone pale, opened his car door and got in, starting the engine as Baylee stepped over to his open window.

"Do you understand me, motherfucker?" she asked.

"You'll pay for that, bitch!" His voice came out as a high-pitched squeak. Baylee reached for him as he put the car into reverse and backed into the road, narrowly missing a truck going by. "You haven't heard the last of me," he snarled, and then roared off, his tires squealing.

*　*　*

The sun was still high in the sky as Clay worked his way up the hill to Lucky Linda's. He guessed that it was not yet five o'clock, a thought that was astounding to him, as his mind was already fuzzy with drink. At least his walking was in a straight line, or so his drunken mind thought.

This made him think of that Leonardo DiCaprio movie, *The Wolf of Wall Street*, where, extremely high on drugs, DiCaprio drives his Lamborghini a mile home from the club. He thinks that he's been careful and done an admirable job, but the police wake him later, showing him his battered car as proof that he'd hit about every obstacle between the club and home in his intoxicated state. That was the good and bad thing about brown liquor, Clay thought. It altered perception and reality as deemed fit by one's subconscious.

Lucky Linda's was crackling along at a hot pace that welcomed him in as one of their own. It was a rough and tumble crowd that hung out at this seedy establishment. The bar itself was just plywood atop barrels in a U-shape. There was a stage, empty now, and a dance floor. There were cheap tables dotting the remainder of the joint. It wasn't worth putting anything nicer in the place as it would most certainly just get broken.

It was a rare night when there wasn't a fight, and if no knives or guns were drawn, it was considered a good night. Clay himself had just the previous year engaged in a brawl here, the last time he'd been in. That had ended with the entire crowd throwing punches, most of them not quite sure why.

Clay spied Murphy at the far end of the U-shaped bar and worked his way through the crowd. A group of men caught his attention, four of them in biker attire, leather vests over black T-shirts and jeans. They looked familiar. Like maybe they'd recently worn skull masks and were handy with a cutlass.

"Clay, me boy, have a seat," Murphy said. "Something catch your eye? Maybe that lovely lass with the spider tattoo on her arm?"

"Murph." Clay sat down in the empty stool next to the man. "How you been?" His words felt thick in his mouth. Had he had three or four of the hefty whiskey drinks? He wasn't quite sure.

"What's the *craic*?"

"Just been down to the Seal Bar." Clay raised his hand to the bartender, pointed at Murphy's glass, and raised two fingers. "What's the *craic* with you?"

Murphy sniggered. "Don't sound right coming from your mouth. Best keep to your good ole English vernacular. Maybe you could get away with 'what's up'."

"What do you know about those four in the corner? The bikers."

Murphy didn't even look that way. There was not much he missed, which was amazing as he drank more liquor than most people drank water in the course of a day. "Been here the past few days. Rumor has it they're staying out on Route 29 at the Town Motel. Why?"

"Four bikers threatened me and Baylee last night with cutlasses. Had masks on, but they looked a lot like those fellows."

"Cutlasses? You mean, like swords?"

"Yeah. Short and fat curved blades with handguards," Clay said. "What's the back of their vests say? Can't read it from here."

The bartender delivered two glasses of Jameson to them, Murphy's drink of choice. Clay drank his down and held out his glass for another.

"*Buccaneers*," Murphy said. "Like the football team."

"Or the pirates," Clay said.

"And skull and crossbones," Murphy said. "Didn't buccaneers carry cutlasses?"

"Yep, I believe they did."

"What've you got yourself into now, me lad?"

Clay shook his head, took his fresh drink, and drained half of it. "Got hired to find some ancient pirate treasure and now pirates are turning up everywhere. I thought it was a bunch of baloney, but now, I'm starting to think there might be something to it."

"There's been whispers in the clamming community as long as I can remember about an old pirate stash somewhere on the coast. Every time I hear the story, it's somewhere different, but one name stays true."

"Black Sam Bellamy," Clay said.

"That'd be the one."

Clay finished his whiskey and raised the glass for another.

"Your kind of hitting the sauce pretty hard, aren't you, me lad?"

"That's the... bowl calling the kettle black, isn't it?"

"Pot, is the correct idiom."

"Idiom?" Clay snorted.

"I lived my life. This is what I have left." Murphy waved at the bar, the people, the world. "You got a lot of life left ahead of you. Stop acting the maggot."

The words hit the brown shield erected around Clay's brain with a clang. He refused to let them in, staring dully at his elderly Irish friend. "I'm going to go talk to those biker fellows," he said. "They're probably better company than you."

He stood up, suddenly angry at Murphy, his words, his truth. He tripped on the stool next to him, earning a black look from the man sitting there staring into his beer. Clay realized he had a fresh Jameson in his hand and wasn't quite sure when he'd ordered it. Last one, he thought, and tossed it back, setting the empty glass on the bar next to the man's beer, staring him down until he looked away.

There were very few people left in Clay's life. Grandpops had been the last of his family. He could count his friends on one hand. And none more important to him than Baylee. The thought of the four men the previous night brandishing cutlasses and putting an ancient pistol to her head of her angered and terrified him at the same time.

Four bikers new in town. Wearing leather with the insignia *Buccaneers*, the name of their gang, their club, and also a term for pirates of the Caribbean.

"What are you fellows up to?" Clay asked, jostling his way into their small circle. "Hey, nice tat." He jabbed his finger into the bicep of a burly, bearded man with an octopus descending down his sleeveless arm.

"Why don't you move on, buddy?" the man said.

"Hey, don't I know you?" Clay asked. "Where'd I run into you? Let me see. Was it at the girl scout fundraiser? No, no, that wasn't it."

"Get lost, buddy. We're having a private conversation." A thin man with narrow eyes and a nose like the edge of an axe gave Clay a slight nudge.

Everything was a bit off kilter, Clay thought. Almost as if it weren't real. The room wobbled around him. The air vibrated. He realized that was his phone. "Just a second, fellows," Clay said, holding up his pointer finger. "I think I got a message."

He took his phone from his pocket and peered at it. Text from Baylee. Hard to read. He held it up close to his face. How is Frank doing?

Frank, Clay thought, had been home all afternoon by himself. He looked at the time on his phone but couldn't read it.

"You're starting to piss me off," Octopus Arm said. "Stinking things up around here. Shove off."

Clay looked back up, re-situating himself to the barroom, away from the comfort of Baylee, concerns for the puppy—swirling emotions of pain, love, despair, and anger kaleidoscoping through his being.

He snapped his fingers, or tried to. "I know where I saw you guys. You were on Oak Street last night, weren't you?"

"You're going to find yourself in a ditch wishing you'd left well enough alone," Axe-Edge Nose said. He grabbed Clay by the elbow. "Now, *get.*"

Clay slashed the man's hand off his elbow with his free arm and then shoved him backward. "Keep your mitts to yourself, Captain Barbossa." He snickered. Then chuckled. Barbossa was the evil pirate from the *Pirates of the Caribbean* franchise.

Then a fist crashed into the side of his head, and he was knocked sideways, stumbling several feet before the wall caught him. His whimsy turned to rage. He pushed himself free of the wall and hit the closest biker in the chin with a punch that came from his shoulder, drove through the man's face and ended up two feet past, a skill he'd learned in football. Don't tackle the man. Tackle *through* the man.

Octopus Arm grabbed him in a bear hug and flung him sideways, toppling him to the floor, and knocking down several other bar-goers. Clay stumbled to his feet as Axe-Edge Nose went to kick him, and he grabbed his foot, twisted, and sent the man crashing to the floor.

A chair crashed into Clay's back, and he again was thrown to the floor, the wood sticky like glue underneath him as he went to rise again. He didn't see the kick that caught him in the ear and spun him back down. He felt a knee in his back and a fist pummeled the side of his head as he squirmed to get free.

And then the pressure was gone. He rolled over to see Westy flinging a biker into a wall, the impact shaking the entire building. Westy turned and hit another man with a smack that rang through the bar like a ship's bell. Axe-Edge Nose charged at him, and he took the man's momentum and threw him across the room and into a table which splintered under his weight.

Four burly bouncers stepped in between them. "The police are on their way," one of them said. "Get gone or get arrested."

Chapter 9

There was a knocking sound. Clay's alcohol-befuddled brain tried to block the sound from pounding into his cranium like some demonic jackhammer. It wouldn't stop. He opened his eyes and tried to get his bearings. He was in his bedroom. It was dark. Clay tilted his head to the side and saw Frank sleeping on a pillow, tiny snores rippling his puppy body.

The knocking was at the front door. Clay groaned, but eased carefully from the bed to not wake the pup. He was in his boxers. A pair of shorts and a T-shirt were on his dresser, and he pulled these on, the knocking steady, insistent. Still, Frank slept on.

Clay slipped quietly through the open bedroom door, pulling it shut behind him, and padded across the outer room to the door. It was still dark outside as he opened the door, a faint recollection of being in a fight starting to filter into his consciousness, enough so that he expected it to be the police there to arrest him. Or worse, four cutlass-wielding Buccaneers. Yet, he didn't bother to grab his Glock or check the landing to see who was there, but just threw the door open in irritation.

"What in the H-E-double-hockey-sticks are you doing, Clay?"

It was Grandpops.

In all his silver fox glory, wearing a ten-thousand-dollar suit, his gray beard tailored to a polished point matching his carefully styled hair. His blue eyes blazed and a faint smile shone from his ivory teeth.

"You're dead," Clay said.

Grandpops laughed, a rich baritone of a boom, and pushed his way past. "Yes, I know, but you're not."

"What are you doing here?"

"Picking up the pieces," Grandpops said. "Putting things right."

"What do you mean?"

"You got any good scotch? Whiskey? Bourbon? Rye?"

Clay stepped to the kitchen and plucked the handle of Glenlivet from the counter. It was maybe a quarter full. Grandpops pulled a glass from a cupboard, the handle from Clay, and poured a bit of the brown liquor. He raised the glass to his lips, leaned his head back, shooting the drink back with gusto.

"Cheese and crackers! That was good," he said.

It seemed that this version of Grandpops had been stolen from some idyllic television show like Leave it to Beaver, *and not the real Gene Wolfe, who was not concerned about throwing the occasional cuss word around.*

Grandpops turned to the sink and went about pouring the Glenlivet down the drain.

"What? Wait. What are you doing?" Clay stood frozen watching.

"Whatever I want," Grandpops said. "I'm dead, remember? One of the perks. But as I said, you're not."

"What's that supposed to mean?"

"That you should stop acting the son of a monkey, is what it means." Grandpops set the empty half-gallon bottle back on the counter. "And start being a real-live human being again."

"It's my fault you're dead," Clay said. "That arrow should've been mine."

"Nonsense, my boy. I was the target, right as rain, and now I'm gone. But you're still here."

"I never should've gone after them like I did."

Grandpops laughed again, but the richness was gone, replaced by a hollow-tinny sound. "The day you stop doing the right thing is the day it is your fault. Don't give me that guff. Time to get back on the hoss, Clay."

"Why?"

Grandpops started to shimmer slightly like the wisp of a campfire and his voice grew fainter. "You know how the elderly go around telling you to not get old and some wisecracker has to say, 'sure beats the alternative'? Well, let me tell you, that isn't the truth, not at all. I moved on when the time was right, before my body and my mind began to fail me completely. It was time, Clay, for me to go. But not you. It is not time for you to go, so stop your doggone crying and get back on the hoss. You got more living to do."

Clay woke with Frank licking his face. The vision of Grandpops strong in his mind. It was time to get back on the 'hoss.' He rolled out of bed and noticed a wet spot. Not the pup's fault. In the kitchen there was an empty handle of Glenlivet sitting next to a forlorn glass.

A cup of coffee through the Keurig while he pulled on shorts and a T-shirt. The sun was just up over the ocean as they went out back to let Frank explore and get some energy out, as well as some pees and poops.

The good thing about day drinking was that it often led to an early bedtime, Clay thought, allowing one to get up the next day and get an early start on things. He touched his face and winced, and the details of the night came filtering back as if through a dark tunnel. Cloutier for lunch with beers. The Seal Bar with too many well-poured browns. Up to Lucky Linda's and feeling the heat, knocking them back, chatting with Murphy. The bikers in the corner. What was their gang name? The Buccaneers. Clay smirked. It was like that *Wild Hogs* movie where a bunch of middle-aged guys pose as a biker gang and get in over their heads. He touched his jaw gingerly. Maybe these guys weren't posers. He dimly remembered getting in a scuffle with them. Outnumbered, he'd succumbed to their onslaught and been in danger of being seriously maimed as he lay on the floor when Westy arrived. The beast. Everybody in town knew to steer clear of his buddy, Weston Beck. Now the Buccaneers knew it, too.

They'd scrammed out of there ahead of the police, the bikers melting into the night. How had Westy known to show up? Ah, yes, Murphy the interfering Irishman had texted. Something to the effect of 'come babysit Clay Wolfe'. This grated, and Clay's cheeks flushed in embarrassment.

He couldn't remember if he'd come home and finished the bottle of brown liquor, dumped it away, or perhaps Grandpops had really paid him a visit.

His thoughts drifted back over the past months. He'd not been a very good friend to anybody. As a matter of fact, Clay Wolfe had become the charity case of his group, treading water, ignoring lifeline after lifeline they threw him, waiting to die. What would Grandpops think of him if he were still here? He'd most likely box Clay's ears and kick his ass. What would his parents think of the man he'd become?

He fished his phone out of his pocket. Texted Westy. **Thanks bud. I owe you one.**

His phone buzzed back. **Time to get back on the hoss, hoss.**
Yep.

"Come on, Frank," Clay said. "Time to become a real person again."

Clay showered, shaved, and applied salve to a few wounds. Then he found some clean shorts and a Bonobos shortsleeve, collared shirt that was his pride and worn only for special casual situations. His head was still a bit fuzzy, but downing four cups of water, and getting another cup of coffee to go was already clearing the cobwebs. The sky was a sparkling sapphire, and he slipped his Ray-Bans on as he carried Frank down the stairs.

There was a market just outside of town on Route 29. Clay put Frank in a reusable grocery bag and went in shopping, dropping items down with the puppy before pulling him out and carrying him on his shoulder as the bag filled, thinking it a poor idea to let the pup run loose in a grocery store. He got bacon, red potatoes, an onion, garlic cloves, mushrooms, eggs, English muffins, and orange juice.

As the top was off the Jeep, he tucked the reusable bag down behind the driver's seat on the floor.

Back in the Jeep, he texted Baylee. Hey. What's up? Can I come over and make you breakfast?

Mm. Came the almost immediate reply. What for?

Because I want to.

When?

10 min.

There was a pause. The little dots on his phone danced and then came her reply. If you don't mind that I'm in my bathrobe just halfway through my first cup of coffee.

Mm. On my way.

On the short drive out to Spruce Island, Clay's mind was filled with images of Baylee springing from the fabric of his memories, emotions, hopes, desires.

Baylee walking into his office just a few days after he hung out his P.I. shingle in town. Dark eyes guarded but confident. A bit on edge. With a hunger to her. There'd never been any doubt about hiring her.

He'd made her a partner and brought her on as another investigator after she'd recovered from a drug dependence caused by killing her husband, or maybe it was the abuse that he'd heaped on her before she shot him in the head that had turned her to anti-depressants.

Visions of the night they'd kissed—on the verge of more when Clive had interrupted them—flittered through his mind, and then Victoria had come up pregnant, bringing their ardor to a grinding halt.

Holding her hand at Grandpop's funeral.

Baylee was standing in her doorway holding a cup of coffee in hand and wearing a jade silk robe with peonies and butterflies decorating it. Her feet were bare. She'd made no attempt to straighten her tangled, honey hair. He liked that. Didn't her hair used to be darker? Clay mused, shaking his head. It was time to pay closer attention to the important details of life.

"What brings Gordon Ramsay to my doorstep this morning?" she asked.

Clay set Frank on the ground who ran toward Baylee, tumbled up the two steps, and past her into the house, presumably in search of Flash.

"If I wasn't quite sure before, I now know what brings me to the threshold of your abode," Clay said, grabbing the groceries. He walked to the bottom of the steps and stopped, looking up at her in the entranceway.

"I do believe you've added a bruise or two and a scrape to your face, Mr. Wolfe."

"Just some old Buccaneer friends, Miss Baker," he said. "Roughhousing around, you know."

"What are you making me?"

Clay let his eyes drift from her eyes down the green-shaded robe to her perfect feet. "Good ole fashion bacon, eggs, and potatoes."

"I was hoping for waffles."

"I'll make you waffles tomorrow," Clay said.

"So this is going to be a regular occurrence?"

"I hope so."

"Come on in." Baylee turned and walked back into the house. "Can I help?"

"I've got it."

Clay went about making breakfast while Baylee sat at the table finishing her coffee. He shared about his tussle. She told him about blowing her cover with Tobias. Frank gave up trying to get Flash to play after a bit and explored until finally curling up and going to sleep.

After they ate, they took the dogs, as well as Ollie the cat, down behind the house to the ocean. There was a bench swing suspended from the branch of a mighty oak tree just feet from the water, and they sat while Ollie hunted, Flash lay in the sun, and Frank tried to make sense of the gentle waves lapping the small pebble beach area.

"You seem different," Baylee said.

Clay shook his head. "I've been in a fog. Knowing that you're in a dark place isn't quite the same as having the ability to escape it."

Baylee nodded. "I know."

Clay looked at her. She did know. She'd been there. "This morning I woke up, and the sun was shining for the first time in a year."

"Why?"

Clay shrugged. "I don't know. It could've been Grandpops coming by in my sleep last night and boxing my ears for me."

"I been wondering when Gene would come by and give you a kick in the ass."

Clay chuckled. "It's like my eyes are open again. The black cloud—"

"Gone," Baylee said. "What do you see?"

Clay chuckled. "All that I have, I suppose. First off, I saw Frank, as he was licking my face."

Baylee chuckled. "He's been good for you?"

"The best. And I was in my bed, in my town, a place I love. I thought of Crystal down in the big house, and grinned, thinking about the first day she came into the office to hire us to investigate who was dealing heroin in Port Essex. She was living in a trailer working at the laundromat folding clothes. I don't think she's changed a whit but now she runs the office with an iron fist and lives in Grandpop's house."

"She sure hasn't cleaned up her mouth at all," Baylee said. "She still curses like a fucking sailor."

"Yes, she does." Clay chuckled. "Then I thought about all the adventures I had with Westy before we went off in different directions after graduating high school." Clay was intensely aware that his leg was pressed against Baylee's. He put his arm around her shoulders and drew her tight, and she melted against him.

"You, Cloutier, Murphy, Westy—you've all been looking out for me this past year, and I've been oblivious to all of it."

"Is that all the thoughts you had of me, Mr. Wolfe?"

Clay had been watching a sailboat tack across the harbor but now he turned his head. Baylee's face was just inches from his own. Her eyes were swirling caramel against her olive-bronze skin. A tuft of honey hair creased her forehead to her cheek.

"No," he said huskily.

"Do tell, Mr. Wolfe, what thoughts have you had of me?"

Clay noticed that Baylee's lips were slightly parted, her teeth very white. "I breathed every image of you I've ever had," he said. "My memories included not only when we were together, but my thoughts of you when we were apart, and I even imagined this moment, right here and now."

"You did, did you?" Baylee said. Her tongue slid over her lips, leaving them glistening in its wake. "Tell me what happens next, then, will you, Mr. Wolfe?"

Clay tilted his head the last fraction of an inch and kissed her. It was pain and torment and euphoria and rapture all at the same time. His hand cupped her neck as his lips met hers in passion, as their tongues danced and explored.

His other hand slid inside her Kimono, under the T-shirt she wore underneath, grasping her breast lightly, his thumb sliding over her nipple teasingly.

Baylee moaned, her arm curled around him in a headlock, her other hand behind him, sliding up his back, her nails grazing the skin deliciously.

It wasn't until a bit later that they made it back to the house, where they engaged in round two, a less frantic, more leisurely lovemaking that increased in tempo eventually to the same frenzied passion and exaltation as before.

Chapter 10

Clay and Baylee were already in the office Monday morning when Crystal came in just before nine. They'd not gotten much sleep, but Clay felt invigorated like he hadn't for quite some time, possibly ever.

"You better have brought Frank in with you today," Crystal said by way of greeting as she entered their office. "There you are, you little fucking cutie-pie."

Frank tumbled across the room and onto her foot, biting the top of her Crocs. She had on a brownish orange patterned top with spaghetti straps that made Clay think of a tablecloth. At least it was a step up from the florescent tube tops she used to wear to work, he thought with a wry grin he hid with his hand.

"Good morning to you, Crystal," Baylee said.

"Yeah, yeah." Crystal picked up Frank and nuzzled him with her face.

"You have a good weekend?" Clay asked.

Crystal looked away from Frank toward Clay and Baylee. "Sure. Where were you all day yesterday? Your Jeep was gone early and never came back."

That wasn't quite true, Clay thought, as he had gone home this morning a couple hours earlier for a shower and a change of clothes and a shave. "I was—"

"You two finally did it, didn't you?" Crystal said, her voice incredulous. "About fucking time."

"What?" Baylee said.

"Don't be an asshole, you two screwed. It's all over your faces. Halle-fucking-lujah."

Clay shook his head and chuckled. "What do you say about getting out of the office for a bit?"

Crystal walked over and sat down with Frank nestled on her lap. "You trying to get me out of here so you two can do the bam-bam in the ham?"

"I don't even know what that means," Clay said. "But no, that's not why. We need you to do some investigative work."

"Now you're talking," Crystal said. "I been wondering when you were gonna tap my hidden talents as a sleuth."

"You know the case Baylee was working?" Clay asked. "Following Tobias Yates around to see if she could catch him with his pants down and report back to his wife, Gina?"

"Yeah, sure. Gina filled out the paperwork with me. Plus, we go to the same yoga studio, nail salon, and hair stylist."

Clay grinned. The thought of Crystal doing yoga increased the grin to a chuckle. "Yeah, well, Baylee seems to have blown her cover."

"Yeah?" Crystal asked. "How the fuck you do that?"

"He may've spotted me in the lobby of The Port in a Storm," Baylee said.

"And then she punched him in the neck," Clay said.

Crystal chortled. "That might've done it."

"According to Gina, he arrived home last night," Baylee said. "She should be here any moment for an update."

As if on cue, the outer door opened with a jingle. Baylee stood and went to greet her, returning a minute later with Gina in tow. She gestured for her to sit next to Crystal and went back behind the desk.

Clay hid another grin as he looked across at the two women. Crystal in her tablecloth top, most likely from Target, to Gina's get-up, dressed like she was ready to go yachting. She had on a tan turtleneck that matched the light jacket and billowing pants made of some breezy material all under a floppy straw hat.

Crystal's hair was dark, curled and big on her head, while Gina's was straight, falling down in front of her just to the top of her breasts, a gleaming golden yellow.

"What have you found out?" Gina asked once she was settled.

"I called to let you know that Tobias did not go to the airport," Baylee said. "And that he went to The Port in a Storm Inn, met with two gentlemen, and then went out on a boat."

"Just him and the captain, you said." Gina sat with her legs slightly crossed, her back straight, and her eyes attentive.

"I spoke with the captain who said that sometimes another woman goes out with them, a woman by the name of Rose. It did not seem to be a pleasure outing, but the captain was tight-lipped and wouldn't share anything further. I did find that Tobias was also staying at the inn, but he appeared to be alone. When I followed him out, he caught on to me, and we had a bit of an altercation."

"Altercation?"

"She punched him in the fucking Adam's apple," Crystal said.

Gina looked sideways at her and raised an eyebrow. "What was your name again?"

"Crystal. Crystal Landry."

"Crystal is going to be taking over the surveillance of your husband," Clay said.

"Did you have a conversation with him about his weekend?" Baylee asked.

Gina tore her gaze from Crystal, who she seemed to be fascinated by. "Not so much. He said the conference was a terrible bore and not something worth wasting my time on."

"So, he is most certainly lying," Baylee said. "But we need to find proof of another woman, if there truly is one."

"You don't believe that he's having an affair?" Gina asked.

Baylee shrugged. "Maybe. But there's more going on than just an affair. Port Essex isn't that big of a place. If he was meeting up with a woman, he'd be taking her down to Portland. Too risky to be seen around town here. I think it may have to do with that boat, and what exactly they're doing on it. It's a salvage boat, that much we know."

* * *

If a passer-by had come upon the five men standing by the ocean in a small turn off in East Essex and looked closely, he would've noticed straight off that one of these men was not like the others, a hipster dandy surrounded by rough trade. The man had black hair pushed back from his forehead, tousled on top, and square, black-rimmed glasses. He had a carefully manicured beard of like color. His shirt was blue with a collar, rolled at the sleeves, with white snowflakes adorning it. He was of medium height and build.

In a different, more urban, environment, he'd blend in like a chameleon, but his hipster look did not jive with the four men he was meeting with, all of whom wore leather or denim vests with jeans, had tattoos, and rode motorcycles. Their facial hair was almost identical—shaven on the cheekbones, a mustache with a thin strip of beard hanging from their chins like a limp beaver tail. Two of them had bandanas. Three of them were thick through the body, while one was thin with a sneer on his face.

They'd met at a small turn-off on the rocky shores of East Essex, and they were the only ones in sight. This was not the tourist mecca that Port Essex was.

"What did you think you were doing?" the hipster, who they knew as Socrates, asked.

"Nothing. We was having a drink, is all." The spokesperson of the bikers, who had a nose like the edge of an axe, shuffled his feet angrily.

"How about the night before?" Socrates asked.

"What about the night before?" Axe-Edge Nose asked.

Socrates stood casually facing the four men, but his eyes were blazing, belying his relaxed posture. "When you braced him and the woman waving cutlasses?"

"How'd you know 'bout that?"

"I know everything," Socrates said.

"We thought it'd be a bit of fun to throw a scare into the fellow and his broad, is all," Axe-Edge Nose said.

"You are not paid to think. You are paid to do as you are told."

"We was letting him know he best be toeing the line, is all."

"Again, you will do as you are told. Not a bit more. I do not need a bunch of idiots messing things up."

A man with an octopus tattoo trailing down his arm stepped forward. "Don't be calling us idiots, man."

Socrates held his gaze from a distance of no more than two feet. "What would you have me call you? Imbeciles? Morons? Nitwits?"

The man's face turned red, and he went to shove Socrates, who deflected the man's arms, stuck two fingers into his throat, and backhanded him, knocking him to the ground, all without shifting his own feet.

"You will do as told or you will be disposed of," Socrates said. "Do you understand?"

Octopus Arm was on his knees, gagging. The other three shuffled their feet, astonishment on their faces.

"I asked a question." Socrates did not lift his voice.

"Yep, got you, sure thing," the men all said.

"You need to leave the Town Motel. I cannot have you found and interrogated by this Wolfe character."

"The dude's a drunk," Axe-Edge Nose said. "Heavy into the brown sauce."

"And his buddy?"

"The one who came and bailed him out the other night?"

"Weston Beck," Socrates said. "Two stretches overseas as a SEAL. Heavily decorated."

"Shit. He was some badass," one of the men said.

"Where we supposed to go?"

"I rented you a farmhouse on the outskirts of town," Socrates said.

"There's a barn. Keep your bikes in there. Don't go into town except for gas. No bars."

"What d'you mean by that?" Axe-Edge Nose asked. "We ain't supposed to go out?"

"You stay there, inside the house, until you hear differently from me."

"What about food?"

"Booze?"

"Broads?"

Socrates smiled lazily, but the emotion didn't reach his eyes. "The place is stocked with food and beer. Keep the drinking within limits. You need to be ready when I need you."

"There was a broad at that joint last night who I was hoping to see. It can't hurt to just go down there all on the quiet and see if she wants to do the Devil's dance with me."

Socrates looked at the man who had a neck wider than his head. "I will supply you with some ladies to keep you company. You keep your head down. Until I call you."

*　*　*

Andy Kozak and Dannie Cox had come into the office at 10:00 a.m. on the dot and were now seated in the chairs across the desk from Clay and Baylee. Crystal had gone off to do surveillance on Tobias Yates, a welcome reprieve from the cussing, even if Crystal did try to clean up her language around clients. 'Try' was the operative word there.

Clay thought that Andy looked quite a bit like Ted Lasso from the Apple TV program, especially the mustache. It might've also been the blue sweater he wore over a white-collared shirt. Bit hot for that, Clay thought, but there was a cool breeze coming off the ocean.

Dannie was staring out the window over Clay's shoulder, looking out onto Essex Harbor as if she might spot the missing treasure. Her hair was blonder than a few days back when she'd first come into the office, or so Clay thought, and he realized that she was quite beautiful, another thing his lethargic self of the previous week had missed.

It was like life had been breathed back into Clay's body, mind, and soul. He was again appreciating the little things in life. The diamond-tipped waves of Essex Harbor, the shops of Commercial Way where he knew most of the owners, the fishing boats going and coming with their catches, the very blueness of the sky, and a pretty woman. Best of all was the stunning, clever, and scintillating woman at his side.

Frank, the puppy, curled on top of his foot and fast asleep, was also a piece of life to cherish, a palmful of enjoyment that made the world a special place. So many things to enjoy, and so little time. It was time to start living again.

Clay had done precious little research on the treasure of Black Sam Bellamy and where it may've ended up, if it indeed existed. He'd been too busy drinking his supposed woes to the bottom of a bottle. Luckily, Crystal had done a bit of digging, sharing what she had with him before going off to tail Tobias.

"What have you found?" Andy asked.

"It's a bit confusing," Clay said. "Are you here for long this time?"

"We took care of what we had to and are here for the duration," Andy said. "Or, at least, until we find the treasure."

"Where are you staying?" Baylee asked.

"Place called Cuddy Cabins," Andy said. "You know them?"

"Sure," Baylee said. "Out past Koasek Park. How do you like them?"

"Little rustic for my taste," Dannie said. "But clean and nice enough."

"What have you found out?" Andy asked.

Clay lay a map of Port Essex including the surrounding area and the harbor on the desk and pushed it across for Andy and Dannie to see. "In your letter, Black Sam states that the treasure is in the village of Winnegance of the Abenaki people. He also states that it is just past their village. Contradicting statements, to be sure, but the real problem is that the village of Winnegance was here." Clay pointed at a spot on the map very close to where they were now, the Abenaki and the English both finding the area first known as Winnegance before eventually becoming Port Essex to be the prime spot for settlement.

"And that is a problem why?" Andy asked.

"The map that supposedly came from Black Sam along with the letter says that the village of Winnegance is on the Sibosek River. Here." Clay moved his finger slightly, but a distance of almost ten miles in reality. "The Winnegance village was not on the Sibosek River."

"The treasure could be just about anywhere," Dannie said.

"The problem deepens," Clay said. "The English bought the land from the Abenaki in 1666 and made their first settlement here."

"Forty years before Black Sam visited the Abenaki and hid his treasure near their village," Andy said.

"But, in King William's War in 1689, the English were driven out, and did not return for forty years," Clay said. "That time period is a blank, as far as I can tell. I haven't been able to find any information at all." Or, he thought, Crystal hadn't been able to dig anything up.

"But the Abenaki could've returned during that time," Dannie said. "And been here when Black Sam sailed into port looking for a place to hide his treasure."

Clay nodded. "Yes."

"Then that could be anywhere along the coast here," Andy said.

"The distance from the original village of Winnegance over to the mouth of the Sibosek River is ten miles," Clay said. "I'd estimate that, given the geography," he traced the jagged coastline, peninsulas, inlets, islands, and more, "that it could be anywhere along a distance of about 120 miles of shoreline."

"Son of a..." Andy said.

"And, if Black Sam did indeed come to this area and hid a treasure, we have no idea how far up the Sibosek River he went. Let's say it's somewhere between here and Wiscasset, that's another twelve miles or so of shore to explore."

"You're saying we're screwed?" Dannie said.

"I would concentrate our efforts in three spots," Clay said. He put his finger on the map. "Black Sam said he sailed up the Sibosek River. He could've been wrong about what body of water he was on. Just west of the original Winnegance village, here, is another body of water that is actually considered a tidal pond. Barlow Pond. Black Sam could've been mistaken. As this is where the original Winnegance village was, it'd be my guess that they'd have returned here when the English were driven out."

"And the other two?" Andy asked.

Clay moved his finger on the map. "The Dunbar River, here, or a little further west, the actual Sibosek River."

"That's a lot of territory to cover," Dannie said, her eyes following the rivers north.

"First, we explore Barlow Pond," Clay said. "If we can't find any of the landmarks, we'll move onto the mouth of the Sibosek River, and then, if necessary, the Dunbar River."

"We're going to need a boat," Andy said.

"I've got a friend," Clay said.

Chapter 11

Murphy had told Westy that the bikers were staying at the Town Motel just outside of Port Essex on Route 29. After he'd slung Clay over his shoulder and carried him out of Lucky Linda's two nights ago, his friend had babbled to him about how these four men had waved cutlasses and blunderbusses at Clay and Baylee the night before. Only he wasn't sure it was them. But he thought it was. Only they'd been wearing masks. Skull masks.

The long and short of it was that Clay had been drunk. Again. And nothing he said could be taken to heart, except that Westy knew Clay well enough to know that, drunk or sober, his instincts were pretty darn good. He'd been on his way over to visit and find out more, but as he drove past Baylee's home on the way off island, Westy had noticed Clay's Jeep parked in the driveway. Interesting, he thought, very interesting indeed.

As Baylee lived only about a mile from Westy, he'd driven past a few more times that day, the last being as the sun was setting just before nine o'clock, and the Jeep hadn't moved. In the morning, as he drove into town, bent upon paying a visit to the Town Motel, the Jeep was gone. Whether Clay left during the night or early this morning, it was hard to tell, but Westy knew in his gut that it'd finally happened. Clay and Baylee had hooked up.

All the more reason, Westy figured, to pay a visit to the bikers who'd threatened them and ask them kindly to leave town. There'd been times over the past year when Westy had thought of smacking

Clay upside the head and telling him to sort himself out. Gene Wolfe's death had been devastating, and Westy understood his buddy's pain, but at some point, the demons needed to be dealt with and some kind of normal life resumed.

It was a good sign that Clay's Jeep had been at Baylee's house all the previous day. As long as Clay wasn't clinging to her as his only lifeline. Dependent on others for happiness was not something that Westy would recommend as being healthy. But he knew that his own wife, Faith, relied on him for safety and stability. He, in turn, counted on her to smooth his rough edges, comfort him through the dark nights when he had a nightmare. Or nightmares. Without Faith, he'd have succumbed to them long ago.

In other words, with the right person, it could be the healthy kick necessary, and Westy knew in his heart of hearts that Clay and Baylee were destined to be together.

The horror that still visited Westy, some thirteen years after the actual events, dated back to a particular mission into the Central Afghan mountains, South of Kabul, back in 2009. He was part of the DEVGRU SEAL operation, a highly classified group tasked with seeking out terrorists and the enemy before they could strike a blow against the U.S. Westy had seen a great deal of action as part of this group, better known as SEAL Team Six. Assassinations, extractions, elimination. He'd killed more than his fair share of Taliban, and possibly civilians, it often being difficult to tell the difference when dropped into enemy territory in confusing circumstances.

This particular objective was to capture and extract a high-ranking Taliban in the Central Afghan mountains. Akhtar Nemat. The man was hiding out in a village, termed a compound by the top brass, and planning an attack on U.S. forces. Nemat had been a key player in the Balamorghab ambush in 2008 and was now said to be plotting something even bigger and more nefarious.

Eliminating him wouldn't solve the problem. What he knew about the planned operation was the essential piece to the puzzle so that the assault could be averted, and American lives saved. He needed to be taken alive. This was not an unusual task. What was unique about this situation was that the man was holed up in the center of the village with his four wives and seventeen children. Extracting him cleanly was an incredibly delicate task and would require absolute secrecy and surprise.

Westy was the troop chief of the Purple Squadron's People Eaters, named after the 1958 Sheb Wooley song, rather than any predilection for cannibalism. Two of the three troops provided support while Westy led the sixteen men of the third troop in the assault on the compound where Nemat was living. They went in at the witching hour, 3:00 a.m., first taking out the outside guards without waking the village or alerting the compound. Or so they thought. When Barney Troop blew the door, Westy was the first one through, leading by example and not by command.

He went down a short hallway and into the main living area of the fortress. Akhtar Nemat was not in the room, but two women and nine children were. Westy had wondered ever since how the man chose which of his wives and children were expendable. They were all strapped with crude vests made of dynamite. One of them must have been wired, as it exploded, the explosion rippling through the room and onto the others, the vests going off like a string of firecrackers, *pop-pop-pop*. One right after another, so close together it was hard to tell the separation.

Westy lost a valuable moment as he froze at the horrific scene when he should've been prone on the floor or back out through the door. It was only after the first body part struck him in the face that he went down. Somehow, the explosions left him physically uninjured.

Within seconds it was over, and he struggled to his feet, ears ringing, sweeping arms, legs, hands, feet, heads, and pools of mush and blood that had rained down on him like some macabre hailstorm of human flesh. There was a girl, perhaps seven years old, whose vest had not detonated, but the damage had been done by the other explosions surrounding her, leaving her limbless, somehow propped upright on her torso, not yet dead, as her screams pierced the ringing in his ears.

Westy shot her in the forehead to stop her pain and then made his way to the door at the back that led further into the abode. There were three men in that room, none of them Nemat, but all with rifles. For the first time in his life, Westy relished killing living beings. When he got to the bedroom, Nemat was there with a pistol held to the head of a toddler who looked barely old enough to walk. There was no way that the man was walking out of that compound, hostage or not, and Westy reacted, lunging forward in a desperate attempt to knock the barrel of the gun aside. Nemat smiled at Westy as he pulled the trigger, the soft skull of the infant bursting like a ripe melon.

They captured Akhtar Nemat, and, angrier than he had ever been before, it took everything he had to not wring the man's neck. There'd been a point where he could've shot and killed Nemat, perhaps saving the child, but the orders had been to take the man alive. It still weighed heavily on Westy's conscience.

Westy never knew what had become of Nemat, or if he'd provided information that saved American lives—or not. In the deepest recesses of Westy's soul, he hoped, not prayed—for he never prayed again after that day—but hoped that the man had spilled his guts and ended up at Gitmo, which was Hell on earth.

But it was not the last child killed who haunted his nightmares. It was the limbless girl screaming, the one he shot and put out of her misery, who woke Westy up sweating in the middle of the night.

Westy had never taken anything for granted in his life, but ever since that day, he'd treated human life like the precious yet fragile entity that it was. He did not take lightly the existence of his wife and son, nor that of his friends. The threat to Clay and Baylee had to be rooted out and stomped on. Hard.

Unfortunately, the man at the desk said that the four bikers had checked out of the motel the previous day. The clerk, who was also the owner, had been happy to see them go as they'd been irritating to the other guests, noisy at night, and rude during the day. He didn't know where they'd gone, only that they were no longer there.

When Westy had asked for their names and addresses, the man had started to bluster that he was unable to do that. After a bit, though, he caught the look on Westy's silent face and had agreed to share the asked-for information. They'd paid in cash, as well as put a large security deposit down, claiming to have no credit cards.

As Westy climbed into his Ford F-150, his phone buzzed with a text from Clay. Friends from New York want to do some treasure hunting tomorrow. Maybe for a few days. You feel like taking us out?

Westy put the truck in gear, called Clay, and put the phone on his lap with the speaker on as he drove off.

"Westy," Clay answered.

"They paying me?"

"Two bills a day."

Westy grunted. "Barely pays for the gas."

"They claim to be strapped for cash. I can cut you in for my percentage of the treasure once we find it."

Westy laughed. "Whatever. You thinking the *Gordana* or the *Freya*?"

"Barlow Pond tomorrow. Let's take the *Freya*. I'm thinking a sailboat would be less conspicuous cruising the coastline than a fishing boat."

"Got you. Saw your Jeep over to Baylee's yesterday."

"Did you, now?"

"A few times. Looks like you spent the whole day there. Maybe the night."

"You know me and Baylee are good friends. And partners."

"You got anything you wanna tell me, *hoss*?"

There was a long silence before Clay answered. "Eight tomorrow morning. Your house or Knox Wharf?"

"I'll pick you all up tomorrow at the wharf." Westy cleared his throat. "Unless you want me to pick you and Baylee up first, out behind her house on my way into town." Westy kept his sailboat moored at his house during the summer and would be going right past Baylee's house.

Clay chuckled. "We'll see you at the wharf."

*　*　*

"What'd he say," Baylee asked, "that made you laugh?"

"Seems he saw my Jeep out to your house yesterday." Clay slid his cellphone onto the desk. "And seemed to be drawing his own conclusions as to what we might've been doing."

"Mm. Did you mention how many times we did what he was assuming?"

"I'd hate to besmirch your reputation." Clay chuckled. "Besides, he wouldn't believe me if I told him."

"Yeah, best you keep that to yourself, anyhow," Baylee said. "I would hate to have my reputation besmirched."

"I did tell all the boys down to the Seal Bar all about it," Clay said, chuckling. "They didn't believe me, much like nobody ever believed in my Canadian girlfriend back in high school."

Baylee put her hand on Clay's knee and slid it up his inner thigh. "You were quite impressive, Mr. Wolfe. Hard to believe you're heading toward forty years of age. Seems you have the vitality of a much younger man, indeed."

Clay reached out, cupping the back of Baylee's neck, pulling their rolling chairs tightly together as he kissed her. She slid onto his lap, straddling him, her hands on his cheeks as she pressed her lips, face, and body passionately into him.

Clay nuzzled his lips down to her neck, and she moaned. "You bring out the young whippersnapper in me, that's for sure," he said.

Baylee sat up straighter, pushing his face between her breasts as she stroked his short hair. "How about we get that young whippersnapper out to play?"

Clay ran one hand up her blouse and unsnapped her bra as his other hand descended inside of her panties to grasp her buttocks. "You don't suppose Crystal will be stopping by, do you?"

Baylee reached her hand down the front of his pants to fondle him. "I hope not."

"How about you lock the front door, and I'll check in with Crystal," Clay said.

Crystal replied that she was bored to fucking death sitting outside the office of Tobias Yates' tech company and wouldn't be back to the office that day. Baylee locked the door.

There was a delicious deliriousness to their desire, Clay mused, as Baylee walked back into the inner office shutting the door behind her. Their words and actions would've been something they mocked if it were in a movie or some Netflix series, but now, in this present moment, he was trapped in a role he never wanted to leave, that of Baylee Baker's lover.

It'd been far too long coming—the seed planted that first day she'd walked into the office a few years back looking for a job. That genesis had sprouted, burgeoned, and grown ripe as the two of them flirted, advancing and retreating like two enemies looking for weaknesses. And they'd found those flaws, the fragility of their inner selves terrified of entering into a relationship that could potentially end in a heartbreak they couldn't handle.

There'd been moments, oh, had there been moments, Clay thought, but for one reason or another, they had never been given in to their desires, but had always managed to curb their appetites and tamp down their longings. But that period of unfulfilled craving had come to an end. Baylee stepped back into the inner office, pulling the door shut behind her. They were on the carnival ride now, and there was no stopping it.

* * *

Crystal had been excited to get into the field and do some real investigative work. That was seven hours ago, and all she'd done was sit in her parked car across the street from the offices of Yates Tech, Tobias Yates' company. She'd recently purchased a laptop, or rather, Wolfe & Baker Private Investigations had bought her one. She had the seat pushed all the way back in her 1977 Firebird Trans Am, a recent purchase—the car she'd always dreamed of. It was black with gold flames on the hood and had a T-top, the identical model that Burt Reynolds had driven in *Smokey and the Bandit.*

The only way life could be better was if Burt, with his dancing eyes and bushy mustache, were sitting next to her in the car. Crystal had been thirteen when the movie came out, and she'd immediately fallen in love with Burt and imagined herself to be Sally Fields. Running away from her life and falling into the arms of a beautiful older man. That was not quite how things had turned out for her, but things were most definitely looking up. The job with Clay and Baylee, as well as their friendship, had been the turning point in an otherwise rocky journey through life.

And she'd found her beautiful older man in Gene Wolfe. That girlhood dream of being Sally Field being whisked off her feet had blossomed, that is, until he'd been killed the previous year by the bolt of a cross bow. Crystal shook her head, banishing those thoughts, and looked back at her laptop screen. Luckily, she'd been able to tap into somebody's wireless service. She'd been researching the Yates Tech Company and Tobias himself, but it was all a lot of gobbledygook to her. That is, until she clicked on the SoLo Do link that was one of the company's subsidiaries.

SoLo Do stood for Soft Love Dolls. The link connected Crystal to a page filled with realistic-looking women dolls with humongous breasts, all of whom had three usable orifices, amazing skin tones, sexy eyes, and, if the copy were to be believed, were perfect life partners for the solo man. Crystal laughed harshly. *Wow.* No wonder it was hard to find a man in today's world, she thought. For under ten thousand dollars you could pick your doll's height, face, hair—including pubic—breast size, nipple shape, skin tone, vagina, eye color, and more. For a bit more, you could get a woman with AI that could speak and vibrate her hips.

Crystal couldn't stop staring at the images of what was considered the perfect woman. Her own tight curls, the crow's feet branching from her eyes, the skin that did the opposite of glowing, her tiny breasts, and rail-thin body—all were laughable next to these statuesque goddesses. Fuck it, she thought, that was it. There was no chance that she'd ever meet a man at the age of fifty-seven, not when a programmable woman of epic proportions was available, one that didn't sass, talk back, or have an opinion. Just the way men wanted their women. She wondered if these soft love dolls could also cook and clean, but neither of those were particular strengths of Crystal's, so it didn't really matter.

It was time to do some recon. Crystal stepped out of the Trans Am, looking at the veins in her legs as she did so, the scuffed and worn New Balance shoes on her feet, and cursed again. Her only knowledge of sex dolls was of the blow-up variety, more of a gag gift than anything else, she figured. She didn't think that Tobias Yates had any idea of who she was, but just the same, she reached back into the car and pulled a baseball cap that said *Trailer Park Boys* from the back seat. Now she was, what was the word? Incognito. Totally fucking incognito.

The sign over the door said merely 'Yates Tech'. The lobby was fairly spartan in nature with two white modernistic looking couches and matching tables. There was a large screen television on both the left and right wall as Crystal came in. A busty woman with large lips in a business suit was talking about the robotics revolution. It took Crystal a few seconds to realize that she was, herself, robotic, and not a real human being.

There was a receptionist sitting behind a black laminate desk with glasses whose frames matched the countertop. She was also very busty, very young, and had a broad smile.

"Can I help you?" she asked.

Crystal stared at her. Took a few steps closer. It was hard to tell. "Are you real?"

The young lady laughed, the sound of wind chimes wafting from her mouth. "Yes, I am a real human. It's a brave new world out there, isn't it?"

Crystal had no idea what that meant. "Do you, uh… I was looking for… do you sell sex dolls?"

"Soft love dolls, you mean. We have only the best. Silicon and not TPE. Very lifelike. Robotics that include speaking, breathing, making appreciative noises, and gyrating are all upgrades, of course."

"Yeah, do you actually have… love dolls I could see?"

"Would you like to see our showroom?" The young lady stood, showcasing long legs and a trim waist that seemed insufficient to hold up her boobs.

Crystal giggled. "You have a showroom?"

The lady pursed her lips and frowned. "Yes. Right this way." She motioned for Crystal to follow her down a hallway behind the desk, opening the first door on the right.

Crystal followed her through the doorway and froze just a step inside. "Holy cock waffle."

The lady frowned at her again. There were armchairs, sofas, beanbags, and a futon with a variety of soft love dolls lounging in various stages of undress.

Crystal counted eleven figures, noting that one was a man in his twenties with washboard abs, a bit of scruff on his face, strong shoulders, and an impressive bulge in his jockey shorts.

"You have male… love dolls?" she said before she realized she was speaking.

The young lady smiled. "Just the one. That's Buck."

"Hmmm," Crystal said. Or maybe it was *Mmmm*.

Chapter 12

The *Freya* cut through the cloudy day with the small band of treasure hunters aboard. She was a forty-foot schooner named after the Norse goddess of love, fertility, sorcery, gold, war, and death. And she was Weston Beck's pride and joy.

Clay and Baylee, after their office interlude the day before, had spent the rest of the day mapping out a strategy for hunting the treasure. It wasn't a very good one as they were largely flying blind, but Clay had always been a believer in the adage that said if you move forward, the way will open.

Clay looked at his friend as he stood at the wheel, directing the *Freya* out of the harbor of Port Essex. This was most certainly where Westy was meant to be, on the high seas, his eyes on the horizon. He wore a faded T-shirt which his arms, shoulders, and chest threatened to burst out of.

There was a slight breeze in their face. Clay looked over at Baylee and smiled. Curled into her lap was Frank. Her hair was blowing in the wind, giving her a mysterious and sexy look that made him want her desperately. There'd be time for that. He thought back to the office sex the day before and then the night of discovery and play that was the delicious nectar of life. He wondered why they'd waited so long to get together and, at the same time, hoped that it wasn't too soon and before they were ready.

Next to Baylee were Andy and Dannie. Andy was looking nervous to be on a boat on the water. Clay guessed that he'd never been on a sailboat on the ocean. Maybe a massive Staten Island ferry lumbering through the water like a small floating village, but a schooner cutting through the waves was an entirely different experience. Dannie, on the other hand, seemed to be relishing the wind in her face as they cut through the sparkling water of Essex Harbor.

Clay's ruminations turned to the new information Crystal had discovered the day before, wondering if it was pertinent, or just titillating. She'd called all excited about her discovery that Tobias Yates made his money from selling love dolls. High-end sex dolls. Realistic in every way other than, perhaps, that they were more flawless than any woman could hope to be. And the newest, most expensive models, were robotic. They had the ability to speak, breathe, talk—and engage in various sexual motions as desired.

He'd brushed off Crystal's discovery and was regretting that this morning. It was not that it wasn't an intriguing tidbit, but did it really matter how Tobias Yates made his money? The truth was, when Crystal called, Clay was still floating in euphoria from making love with Baylee in the office, and he chided himself now for not giving Crystal the pat on the back that she deserved for her sleuthing.

When he told Baylee, she'd kicked herself for not uncovering that in the short time she'd been on the case. Clay took out his phone and texted Crystal that she was doing fantastic on her first foray into the field and to keep up the good work, making sure to pass on any new developments. He ended with a promise that the three of them would get together either later today or tomorrow to share notes.

There was a building excitement suffusing the sailboat. They were, after all, searching for pirate treasure. Clay hadn't felt this good in some time. He'd woken early to return home to shower and shave and give Frank a chance to play outside while he drank his coffee and checked email on his phone.

"Are we heading out to sea?" Andy asked.

"No," Westy said.

Clay smiled. His buddy was not the most talkative. "We have to go out and around Spruce Island to get to Barlow Pond. The bridge is too low for us to pass under."

"That's where I live," Baylee said, pointing to shore. "See that swinging bench behind that small beach? My house is right up the path behind there."

Clay thought about the lovemaking they'd engaged in on that swing just the day before yesterday. Wow, he thought, just the day before yesterday.

"That's a gorgeous spot," Dannie said. "You'll have to have us over for a cocktail some afternoon."

"For sure," Baylee said. "You can meet my dog and cat."

"Maybe after we find the fire opals," Andy said.

They all were quiet, contemplating their quest, as they sailed out past Westy's home on the end of the island. He didn't bother mentioning that it was where he lived.

"Have you looked into the laws about the recovery of treasure?" Clay asked. "I mean, I'm sure you have, but they seem quite complicated."

"The Treasure Trove laws give the ownership of found riches to the finder," Andy said. "And Maine is one of the states that adheres to that."

"At this time, however, that only applies to gold, silver, or paper money," Baylee said.

"The intention of the law includes gemstones," Dannie said.

"The laws are vague concerning trespassing," Clay said. "And Maine has also passed legislation that half of found treasure belongs to the township where it is found."

"Not to mention taxes that will be assessed on this found treasure," Baylee said.

"Only if we report the discovery," Dannie said quietly. "Then all the complications become moot."

Clay was fairly certain that not reporting found treasure would be breaking the law, but he wasn't aware of how serious those consequences would be. This made him think of Grandpops. The silver-haired fox had been one of the best legal minds in Maine, if not New England, and had always been his go-to for legal questions. He'd tried to dig into the convoluted language of understanding found treasure in the state of Maine, but every new passage seemed to contradict the previous, and the whole exercise had left him shaking his head.

"The Winnegance village was located roughly off to our right, just ahead there," Baylee said, pointing. They'd reached the mouth of Barlow Pond, a tidal body of water that was as much an inlet as a pond.

"And we're looking for a rock formation that looks like a church bell," Andy said.

"Kind of like trying to imagine clouds into specific shapes," Westy said. "More creativity than reality."

They cruised the shoreline of Barlow Pond, first up the right side, around the back, and down the far side. They determined there were three possible rock formations that could be considered in the shape of a church bell. The directions then stated to go around the corner, climb to the top of the bank, and find a pine tree taller than all the rest, back toward the village at a hundred steps. Clay doubted very much that the tallest pine tree from 1717 was still standing.

They decided that traveling back down Barlow Pond a hundred steps was the wisest course of action. Going slightly inland. The map then directed them to go twenty paces back toward the river which, in this case, was actually a tidal pond, and look for a rock shaped like a heart. A granite boulder. The five of them fanned out looking for anything that might resemble the shape of a heart. At the first stop, they came across seven possibilities, but upon wrestling the boulders loose, found no catacombs underneath.

As they crowded into the dingy to go back to the sailboat on their way to the second possible rock formation shaped like a church bell, Clay looked at the time. Two p.m. It was going to be a long and frustrating day at this rate.

He pulled out his phone and texted Cloutier asking if she'd be willing to get together later to talk about the article she'd written a few years back. It looked like they were flying blind and would need more information. It was one thing to be sifting through evidence, but quite another when it was over 300 years old. Clay had always liked history, but he was beginning to realize that he was outside the realm of his expertise.

*   *   *

Crystal called Gina Yates at 4:00 p.m. to ask the woman if they could get together to chat after Tobias, the husband, was home for the night.

Thus, after Crystal tailed Tobias to his home on Townsend Island just after 6:00 p.m., she circled back to the Pelican Perch. She secured a high-top table on the corner of the deck and ordered a margarita. She only had to wait twenty minutes for Gina, who'd told her husband she was picking up Thai takeout for their dinner, to show up.

Crystal waved her over. "Gina," she said as the woman walked up.

"I'll have a glass of chardonnay," Gina told the waiter as she sat down. "You're the receptionist who had me fill out the forms when I first came in to hire Wolfe & Baker to investigate my husband. Now, you're the P.I. in charge of my case. Odd."

"I am also the lead investigator for the firm, as well as tending to my administrative duties." This was a bit of a stretch, but she had been in the field before, and what was a title, really?

"Did you discover something about my husband?"

Crystal had never much believed in subtlety. "When you expressed concern that your husband might be having an affair, was that with a human being or a sex doll?"

Gina laughed gently. "You're referring to his company, I take it?"

"Yeah. SoLo Do. The soft love dolls that he makes to be fuck toys."

"Companions for the lonely, is what he says," Gina said, taking the arriving glass of wine and sipping from it. "But yes, you are right, they are fuck toys."

Inwardly, Crystal nodded. There was a bit of bite and toughness to Gina Yates. "So?"

"You're asking me if I hired your firm to investigate whether or not my husband is having an affair with one of his creations?" Gina leaned forward over the table. "Have you ever been married, Crystal?"

"Sure," Crystal said. She didn't mention she'd turned him into the police for dealing drugs, as much to protect their kids as to get rid of him. "What of it?"

"Did you own a vibrator at the time?"

"What?"

Gina smiled. "The question is simple. Did you own a vibrator at the time?"

"Yeah, I guess I did."

"And did your husband consider that cheating? That in your underwear drawer at the top of your dresser you had a sex toy to meet your sexual needs?"

Crystal thought back to the piece of shit who'd been her husband. The man who met few if any of her sexual needs, or any other needs for that matter. The man who'd occasionally hit her, threatened her children, and was usually too high on drugs to even engage in bad sex with her.

"The answer, Crystal," Gina said, "is that there is no real difference between the sex dolls my husband makes and a vibrator. For years, it's been acceptable for women to buy, own, and use a sex toy to achieve satisfaction, while men visit with prostitutes and mistresses for the same thing. If anything, my husband is merely leveling the playing field in his business practice. Does he bring his creations home? No. Would I be upset if he did? Not in the slightest. I'd be happy that I'd not have to succumb to his desires. I almost ordered his latest, Christine, as a birthday present for him a few months back."

"Because that was when you first became suspicious that he was cheating on you?" Crystal asked. She thought she remembered which doll was Christine. If she were right, it looked nothing like Gina, but had dark hair, was short, and had those humongous breasts.

A man came over and stood silently until they looked up at him. "Can I buy you ladies a drink?"

"No, we're fine," Gina said.

"My name's Alan."

"Fuck off, *Alan*," Crystal said. He wasn't bad looking, she thought, but she was more than certain that his interest was not in her.

Gina laughed as the man moved on to the next potential victim. "I think I'm going to like you," she said, raising her glass, to which Crystal clinked. "Yes, that was when I first thought he might be screwing around on me, so I thought about getting him Christine, who he couldn't talk about enough, how perfect she was, how beautiful she was, how lifelike, yadda, yadda, yadda."

"Probably should've gone ahead and done it," Crystal said.

Gina picked up her wine glass, looking coolly over the rim, an appraising and thoughtful glance. "You're assuming I want my husband satisfied at home. Maybe I'm tired of him." She finished the glass and set it down on the tabletop.

Crystal nodded. "Amen, sister. Sometimes it's time to pack their fucking bags and send them on their way."

"I'd guess you've had a few rough Joes in your life," Gina said.

"What do you mean?" Crystal asked.

"Men who treated you like shit. People who stomped all over you."

"I've known some real dickheads," Crystal said.

"My uncle started molesting me when I was ten," Gina said. "When I was seventeen, I put him in the ER. Joined the Army to avoid jail. Served eight years."

"You were in the motherfucking Army?" Crystal said.

Gina smiled. "My dream was to open my own health club. I had some money saved up from the Army, but not enough, and my credit wasn't worth shit. I met a guy who was interested in financially backing the venture, that is, if I slept with him."

"Pigs," Crystal said. "What'd you tell him?"

"I spent two years putting up with his pathetic concept of sex while I got the health club up and running. *GI Gina's*, I called it. It was a real hot club, down in Savannah. People were breaking down the doors to get in."

"What happened?"

"When I stopped being the arm candy and sex toy for Brett, he pulled the rug out from under me. It seems the whole thing was in his name, and I… long story short, he kicked me to the fucking curb with nothing."

"How'd you end up here? In Port Essex? With Tobias?"

"That's a story for another day," Gina said. "I just wanted to let you know that you and me didn't come from all that different of places."

"When this is all over, I'll tell you a couple fucking yarns that will make your fingernails bleed," Crystal said.

"What about this other woman, then?" Gina asked. "Rose, I believe Miss Baker said her name was. What of her? Have you found out anything more?"

"No." Crystal finished her margarita and contemplated another one. "I'm going to suggest that we not charge you for sitting outside your husband's business when he's at work. That seems like a waste of your money. How about I tail him to work in the morning, come back during the lunch hour to see where he might get off to, and then return to pick him up at the end of the day? That'll give me more time to look for the redhead and investigate what your husband might be doing going out on that boat."

Gina stood up. "I hired you to find proof of my husband's infidelity. How you do that is up to you. I gotta run and pick up the takeout to bring home to the bastard. Sooner, Crystal, would be better than later. Do what you have to, but find me something."

*   *   *

Cloutier texted Clay that she'd be at the newspaper until midnight and that he could stop by anytime. They didn't get back from their futile search for treasure until almost nine. Baylee had to get home to Flash and Ollie. She took Frank with her. Her friend Tammy had stopped by to feed them and take them out to stretch their legs at five, but still, they were not used to spending all that time alone.

Sally, the receptionist at the *Port Essex Daily Register* was still at her front desk, which was odd for this late at night. Clay figured there must be a time crunch that required all hands-on deck for the following day's publication. She had a dog who was just over two years of age, and Clay took the opportunity to share that he had a new puppy, and perhaps get some advice. She was not much of a bearer of good news, as she said that her Lab was still chewing pretty much everything in sight.

The newsroom was about a dozen desks, one side being marketing, and the other being news. The production team was housed in the back with the printing presses. Four people other than Cloutier were silently clattering away on their keyboards. Two of them had headphones on, most likely drowning out any noise with music.

Clay sat down across from Cloutier and pushed a piece of coffee cake from that morning's diner run across to her. He set a fresh cup of coffee next to it that he'd brewed at home when he picked up the pastry.

"Ah, you're a saint," Cloutier said, ripping a chunk of the delicious breakfast dessert off and washing it down with the hot brew. "The coffee in the pot here is starting to resemble mud on a chilly autumn day."

"Just from my Keurig at home," Clay said. "Can't get a good cup of joe anywhere this time of night."

"What can I do you for this evening? You said you wanted more information on that Etchemin woman?"

"Yes. My clients and I are sailing blind on where the supposed treasure might be buried. The map, letter, and facts don't match up."

"You're telling me that I might be the key to you finding a treasure trove worth millions? What's in it for me?"

Clay chuckled. "Besides the coffee cake?"

Cloutier shrugged. Nodded. "That's a start."

"Make for a pretty good follow-up story to the one you already did," Clay said. "You know, if you were able to connect the dots and had the treasure from Black Sam Bellamy discovered right here in Port Essex, where that woman—what'd you say her tribe was?"

Cloutier tapped her keyboard. "She was of the Chbo So Clan of the Etchemin People."

"Yeah, can you imagine that follow-up story? The big wire services would gobble that up."

"You give me first crack?"

"Absolutely."

"And you and Baylee take me and Denise out to a fancy dinner?"

"If you help me find this lost treasure, your wish is my command."

Cloutier chortled and shook her head. "No. You buy the dinner regardless of whether or not you find any pirate booty, which is more likely than not just some local legend."

Clay held out his hand. "Deal."

Cloutier ignored his hand, again searching on her computer. After a bit she muttered under her breath, stood, and walked to a filing cabinet in the corner. "Think that was back when all my notes were handwritten."

"You said Black Sam built a fort next to their village. Was that the Winnegance village?"

Cloutier shook her head. "No. Winnegance was the Abenaki. The Chbo So were a clan of the Etchemin."

"I've never heard of any village other than the Winnegance in the area," Clay said.

"They were just a clan," Cloutier said. "An extended family of a larger group that set up an encampment in the area. Not quite sure where, but maybe, if the woman is still alive, she can be of help."

"Still alive?"

Cloutier sighed. "Yeah, she had to be in her eighties, at least, when I spoke with her ten years ago. She looked like just flesh and bones, thin as a string bean, but her eyes, mind, and tongue were sharper than the black keys on a piano."

Clay had little idea what that meant. Music was not really his strength. But he had a notion that Cloutier was suggesting that the woman still had full use of her faculties.

"Ah, here we go," she said, pulling a spiral bound notebook from the cabinet. She flipped through the pages. "Niben Glenn." Cloutier scribbled on a piece of paper. "She didn't have a phone but here's her address."

Chapter 13

Baylee pulled into Niben Glenn's driveway at 10:00 a.m. on the dot. Clay had thought that an elderly woman would be more receptive to speaking with another woman, rather than a man. He didn't mention that Niben, being a Native American and thus sharing Baylee's heritage, might be a better match as well. Baylee knew he'd been thinking it, of course. Truth be told, she agreed, even though she'd rather be out on a sailboat cruising up the Dunbar River than pulling up to a ramshackle trailer in the woods somewhere in Edgecomb.

Yesterday had been glorious, Baylee thought, even if they'd come up empty on the treasure, or even any possibilities of treasure. They'd moored and searched the three possible locations, and then a fourth, without any luck at all. There'd been seven granite rocks that with a very creative imagination could've been considered heart-shaped, but there'd been no catacombs or tunnels or openings underneath any of them.

All the same, it was like a vacation day—sailing and hiking— and with Clay. She blushed, thinking of their new phase of carnal delights. When she and Clay were together now there was a giddiness that she couldn't quite control. She felt like a door had been unlocked and the hopes and desires within, previously so carefully guarded, had been loosed into the wild. Now, by herself, it was hard to believe the things she'd said and done with Clay, but there was a lusciousness to her being that she was currently incapable of controlling, and quite frankly, had no desire to.

They'd always had a great connection, right from the day she'd walked into his office looking for a job, trying to rebuild her life after a tumultuous childhood leading into a disastrous marriage which ended up with the bastard dead at the end of her smoking gun.

Clay knew her. He got her. He didn't judge her. Over the past few years, they'd shared every dark secret, every buried failure and loss. Baylee felt a connection to Clay that she'd never experienced with anyone else. At one point, she'd felt the security a daughter feels with her mother, but that was before Mom slept with her boyfriend when she was still in high school.

The only friend of any worth she'd ever had prior to Clay and the group she'd become part of through the P.I. firm was Tammy. She'd never shared the deepest secrets of her past with anybody at all, not even Tammy. Not until Clay. Their bond was forged in difficult beginnings, for he'd been orphaned at eight, and that mutual yesteryear of rawness brought them together.

Of course, she'd been madly attracted to him right from the start. His blue-green eyes were damn sexy and promised intrigue and mystery. His sandy blond hair was always slightly tousled, which she suspected was carefully crafted, as was his seemingly permanent facial scruff. He was slender yet muscular. Gentle but tough. Thoughtful and spontaneous.

And an emotional train wreck as far as the ability to have a deeper relationship with a woman beyond one of a raw sexual nature. On his way to the big 40, Clay had never been with a woman for longer than six months, and usually, not even that. All that seemed tied up with his unresolved feelings of loss and abandonment after the death of his parents and grandmother at the vulnerable age of eight, all perished in a senseless car crash.

Baylee smiled to herself. Now, they were like two trains crashing into the other, and it was either going to be a beautiful union, or a horrific disaster. They'd avoided these particular tracks for the years they'd known each other, afraid of destroying their friendship, but that, too, was now behind them. There was no turning back from the erotic commingling of their bodies that symbolized the intense fusion of their beings on a deeper level. Goddammit, she thought, they were in an actual relationship.

Baylee sat staring into space for a few moments, smiled, shivered with pleasure, and got out of the car, grabbing her phone from the seat in case she needed to record any of the conversation with Niben Glenn. The trailer was ancient looking, and it appeared that repairs had been made using duct tape on more than one occasion. There was a wooden awning in front that leaned precariously to the side, tilted, skewed, and totally rickety by all appearances.

Unfortunately, it was underneath this perilous roof that Niben Glenn sat in a rocking chair. A blanket covered her lap and legs, even though it was close to 80° already this morning. Niben had a faded scarf on her head and tied under her chin with snow-white hair poking out in tufts. Her face reminded Baylee of a prune—the skin dried from within and carved into countless wrinkles. Her eyes were mere slits, and her nose was lost in the roadwork of her face. For the first time, Baylee realized where the term 'old prune' came from.

"Mrs. Glenn?" Baylee said, stopping just short of the dicey overhang.

The woman stared back through the slits of her eyes and kept rocking.

"Are you Mrs. Niben Glenn?"

"Ain't been a Mrs. for some forty years now." Niben's voice was low, coarse, and sounded like it was being dragged over jagged glass. "Niben will do just fine. That Mr. Glenn was no-account and left me with nothing but a name that don't fit all that well."

"My name's Baylee Baker, and I was hoping you might help me out with something."

"Settle your feet, youngster." Niben nodded her head to the side where there was a white plastic chair, one arm gone, crooked, and probably entirely unsafe to sit in.

Baylee looked at the chair. Looked at the awning. Looked at Niben. Shrugged. She stepped forward with tentative steps and sat as gently as she could. "I was given your name by Marie Cloutier of the *Port Essex Daily Register*," she said.

When the old woman didn't answer, Baylee continued, "I was hoping you might be able to answer a few questions about the Chbo So."

Niben's eyes crinkled slightly. "You got Etchemin in you?"

There weren't many people who recognized Baylee as having Native American blood on such brief acquaintance. "Abenaki. Through my father's side," she said. Bastard, she thought.

Niben nodded. "Lot of us folk have a hard time with things. Don't you think badly on him."

Baylee twitched slightly, wondering if the old woman had read her thoughts. "He's dead. Didn't give me or leave me much but my name, as you said."

Niben cackled. "Menfolk ain't much good for any more'n that, truth be told. Got it so easy, they do, and spend most of their time bellyaching at how hard they got it." She spat a stream of tobacco juice into a pot to the left of her feet.

"Not sure his blood even flows through my veins," Baylee said.

"Yet you got *Alnambak* inked onto your forearm."

Baylee flipped her arm and looked at the tattoo. *Real People.* The Abenaki had called themselves *Alnambak* which translated to Real People. Not monsters, animals, or other people, but real people. "For a while after my father died, I read everything I could about his people. They made a lot of sense to me. Their spirits are more practical than God. Their symbiotic accord with the natural world. The simplicity by which they lived. Their sense of family. These all made sense to me. They *were* real people. The Real People."

"Not they, youngster, but you."

"I know nothing of my Abenaki ancestry. My father never shared it before he left this world behind."

The old woman put her hand over her heart. "You know your family here."

Baylee fought a tear in her eye from forming, willing her eyes dry as she stared wide-eyed at this person who'd thrown a spear into the very core of her being. Thoughts and emotions she'd never even shared with Clay, mainly because she'd suppressed them herself, came swirling forward, trying to break through.

"The article in the paper said something about the Chbo So Clan living in the Port Essex area during the time after they'd driven the Europeans away," Baylee said, trying to put the conversation back onto firm footing. "That after King Phillip's War and before the Europeans reappeared in the 1730s, a clan known as the Chbo So lived somewhere in this area."

The old woman rocked in her chair, staring up over the trees into the sky, apparently lost in thoughts and memories.

"Do you know anything about this?" Baylee asked after several long minutes.

"It was a difficult time for my people," Niben said. She spit a stream of tobacco juice into the pot at her feet. "We'd grown used to the weapons and tools of the white people, and then all of a sudden, they were gone. We had to go back to hunting the old way. The Abenaki were growing in numbers and strength and absorbing the Etchemin."

"I believe the Abenaki returned to their village, Winnegance, down by the harbor, where Port Essex is now, for the fishing." Baylee shifted her chair so she could look Niben in the eye. "But was there another village?"

"My ancestors were the Chbo So," Niben said, nodding. "Soon after the time you speak of, they were gobbled up by the Abenaki, killed by white disease, hunted down for scalps, and destroyed by the white hunger."

"All of that was mentioned in the article in the *Port Essex Daily Register.*"

"The time you speak of was the last period in which the Chbo

So were still a clan. A family. Brothers. Sisters. Wives. Husbands. Aunts. Uncles. Grandfathers and grandmothers. Children. All living together as a clan. Chbo So."

"Do you know where they lived?"

Niben spit in the pot. Then she tilted her head to look Baylee square in the eye. Her eyes were filmed over slightly, but a light shone through that bespoke vibrance. "They lived on the river, away from the Abenaki, who they were friendly with, but they were their own people. They were the Chbo So Clan of the Etchemin."

"What river?"

"They lived on the banks of the Sibosek River. Right up until the white devils returned and drove them out."

Baylee reflected on the time her people had lived here on the shores of the Atlantic Ocean. In the time before the Europeans had arrived with their steel tools, weapons, and disease. A simpler life, certainly. Real People.

A whistling noise interrupted her reverie. Niben had fallen asleep and was snoring, the ripples vibrating her frail body, her face in perfect, peaceful repose.

* * *

Socrates sat in his Ford F-150 on the side of the road overlooking the Knox Wharf. If nothing else, he was a chameleon, able to blend into wherever he was with ease. The trick was to understand the locals. The second day here in Port Essex he'd gone to a dealership out on Route 1 and bought the truck. A Ford. Not a Chevy. Not a hybrid. A Ford.

Even though it was warm, he had on a light flannel shirt and jeans. This was the dress of not only the locals, but of the hipsters who'd slowly insinuated themselves into the life of the town of Port Essex. Now they were an established segment of the population. It didn't hurt that the long sleeves and collar helped hide his tattoos.

He'd followed Clay Wolfe from his home to his office and then to the marina where, for the second day in a row, he'd boarded the sailboat of his good friend Weston Beck. Today, the woman, Baylee Baker, had not been with him. Socrates was aware that Wolfe had spent the night at her house for the third night in a row, only returning home in the early hours to prepare for the new day. They'd both been to the office, but when Clay left, Baylee had stayed behind.

It'd been a dilemma whom to follow, but he'd decided to stick with Wolfe, who'd gone to the marina and met with the New Yorkers, Andy and Dannie they were calling themselves. Andriy Kozak and Daniela Cox were their given names. He'd investigated them at length in the early morning hours, sitting at the kitchen table of an otherwise graceless rental unit he'd taken for a single feature — the best high-speed internet that Port Essex had to offer.

It was these two who Socrates was most interested in. It was they who had brought him to Port Essex, or the reason he'd been hired, anyway. His employer was paying good money to find out what they knew of a hidden pirate treasure. At first, Socrates had scoffed, but the story had been supported by his research. Now, he was starting to believe that there just might be a treasure hidden away in or around Port Essex. And that was very interesting.

There was no way that the two New York antique dealers were going to walk away with the treasure. The woman had been born with a silver spoon in her mouth, Socrates had discovered, but seemingly, had had it taken away. Too bad for her. The man, Andy, was just some putz, toiling away at a failing antique business from nine to five, home to watch game show reruns, and then to bed in preparation of doing the same old thing again the next day. That is, until he met the more exotic Dannie, when everything had changed for him.

No, there was no chance that these two fobs were going to walk away with Socrates' treasure, as he'd come to think of it, it being equally unlikely his employer would reap the rewards.

While that person was paying him very well, that paycheck was not going to allow him to retire to the life of leisure and wealth that was his destiny. He wasn't meant to be slumming in this shithole, redneck bikers his boon companions. He'd done that before, when he was young and drunk on power—or just drunk, period. He'd since grown out of it. If he had to hear one more person with too many drinks in them complain about their job or their old woman, he was going to kill somebody. Literally. Life had a way of boiling his blood, and, while he found release in shagging some bimbo, whether picked up in a bar or paid for on the street, it wasn't the same thrill as rubbing out the life of a human being.

If the fire opals really existed, Socrates meant to take them for himself. He'd be able to buy himself a house in Paris, another on an island in the tropics. He'd enjoy the finer things in life and hire nothing but the most beautiful of escorts. No more trollops from the streets. No more rednecks and drunks and boring people with their mundane lives.

After the sailboat motored out of the harbor, Socrates put his binoculars down. It was time to rent a fishing boat. Something innocuous. But he needed to know where they were going. The problem was that he didn't know the first thing about boats. However, he reasoned, if he was going to have a house on an island, it seemed a good time to learn.

Tobias Yates also went out of this same marina, not that he'd been out for several days, Socrates knew. Not until the next time he lied to his wife about attending a conference and instead hooked up with the redhead on that salvage boat. Socrates wondered if the two of them did dirty things together or if they were just business partners. He'd always been fascinated by redheads. They were fiery, in and out of the sack, he'd found, and he liked that.

It'd be best to not rent the boat here, Socrates thought, as he might be noticed. No, better to get it elsewhere and be sitting in it out off Spruce Island with a fishing line in the water when the *Freya* came motoring by. From there, he didn't know which way they went, but he certainly meant to find out. He'd rent a boat for the week. And he'd find somebody to take him out, someone who'd keep their trap shut for the right amount of money.

That Daniela Cox was one smoking hot woman, Socrates thought, and she might be the weak link. Socrates figured he might be able to get her to share some information with him and have some fun with her at the same time. Of course, then he'd have to dispose of her, and the anticipation would be gone. It might be better to wait a few more days and see what happened. Then he'd grab her, shake her tree, have his fun, and feed her to the fish.

Chapter 14

"Are you and Baylee more than just business partners?" Dannie asked.

Clay looked at her, surprised by the question. Today they were exploring the Dunbar River which went up the east side of Townsend Island and then cut inland for a few more miles before petering out into a shallow creek.

"We are close friends," he replied, hedging a bit. He wasn't quite ready to share with this complete stranger, a client, that he'd recently began having sex with Baylee and thought that he might have jumped off the precipice into love. "Baylee is good people."

They'd woven their way through a myriad of islands, deciding to look for a rock formation shaped like a church bell until they'd entered the mouth of the Dunbar River. Not two hundred yards into the river, they'd come across their first possibility. They'd broken into pairs—Westy with Andy, and Clay with Dannie—for the search for the tall pine, which was more than likely long gone, and more importantly, the heart-shaped rock that was the doorway to the catacombs and the treasure.

Dannie paused and looked sideways at Clay. "She mentioned something about a run-in with some bikers the other night."

Clay stopped, turned, and faced Dannie. He again realized that she was quite a beautiful woman, but not in a fragile, damsel-in-distress sort of way. She wore a navy-blue tank top that showcased muscular shoulders and arms. "You know any reason why our association with you might lead to us being threatened?" he asked.

Dannie laughed drily. "Other than the fact that we've hired you to help us find a lost treasure that is most certainly worth millions, and likely much more? And that this ancient pirate booty is the property of whoever finds it first?"

"Okay, point taken." Clay didn't mention that this was a point of contention. As far as he could tell, the property owner, and the local, state, and the federal governments all had their paws out wanting a cut of whatever was found. "Let me rephrase. Do you think that the threat was related to our business together?"

"Four men with skull masks menace you with cutlasses and blunderbusses, weapons favored by pirates. I'd certainly guess that it is all related." Dannie's eyes glinted hotly. "I just don't know how they know about it. We've kept this under wraps. You're the only people we've told about the map and the letter. Yet here they are."

"Did Baylee also tell you that I had a confrontation with a group of men I surmised might be the bikers who... sent us a message?"

"The Buccaneers," Dannie said. "She said you got your ass kicked."

"She did, did she?" Clay chuckled. "I did okay for a bit."

"Sounds like a different way of saying you got your ass kicked." Dannie bent to tie her boot. "You done anything about them?"

"Like what?"

"Seems to me it'd be a good idea to know where they're at."

"They were staying out 29 at the Town Motel," Clay said. "Westy swung by there a couple days back, and they'd checked out. Hopefully back to whatever rock they came out from under."

"Somehow, I doubt that."

"Back to how anybody knows you're here looking for a long-lost treasure." Clay sat down on a rock. "You can't just leave your life behind, and nobody misses you."

"We have an antique shop in Queens. We told people, as well as put up signs, that it was closed for renovations. We told our family and friends we were going on an antique crawl. Searching for pieces for our shop. Not unheard of. Many of the bigger places get estates brought to them, but us? You've seen the television shows like *Antique Road Show* or *American Pickers*, I'm betting. That's what we do."

Clay hadn't ever watched either show, or any show about antiques, but had flicked past them, pausing long enough to get a bit of flavor of what they were about. "And you can't think of anybody that might've been… skeptical about your real motives?"

"No. Certainly not a motorcycle gang." Dannie began picking her way through the rocks and scrub brush of the shoreline again, and Clay followed. "What do you know about these… Buccaneers?" she asked.

Clay let out a long breath. "Not much," he admitted.

"Seems like it might be important to find out more about them," Dannie said. "Not to tell you how to do your job."

Clay chuckled. "Point taken. Been stretched a bit thin." Which was true, with Crystal out of the office following Tobias Yates around, and with him escorting Dannie and Andy on a treasure hunt the past few days. He studiously avoided thinking that his dereliction of duty was also the result of his newfound amorous relationship with his partner.

"Got a contestant over here," Andy called out, and they veered in the direction of him and Westy.

There was a rock that looked almost exactly like a heart. Unfortunately, it probably weighed 500 pounds. They'd brought pry bars and shovels. They set about moving some of the smaller rocks from the lower side, before setting up behind the boulder, Westy and Dannie manning the pry bars, and Clay and Andy pushing with their hands.

It wasn't unlike getting a car unstuck from the snow, Clay thought, as they rocked what they hoped was a monolith marker to the entrance of catacombs within which lay buried treasure. On the fourth try, the boulder rolled, then picked up speed, and went crashing down to the water's edge where it came to rest.

Nothing. They used the shovels, pry bars, and picks to dig into the ground, hoping to find something, anything, but there was nothing.

"I think we've pretty much covered this area," Clay said. "Back to the sailboat?"

The four of them picked their way back to the sailboat, which had been moored to a tree on the shore.

Chapter 15

Clay was the first one to arrive at the Pelican Perch. He was meeting Baylee and Crystal here for dinner, on the firm, as they would be working. That was always the excuse, but this time it was for real. They'd gone in three different directions all day, and updates on what'd been found were necessary.

He slid into the bar. That new fellow, Silas, was behind the bar. "Hey, do you think I can get a hold on the table over in the corner?" Clay asked. "I'm meeting a couple people here in about twenty minutes for dinner."

"Heard tell you locals get special privileges," Silas said. He finished wiping a glass. "Can't even kick you out for beating the bejesus out of somebody, so I guess we can hold your table for you." He pulled out a sign that said reserved and was held by a pylon, much like one on the side of a dock, or a pelican perch. "Throw that on the table. Can I get you something?"

Clay had wrestled with this all the way over. He hadn't had a drink in three nights. He could feel the powerful pull of the brown liquor. "Glenlivet. Single. Neat." He stepped back to the table and put the reservation placard down, returned to the bar, and sat.

"Haven't seen you around," Silas said, putting a glass in front of Clay and pouring a healthy stream of scotch into it.

"Busy working a case."

"A case?"

"Yeah, I'm a P.I."

Silas raised his black eyebrows, his glasses ascending as well. "You mean like Marlowe and Spade, man? That's cool."

"Some of the time," Clay said. "That fellow I got in the tussle with, he been in?"

Silas pursed his lips, shook his head no. "Why d'you ask?"

"No reason. Just wondering."

"Does he have something to do with the *case* you're working on?"

"No, not at all." Clay thought back to the comment by that fellow, Roderick, asking about the inhabitants that lived in Port Essex before the Europeans. Which meant the Native Americans. Who were tied in with Black Sam Bellamy. And the treasure. "How about a group of bikers called the Buccaneers?"

Silas seemed to ponder that while he dried a glass before shaking his head. "No, man, can't help you out there, either."

"They seem to be more the sort to hang out at Lucky Linda's."

"I'll look out for them. Whatcha want with them?"

What indeed, Clay wondered. "Not sure. Can you let me know if you see them?"

"You want me to text you or something like that?" Silas asked. "Like some sort of secret operative?"

Clay chuckled. "Nah, nothing like that. You're here most nights, it seems?"

"Yeah, I got the noon to ten shifts during the week. I'll let you know, man."

"Thanks. Where were you before you came here?" Clay asked, finishing his drink. It wasn't much liquid, after all.

"I bounced around Europe for a bit working under the table. Last place was in Spain. Cádiz." Silas grabbed the bottle of Glenlivet. "You want another?"

Clay put his hand over the glass. "Nope. How about a cranberry and ginger ale?"

Silas raised his eyebrows. "Tell me," he said grabbing a new glass, "are you and that lady with the pretty face and eyes that you had dinner with the other night an item?"

"What's it to you?"

Silas set the cranberry and ginger ale on the bar in front of Clay and held up his hands. "No offense, I just noticed she didn't have a wedding ring, is all. But if you two are hooked up, well, then, I'll look elsewhere."

Clay had no doubt the man was successful with the women. He was young, virile, handsome, and privy to many a secret and lonely face. And there was always something romantic about the wandering rambler type. How did one go about saying to another dude that you're with a woman, heart and soul?

"We, um, are romantically involved, as well as business partners," Clay finally said.

"No shit? Double the partner, so to speak. Good for you, man, she's a fine tamale."

Clay took a drink, his thoughts turning to Baylee, as Silas went off to serve up a tray of drinks to a boisterous crowd down the bar. Caramel, he thought, was the best one-word description of her. Skin, eyes, and hair. Rich and sweet. That was Baylee. Certainly not tamale, but he appreciated that Silas was impressed with her beauty, a glow of pride that he couldn't quite tamp down. That beautiful and desirable woman was his, as long as he didn't screw it up.

As if on cue, Baylee walked in along with Crystal. Clay got up to join them and guide them to the table.

*   *   *

Socrates stole a white panel van. The type of vehicle your parents told you never to climb into, even if the occupant was offering candy. Well, he thought, a grin creasing his features, it wasn't like he'd even boosted the vehicle, as the keys had been sitting right on the front seat. Maine. The way life should be. If you're a criminal, that is. It was a place where the keys to the kingdom were handed over to anybody wanting to abuse the system. Or, in this case, the keys to the abduction mechanism.

He'd fully planned on having to hot-wire the vehicle, finding it parked in back of a locksmith shop, a shadowed corner perfect for what he needed to do. He parked down the street at the empty market parking lot, the store having closed at nine, and walked back with a small satchel containing the things he'd be in need of that evening. There was nobody in sight, no cameras on the building, which was shielded from view by trees, and no cars on the quiet street as he slid onto the seat. And sat right on the keys.

With a curse, he pulled the keys from underneath his butt, and then laughed. Too easy. The van rumbled to life with no complaints, which was important, for it wouldn't do to borrow a vehicle that would fail to start when necessary. Or run out of gas. Socrates looked, nodding when he saw that there was half a tank. He drove away from his ultimate destination, finding a quiet road to pull over in order to assess his acquisition for the evening.

All the lights worked. He even propped a stick against the brake to make sure that those lights were in good order. It wouldn't do to be pulled over with a woman zip-tied in back because of a faulty license plate light. He opened the back. There were shelves on either side full of equipment, presumably the tools and gadgets necessary for a locksmith. More importantly, these shelves were securely attached. Socrates attached four restraints, two on each side, about five feet apart.

Back in the driver's seat, he checked the time on his phone. It was 11:00 p.m. It was time to get moving. He pulled into The Port in a Storm Inn twenty minutes later. A novice would've been nervous and shown up too early. Experience taught one patience and timing. For the past two nights, Daniela Cox had come outside at exactly 11:30 to smoke a cigarette. Humans were creatures of habit, Socrates knew, and he was hoping there was nothing to upset this routine on this evening. Or that the past two nights had been an abnormality.

Either way, it was no big deal. If she didn't show, he'd drive the van back, remove the restraints, drop the keys on the front seat, and walk away to fight another day. Socrates hadn't stayed alive this long by allowing his thirst to make him foolish. In the back of the inn there was a small parking lot and a door for guests. He backed the van into the space next to the door, which was reserved for loading and unloading service vehicles.

Socrates got out of the van, went to the rear, opened the doors, and grabbed a toolbox. He had garnered himself a room key earlier and had access to the door. It was easy when you knew somebody, especially one of the maids, a young woman he'd shared a bed with at the inn a few times during her break, all on the dime of the owners, of course. He could cut the wire to the security camera, but that might raise suspicion. A simpler solution was a narrow splint that stopped the camera from rotating to the left side of the door, covering the space where Daniela had gone the last two nights.

Right inside through a door to the left was a stairwell with a small glass window a cubic foot in diameter. Socrates stepped inside, setting the toolbox down. Hopefully nobody would be coming down or up the stairs.

When Daniela Cox came through the first-floor door into the vestibule, Socrates stepped carefully to the side, watching the outer door through the small window. He gave her time to light a cigarette, and then he picked up the toolbox and exited the stairwell and the building. She was standing off to the side, about ten feet from the rear of his van, not perfect, but doable. Socrates nodded to her, and then went and opened the back of the van, sliding the toolbox to the side. He made sure the zip ties were accessible but not in the way of a thrashing body.

He turned, placed a cigarette in his mouth. This would be like candy from a baby, and not even giving them treats to climb into the creeper van. Some broad smoking a cigarette who bought and sold antiques for a living. It would be the simplest of snatch and grabs. The camera was stuck facing away. There was nobody in the parked cars, no late-night revelers coming home from cocktails on the town, and no smokers. The inn didn't allow dogs, which was a plus.

Daniela was looking at him, her blonde hair tousled, wearing a sleeveless black blouse of some lacy material, cut low. Socrates wondered, not for the first time, if she came out here to smoke after having sex. Three nights in a row, if that were true, he thought, a grin spreading onto his face. Good for Andy. She was quite the looker, that was for sure.

"Hello," he said. "You got a light?" He took two steps toward her. Only three more steps would put him in reach.

Daniela looked warily at him. He imagined that it wasn't the first time some guy had hit on her as she smoked a cigarette in a dark parking lot. It must be tough being a woman, Socrates thought, having to constantly look out for creeps that were always trying to get into their pants, either through invitation, or by more heinous means.

"No, really, I lost my lighter somewhere," he said. "Give me a light, and I'll be on my way. I'm not here to bend your ear. I just want to get home to my girlfriend and be done for the night." He took another step closer. Two more. Still, nobody around.

Daniela held out a lighter. Socrates sidled forward and grasped her wrist and went to punch her in the jaw, just enough to stun her, not really meant to do any damage. Just make her malleable as he steered her the few steps into the back of the van and secured her to the floor and put a gag in her mouth.

Her left hand slapped his own hand free of her wrist with a numbing ferocity as she moved sideways out of the path his right cross, her hand hitting him at the elbow and using his momentum to slam him into the wall.

Socrates turned as a kick slammed him into the chest and back into the wall. He grabbed her foot, twisting and shoving her backward. Daniela toppled to the ground, rolled, and came to her feet with surprising agility as he went after her. He struck with his left palm, striking her in the chest and making her stagger backward.

Daniela stepped around the front of his van as he followed, giving him a chop to the side of the neck that he deflected with his shoulder. He lunged at her as she sidestepped, his face meeting another blow that crashed into his cheekbone.

This was not going as planned, Socrates thought, realizing that this was no fragile damsel in distress to be plucked, but rather, a dangerous foe with martial art skills and possibly other training.

His anger bursting forth with a raw violence as his instincts took over, he now fought to escape rather than capture. Socrates jerked his elbow back into her side, spinning as he did so, hitting her a glancing blow, knocking her sideways. He sent a roundhouse kick her way, which she blocked with a forearm, but it still knocked her tumbling over backward.

Socrates took that moment to turn and run.

Chapter 16

Clay was lying in Baylee's bed, awake, and thinking about getting up to go home for a shower and change of clothes, when his phone buzzed on the side table. Actually, he'd been wondering if it was too early in their relationship for him to keep some toiletries here and maybe a few clothes. Baylee had opened him up a new toothbrush the second night, but so far, that was all.

He swung his legs free of the bed, grabbing the phone, so as not to wake her. In doing so, he uncovered her back as it tapered down toward her still hidden rear end. Clay eased the covers a little further, looked, shook his head, breathed out, and pulled them back over his partner. Naked, he carried his phone into the hallway before answering.

Two minutes later, he was back, sliding into bed behind Baylee, his arm draped over her, his other hand on her shoulder.

"Who was that?" she asked.

"Just somebody telling me I could go back to bed with my raving beauty."

"Mm. Scratch my back." Baylee pressed back against him. "Raving like stark raving mad?"

Clay chuckled. "I guess kind of. Crazy gorgeous."

Baylee snickered. "Aren't you the smooth one, Mr. Wolfe. What is it that you want from me?"

He kneaded her shoulder gently. "Just this."

She wiggled against him. "Nothing more?"

Her phone buzzed. She picked it up, looked at the screen, tensed, and put it back down.

"What?" Clay asked. "Something wrong? Who was that?"

"First, you must tell me who it was that told you that you could rejoin your... raving... beauty in bed."

"Andy Kozak. He said that him and Dannie were unable to come out on the boat today, that something had come up."

"Did you tell him about finding out about the Chbo So Clan settlement on the Sibosek River?"

Clay ran his thumb down her spine and massaged the hollow of her lower back with a steady circular motion while his other hand caressed her thigh. "I told him we had some news, but we'd share it with them tomorrow once they'd taken care of whatever they had to."

"I suppose we can spend the day doing some more research on the Chbo So."

"Hmm. Maybe later."

"You should have mentioned it on the phone."

"Had other things on my mind," Clay said. "I'll call him later when we know more."

"You didn't feel like chatting?" Baylee reached a hand back and draped it on his hip.

"I thought it best to deliver that information for face to face."

"And that decision had nothing to do with me naked in bed?"

Clay chuckled softly, his lips brushing her ear. "Maybe. Your turn. Who was texting you at this time of the morning?"

Baylee slid her hand from his hip and grasped him firmly. "Nobody important."

*   *   *

"What are you doing?" Crystal said into the cell phone.

"Making a tree fort for Joe," Westy said. "Not that it's more than two feet off the ground."

"You feel like a sailboat ride?"

"The New Yorkers canceled us today."

"This is something different."

"Yeah? What?"

"Is the *Freya* moored in your backyard, so to speak?"

"So to speak. Talk to me."

"I'm on my way there. Five minutes."

"You chasing after another lobsterman?" Westy put the hammer down and went to the garage. Joe was at day camp and Faith was at her part-time job as a tattoo artist. Before Joe, it'd been a full-time gig, but now she only took a select number of clients.

"I'll tell you when I get there. Fucking driving and talking is not something I do well."

Westy hung up, put the phone in his pocket. He grabbed a scuba tank and carried it down to the dingy on shore. The rest of his gear was on the *Freya*. Except for a gun. He went inside, got his Sig Sauer out of the locker, and stuck it in his waistband. Depending on what Crystal said, he could always add more weapons to the pistol, as his gun cabinet was actually more of an arsenal.

He heard the car in the dirt driveway and went out the front door and met Crystal as she climbed out of the vehicle. "This business or personal?" he asked.

"Guy I'm following for Clay and Baylee," Crystal said. "Just got on some big ass boat down to Knox Wharf and was getting ready to cast off as I drove away."

Westy measured the statement. No need of anything more than a pistol, he figured. "Okay, let's go. My day is open."

"Clay told me. Said to call you."

The two of them walked around the side of the house. "Hey, okay if I go inside?" Crystal asked. "I gotta piss like a racehorse."

Westy smiled. "Go ahead. But hurry up. They should be coming along soon. Boat got a name?"

"The *Coronado*," Crystal said over her shoulder as she went inside the back door.

The binoculars were on the *Freya*, Westy thought, but they should still have a few minutes before the *Coronado* came into view. Unless it was headed around the Point and up the coast.

He'd untied the dingy and was holding onto the short dock when Crystal came out of the house and crossed the backyard, past Joe's partially constructed tree fort, and climbed in next to him.

"Phew," she said. "The dragon has been drained. Let's go follow the doll-fucker."

Westy shook his head, waiting for her to settle, and steered the small boat away from the shore. "You want to explain the second part of that statement? Please, not the first."

Crystal laughed. "Tobias Yates makes sex dolls for a living." She told Westy about his company and the prototypes as they motored the short distance across the cove to the *Freya* and climbed aboard.

"And we're following him why?" Westy asked as he grabbed his binoculars to scan the harbor between them and Port Essex. The water was dotted with numerous vessels, pleasure craft and working boats of every size and make.

"His wife hired Baylee to find proof that he's cheating on her so she can rip up the prenup." Crystal sat down with a sigh. "See anything?"

"Got him. Coming this way." Westy went and released the lines to the mooring. "The *Coronado* is a salvage boat. Not exactly a romantic yachting experience for a successful sex-toy entrepreneur and his mistress. Is she the redhead?"

"Not actually sure they're doing the horizontal bop or not," Crystal said. "But that is the Rose Ryan we was talking about the other night."

Westy turned the engine on and spun the *Freya* around in a slow circle. "And he's taking his ladylove out on a salvage boat why?"

"I believe they might just be treasure hunting," Crystal said. "Same as you, Clay, Baylee, and the fucking New Yorkers."

"And I thought I had a day off from playing pirate," Westy said. He pushed the throttle forward and motored the *Freya* out at an angle away from the *Coronado*. "You think Tobias is looking for Black Sam Bellamy's fire opals?"

"Quite a coincidence," Crystal said. "What happened to the New Yorkers? Clay didn't say, only that they canceled for the day."

Westy shook his head. "Just that something came up, and they couldn't make it today. Didn't want us going out without them. Guess they're afraid if we find the treasure, not that I think there really is one, that we'll not be good sharers."

Westy cut zig zags through the water ahead of the *Coronado*, sometimes the best way to covertly follow was to stay out in front. He hadn't spent much time alone with Crystal over the past few years, but knew that this rough and tumble woman had become an important part of Clay's life, and thus, relevant to his own life.

He knew that she'd been a heroin user for years. Was that worse than the years he'd spent killing people? Of course, he'd been doing it in the name of preserving democracy, and sometimes he almost believed that, while Crystal had been escaping the reality of the hand she'd been dealt in life.

"Might be headed out to Gorges Island," he said. The strip of land about six miles off the coast of Port Essex loomed in front of them. Almost on cue, behind them, the Coronado cut its engine and drifted to a halt. "Take the wheel. Might want to come around in a minute or so."

Crystal stepped up and manned the steering, turning the sailboat through a wide U so it was almost facing the *Coronado*. She'd been involved with her fair share of lobstermen and fishermen in her years and was comfortable in a boat. "What are they doing?" she asked.

"Putting on scuba gear," Westy said, his binoculars steady in his hands.

"Seems to me they might be looking for something."

Westy laughed. "Ya think?"

"Haven't you been trawling the coastline looking for those fucking fire opals?"

"Yep. Guess they could be looking for something different."

"Could be just a coincidence," Crystal said. "Was it my imagination, or did you bring an oxygen tank out when we came?"

"That I did."

"You going to go down and see what they're up to?"

Westy put the binoculars down and looked at her. "Very little visibility and another diver would stick out like a sore thumb. Maybe we'll just mosey over to the *Coronado* and keep Adam Dube company until they come back up."

"Adam Dube?"

"He's the captain." Westy took the wheel back form Crystal and headed toward the *Coronado.*

"And then what?"

"Why, I suppose we'll ask them what they're looking for."

Adam wasn't all that happy about Westy tying up and boarding his boat. But, like most people in town, he knew Weston Beck, and he wasn't enough of a fool to complain too insistently. Crystal was quite excited, suggesting it was like pirates attacking and boarding a merchant or treasure ship, jumping onto the deck with a flourish, and yelling out something about 'where are the wenches?'

Not much conversation was had, Adam claiming that he knew nothing of what they were looking for, that he only captained the boat. They had just over an hour wait before Tobias Yates and Rose Ryan emerged from the dark water below and clambered back into the salvage boat.

"Who the fuck are you?" Tobias asked as soon as his mask was off.

"We're pirates," Crystal said. "Here for your booty."

Chapter 17

Westy and Crystal arrived back at the P.I. office just past two in the afternoon. They were currently seated in the two chairs across the desk from Clay and Baylee. Clay was careful to keep his happy smile from lighting up his face and drawing attention away from the business at hand.

"What'd you find out?" he asked. "Anything good?"

"What have you two been doing all day?" Crystal asked. "While me and the SEAL been out doing your job?"

"Trying to determine the exact location of the Chbo So Clan," Baylee said.

"Is that like some kind of martial arts shit?" Crystal asked.

Clay chuckled. "Baylee spoke with a woman named Niben yesterday who told her that there'd been an extended family of the Etchemin People living over on the Sibosek River, most likely about the same time Black Sam sailed his ship up the river to hide his treasure."

"If we can pinpoint where they were encamped," Baylee said, "then we are darn close to where the opals might be."

"Looks like you might be barking up the wrong tree," Crystal said.

"Why's that?" Baylee asked.

"What'd you find out?" Clay looked at Westy.

"Your pals Tobias Yates and Rose Ryan shared a story with us," Westy said. "Might or might not be true."

"Let's have it." Clay had never known anybody with a memory for conversation as good as his buddy's. "I like a good story, now and then."

Westy stared out the window overlooking Port Essex Harbor with a far-off look that Clay knew well. Once, when asked, Westy had told him he was organizing the pieces in his mind before speaking.

"The story begins on Gorges Island back in the early 17th century when it became a fishing hub," Westy said, his eyes still looking out, almost as if he could see the thin spit of Gorges Island hidden off behind the Point. "It was first inhabited by Europeans in 1608. As a matter of fact, they supplied an entire ship of cod to the Pilgrims in their spring of need back in 1622. Along with the rest of the white people, they were driven away during King Phillip's War, but in the spring of 1717, there were sixteen men using two shallops and several sailing vessels to fish for cod, stations to dry cure it, and then ship them off to the Antilles and the Mediterranean. One of those men was the ancestor of Rose Ryan. He kept a diary, which she recently found."

"What's a shallop?" Baylee asked.

"A two-masted boat with oars that can carry maybe a dozen people," Westy said.

"And Rose Ryan just found this diary in her possessions, much like Andy Kozak found the map and description in a King James Bible?" Clay said. His voice dripped with skepticism.

"I'm just telling you the story I heard," Westy said. "In April of that year, as you know, Black Sam Bellamy sailed past Gorges Island and to the Winnegance village. On his way back toward Cape Cod, two days later, he stopped in at Gorges Island. He told them that if they kept watch for strange interlopers sailing into the area, that he would make them rich beyond their wildest dreams. He promised to be back within the week, planned on starting a democratic republic, and meant to include any pirate who cared to join as well as the fishermen of Gorges Island.

"A week went by and he didn't return. Then a month. The fishermen were severely disappointed, their dreams of grandeur dashed, a life of brutally hard work fishing year-round in the harsh Maine climate being their reality. And then an Indian, their word, not mine, with no description of what tribe written into the diary, came to the island one day to trade.

"During the negotiations, the Indian mentioned that Black Sam had hidden something in the rocks above their village, but they did not know what, but would search for this hidden item if the fishermen of Gorges Island were interested in trading guns, ammunition, and steel for whatever it was.

"After the Indian departed back to the mainland, the fishermen held a council, in which it was voted to do no nothing, the main reason being their fear of Black Sam. A week later, they heard from a passing sailboat of the shipwreck and death of the pirate captain, and they voted again. This time, it was decided to go in search of whatever had been hidden away near the Indian village on the mainland.

"Twelve of the men took one of the shallops, while the other four remained behind to man the palisade fort and keep lookout. Two days later, there was a storm, and the next morning, the four fishermen found the debris of the shallop washed up on the shore. Three bodies were recovered. There were no survivors and no treasure to be found. It was determined that the shallop had gone down in the storm on its return journey from gathering the treasure. It now lay somewhere on the ocean bottom.

"The four men hung on for six weeks, hoping the treasure would wash up on shore, during which time they paid a visit to the Indians on the mainland who said that their friends had come, spent the night above their village, and then rowed out of the harbor just hours before the storm, presumably with what they'd come looking for.

"And then the rumor came that the pirates Benjamin Hornigold and Edward 'Blackbeard' Teach were coming north to avenge the death of their compatriot, Black Sam. Even though they'd had nothing to do with the natural disaster that sunk his ship, the four fishermen decided it was time to get off the island. They hopped a ride to Monhegan Island, and from there, got passage back to Ireland.

"This was all written down by Walter Ryan, the ancestor of Rose, in a diary that she uncovered a few years back. At first, she did nothing with it, but it was always there, at the back of her mind. When she met a man on a business trip in Dublin who was from Port Essex, Maine, six miles from Gorges Island, she shared her secret with him. The two began a communication, and when Tobias agreed to finance the search, Rose arranged to come to the United States. She's been here about a month now."

"And Tobias hasn't shared all of this with his wife?" Baylee asked.

"He wanted it to be a fucking surprise," Crystal said. "Sort of like springing a diamond on some broad with no forewarning. He wanted to take her out to dinner one night, wine and dine her, and at some point, casually say, 'Honey, we're rich beyond our wildest dreams.'"

*   *   *

Clay and Baylee were waiting for Andy and Dannie to come down to the bar at The Port in a Storm Inn. The few tables had been filled with tourists, seemingly just now eating and drinking their lunch in the midafternoon. There was a low hum of noise, this crowd refueling for another night, perhaps having just gotten off a charter boat or back from a hike, or more likely, shopping along Commercial Way.

There were few windows, which was a shame, as the back wall behind the bar faced the harbor and would've had stunning views. Clay supposed that would've caused the dilemma of where to stack the liquor bottles that lined the shelves there. You can't have it all, he thought, grinning wryly, either a view or alcohol, one must choose. The bar was made from walnut, polished to a shining gleam, and the bartender sported a red bow tie with white stars on it. Much fancier than the more comfortable Pelican Perch.

"Interesting that Port Essex is host to two different treasure seekers, and they both have taken up residence here," Baylee said. "At The Port in a Storm."

"I guess a port in a storm would've been helpful," Clay said. "For the fishermen of Gorges Island and Black Sam Bellamy."

Baylee chuckled at the thin witticism. "What do you think we should tell Gina Yates?"

"You mean, is it good news that her husband is not having an affair but is merely secretly searching for a lost treasure with an Irish lass without telling Gina?"

"I suppose she's paid us to find the truth, and we're obligated to share that truth." Baylee took a sip of her frozen mocha. "And that most likely will be the end of it."

"Yep." Clay swiveled his eyes around the room. No Rose. No Tobias. But he did recognize the fellow in the corner, sitting at a table by himself, a hamburger in his hand. The fellow he'd had an altercation with. Rod, or something like that, Clay thought. "We'll let the two of them sort out their own affairs. That way we can concentrate on helping Andy and Dannie find the fire opals."

"Sort of throwing some gasoline on the fire to distract Tobias in his search for the treasure while we hunker down and see if we can't find it first?"

"Just doing the job we were hired for," Clay said. "If that muddies the waters, so to speak, so be it." He felt his sixth sense tingle, his eyes flickering sideways. Roderick. That was his name. With some sort of Hispanic last name. The man seemed to be staring at them. "The guy over in the corner seems to have an abnormal preoccupation with us."

Baylee took her time, picking up her drink and taking a sip through the straw from the mason jar, allowing her eyes to search out the corner as she did so. Her lips twitched, a dribble of the chocolate sauce running down her chin.

"Sorry we're a bit late," Andy said, coming up on Baylee's side of the table, Dannie in tow. "I had a phone call just as we were about to come down."

"No worries," Clay said. "I believe that table there," he nodded, "just opened up. Should we grab it?"

Once they were settled, Clay snuck a glance back to the corner, but Rod was gone. As if he'd never been there. He'd been replaced by an Asian couple.

"What happened to you?" Baylee asked.

Clay looked back to his present company and realized that Dannie's eye was discolored and there was a scrape on her cheekbone.

Dannie snorted. "Quite embarrassing, really. Last night, I went out for a smoke at the end of the night. I'd thought it'd be pretty to walk out on the dock behind the inn and see the moon out over the harbor. Long story short, I tripped over what I think was a lobster trap and smashed my face into a piling."

"That's why we had to take a raincheck today," Andy said. "I think she had a bit of a concussion even if she refused to go to the hospital."

"Urgent care closed at 7:00 p.m." Dannie snorted again. "Wasn't going to drive all the way to Brunswick for a bump on my noggin."

Both Andy and Dannie ordered vodka on the rocks. Clay wasn't sure if that was the best idea with a possible concussion. He felt the tug of wanting to order a drink other than coffee, perhaps an Old Fashioned, but refrained.

"You said you had something to tell us?" Andy said. "A new development in the treasure hunt?"

Clay tore his thoughts from brown liquor. His eyes flickered around the room, but there was no sign of Rod. He looked at Dannie's black eye. Where to start?

"We've come across two pieces of information," he said. "There was a Native American village on the Sibosek River that matches your map and directions better and so might help us find the church-bell shaped rock."

"Fantastic," Dannie said. "Where was this village?"

"We're not quite sure, to tell you the truth," Baylee said. "We're still working on that."

"But the second development very well might negate the need to do that," Clay said.

"What's that?" Andy asked.

"We have learned that the fire opals might be on the bottom of the ocean floor."

Clay went on to fill them in on the story Westy had relayed, omitting names, and probably not in as much detail as his buddy had done, but he passed on the gist of it. The treasure had been moved and very well might be anywhere, depending on currents and tides.

Chapter 18

Clay and Baylee parted from Andy in the parking lot. He was driving to Damariscotta to have dinner with a friend while Dannie was going back to the room to lie down and rest her concussed head.

Clay and Baylee had walked down to the inn and were now on their way back to the P.I. office, it being actually quicker to walk than drive down Commercial Way in the heart of the summer. It was approaching five o'clock, happy hour time, but it appeared that many of the pedestrians had started their jubilation some hours earlier.

These revelers were mixed in with shoppers, mostly women, carrying cavernous bags down the narrow sidewalks, sideswiping others as they went, oblivious to their oafishness. Families, with children licking ice cream cones, wended their way through the obstacles of party-goers and gung-ho shoppers, all trying to avoid being knocked into the street, which was luckily locked in gridlock and not as dangerous as if the cars were traveling at a higher rate of speed, especially seeing as more than likely many of the drivers had started their happy jubilation some time earlier, as well.

Clay's phone buzzed with a text from Murphy. Got some info for you.

Clay paused to text back. You at Lucky Linda's?

"What's up?" Baylee asked, stopping and turning back to him on the crowded sidewalk.

A thumb's up emoji came back from Murphy as a woman laden down with shopping bags jostled past Clay, giving him the stink eye as she did so. Baylee stood her ground and stared the woman down, making her take a wide berth around her.

"Feel like swinging by Lucky Linda's?" Clay asked.

"A bit early, but sure," Baylee said with a smirk.

"It's always too early to stop by L & L." Clay resumed walking.

"I take it that was a certain Irishman."

"Aye, lassie, that it was."

Baylee fell into step beside him. "I'm not sure I quite like being called a dog's name."

They turned up the hill. "To be fair, Lassie was quite a brilliant dog."

Baylee batted him in the arm. "What'd the wee Irishman want?"

"Said he had some information."

"Couldn't he just text it to you?"

Clay chuckled. "Information is shared by Murphy only with the purchase of a double Jameson."

"In which we must also indulge," Baylee said.

"I told you right from the get-go that being a P.I. is tough gig sometimes."

Baylee snickered. "If you enjoy your work and are good at it, you will prosper. Isn't that an adage or something?"

"If it isn't, it should be."

The bartender eyeballed Clay as they came through the door. The place was filling up, the day crowd overlapping with the happy hour patrons, all mixed in with a few tourists either slumming or lost.

Murphy was on the right side of the U-shaped bar and Clay sat down on one side of the wiry and wrinkled Irishman with the sparkling blue eyes and Baylee on the other, lucky to have gotten seats.

Clay raised three fingers to the bartender who was still glaring at him. "Three double Jameson's. One neat, two with rocks."

The bartender finished drying the glass in his hand and set it down. "Usually, you start a fight in here. You're banned at least until the bruises and scrapes on your face heal up."

"Ah, Danny-boy, ease up," Murphy said. "Those lads were bad news. And not from around these here parts. Stop acting the maggot."

"Haven't seen you in here much," the bartender said, grudgingly putting two glasses on the bar to which he added ice cubes. "'Cept when you're causing a ruckus." He poured a liberal dose into Murphy's almost empty glass and then made a point of measuring Clay and Baylee's liquor with a shot glass so as not to give them a drop more than a double.

"Just trying to protect the Linda's good name and weed out the trash," Clay said. He took a belt of the Jameson. "Matter of fact, you should be paying me, not criticizing me. Doing you a service and all."

The bartender snorted and walked off down the bar.

"What do you got for me?" Clay turned to Murphy.

"See that lass across the way?" Murphy asked. "Sitting by herself with her head down and dark glasses on?"

"Yep. What about her?"

"Lovely lass, she is, but sometimes she turns tricks to pay the rent, put food on the table for her three sons."

"Girls gotta do what a girls gotta do," Baylee said.

"You get a bit closer, and you'll see her face is all marked up," Murphy said. "And I'm betting that's not the all of it. See how stiffly she's sitting?"

"Tough profession," Clay said. "No doubt about that."

"Men can be real asshats," Baylee said.

"She said she got a phone call from some dosser. Offered to pay her, as she said, real good money, for a night of work. Didn't say that there'd be four of them." Murphy took a sip of his Jameson. "Bikers, she said they were. Four of 'em. One of them had a vest on with the name Buccaneers on the back."

"Interesting," Clay said. "Think she'd talk to me?"

"Told her I had a friend who'd gotten in a tussle with those same lads the other night and would love to follow up with them on some unfinished business. She was mighty interested in that line of thought."

Clay stood up, drink in hand, and Baylee went to follow, but Murphy grabbed her arm at the elbow. "Stay and keep me company," he said.

Clay walked around the bar and slid into the seat next to the woman. "Mind if I sit here?"

"Murphy said it was you." The woman nodded at the seat next to her. "I been following all your doings in the *Register*." Below the blackened eye and scraped cheek was a pretty face with a pert nose and full lips.

"Clay Wolfe." He held out his hand, and she took it firmly.

"Annette. Used to be Annette Williams when we were back in school together."

Clay took a second look. He knew her. She'd been popular, not of the cheerleader variety, but was one of the in girls back in school. Same straw-colored hair and freckles and filled out some since high school, but it was Annette Williams, who he'd had a crush on for several years of school. She took off her sunglasses and revealed her sparkling blue eyes.

"You might want to close your mouth," she said. "Who knows what's floating through the air in this joint."

Clay realized his jaw had swung agape, and he snapped it shut. "I haven't seen you since the graduation party out to the quarry," he said. They'd shared drinks by the fire, and at times, Clay thought it might evolve into something more but hadn't. They'd gone their separate ways that night never realizing how long and how much would pass before seeing each other again.

"Yeah, well, I was working on my uncle's fishing boat all summer, and then you went off to college and were gone for, what, like fifteen years?"

Pretty much, Clay thought. He'd come home to visit with Grandpops but had tried to leave Port Essex behind, thinking it was a Podunk town, and he was meant for the big city. There was something about city life that had never jived with him, and when his Grandpops had taken a tumble, he'd returned home and not left again, the best decision of his life. This was his town. Who he was.

"You look good," he said. "Other than the black eye and scrapes."

"Same could be said of you," Annette said, and they both laughed.

"No, but seriously, you look good."

"You're sweet," she said. "Always had a soft spot for you. You were one of the nice ones."

"Murph said you have three boys?"

"Took up with some guy from down to Portland and married him. Only good part of him was those three boys. Best thing that happened is he up and disappeared off the face of the earth one day. Although, it ain't easy supporting growing boys as a hair stylist. On occasion, I have to supplement my income." Annette touched her face gingerly with her pointer finger. "Work hazard, you know."

Clay reached up to his own battered visage. "Me, too."

They both laughed.

After a few seconds, Annette's eyes clouded, and her face went grim. "Murphy said you had a run-in with the same guys who did me."

Clay nodded. "If it was four fellows with poor hygiene and vests that say Buccaneers and have a hard time pronouncing words, then, yes."

"Three of them heavy-set, one thin guy with a nose like a wedge," Annette said. "And mean eyes."

"One of them had an octopus tattoo dangling down his arm."

Annette nodded. "That'd be the same bastards."

"They threatened me and my partner with cutlasses and old-style pistols one night on the road, so when I saw them in here, right over there," he jerked his chin toward the corner behind them, "I thought it would be a good time for a chat."

"Murphy said you weren't done talking to them."

"Not by a long shot. You know where they're at?"

Annette sighed. "Fellow who called me and set it up said the gentleman, his word, who wanted to… engage my services, didn't want me knowing where he lived, and that I'd have to be blindfolded for the drive out there."

"And you agreed to that?"

"He was paying well. Very well."

Clay nodded. "Go on."

"He had me park out back at Koasek Park, you know, where everybody used to go parking back in the day. There's a bench off to the right, and he told me to meet him there at ten o'clock at night. Came up behind me, told me to not turn around, and blindfolded me. Led me out to the road where he must've parked his car. It only took about fifteen minutes to get to where we was going. He led me inside. It was all a lie. It wasn't some married gentleman cheating on his wife but four pigs who took turns having their way with me, and in between, slapped me around." Annette sniffled, cleared her throat, and turned her blazing eyes toward Clay. "You know, I figured I just had to get through it, but when they'd all had their turn, and I asked if I could go, they just laughed at me. Said I'd be there for a while. As their sex slave. When I argued, they beat me, when I fought back, they beat me worse and tied me up."

Clay put his hand on her shoulder. There was nothing to say. Tears had started sliding down her cheeks.

"I got my boys I had to get home to," Annette said. "When the thin guy came back for a second helping, I played along, pretended I was enjoying it, that he was some big stud, you know, and then when I got the chance, I made a run for it. Came out the back door of the house and right into the woods. They came out calling and looking for me, I could hear them behind me as I ran, naked through the woods. But they was drunk and in no shape to come after me. I figured they might roam the streets looking for me, so when I found a road, I followed it but stayed in the woods, you know, until it came to a crossroad, and I was able to read the sign. It was the Old Narrow Ridge road that runs between East Essex and Essex."

"Was that the road the house was on?" Clay asked.

Annette shook her head. "Can't be sure. I was stumbling through the woods for more than an hour. Maybe two. It was up that way, anyway."

"How'd you get home?"

"Just before the sun came up, an old truck came rambling down the road. I figured they wouldn't be driving some old jalopy like that and flagged it down. Nice old geezer had a blanket behind the seat to wrap me in, wanted to take me to the police, call an ambulance, but I wouldn't let him, you know, as I don't want the town, my boys, to know that I turn the occasional trick and fuck somebody for money. Police would've probably thrown me in a cell, what with that new chief they got and all. I finally convinced the old guy to just take me back to my car, and I drove home in nothing but a blanket. Got into my trailer before the boys even woke up for the day."

"Did you get any names?"

"The thin one was named Lonnie. Another one was Jerry. That's all I know."

"And they're staying in a house up around the Old Narrow Ridge road," Clay said. "That'll give us something to look for. Can't imagine that four dudes on motorcycles have gone unnoticed. Somebody will point me in the right direction."

"They ain't got no respect for anybody or anything," Annette said. "You make 'em pay for what they done, or you tell where they are, and I'll take care of it my own self."

"One way or another, amends will be made."

"I hear you still got Weston watching your back," Annette said. "And that he was a SEAL for a bit."

"Yeah, that's right," Clay said.

"You bring him along when you go looking for those monkey fuckers," she said. "He'll know what to do."

* * *

Socrates sat in his gray, 2008 Buick Regal. There were no dents or scratches that would attract attention. Nine out of ten people wouldn't remember even seeing a car like this. That was the point.

It was eleven at night. He was pulled over to the side of the back road from Damariscotta to Port Essex. Waiting for Andy Kozak. Right about now, the man would become aware of a group of motorcycles on his rear bumper. Socrates visualized the scene, two bikes pulling out and passing Andy on the straightaway. As if on cue, he heard the distant rumble of Harleys in the air.

If the man was smart, he'd slow, and wave the other two to pass, joining their comrades in streaking away into the night. He'd be surprised when they didn't take him up on the offer, barely noticing that the two in front were not flying off into the distance, but in fact, had slowed done in front of him. The rumble grew deeper, angrier, approaching the curve beyond which Socrates waited.

He could see the headlights flashing on the telephone poles, and then the small caravan swept around the corner, barely moving, before coming to a complete stop next to Socrates. He stepped out of the car, his GSh-18 9 in hand, the 18-shot 9 mm comfortable in his hand. The pistol was made for short work and could pierce body armor, and thus, would easily shoot through a car door if necessary.

It was not. Andy Kozak's eyes got very large in his head, his mouth opened and shut, and it looked as if he was briefly contemplating running over the two motorcycles stopped in front of him. It would've been better for him if he had tried. Of course, Socrates would've shot him immediately in the head, and he'd be dead. But that was still better than his future if he succumbed to the menacing pistol and surrendered.

As it was, Andy allowed himself to be persuaded out of the car. Socrates put zip ties around his wrists, sat him in the passenger side of the Buick, and snapped the handcuffs to the chain he had attached to the underneath of the seat. And then Socrates drove off down the road. The Buccaneers would dispose of the car, there being a spot just a hundred yards up where it could be driven off the side to go tumbling down into ocean below. It wouldn't escape detection for long, but that didn't matter, for Andriy wouldn't be around much longer, either.

He drove to the rental house where the Buffoons, as he'd taken to calling the Buccaneers, had been staying for the past few nights. By the time they arrived, he already had the tarp spread out over the living room floor. From a chain slung over the center beam of the farmhouse, hung Andy Kozak, stripped naked. Ankle chains attached him to the floor, his body stretched taut.

"Who are you?"

"What training does your partner, Daniela Cox, have?"

"Who do you work for?"

"What is your real name?"

Socrates went to the ottoman table where a toolbox, gray metal, sat. He opened it, rummaging around until he pulled out a clamping tool, a dull-ugly gadget. "This should do the trick," he said, opening and closing it. "How big are your balls, Andy?" He walked back over with the clamp stretched wide. "Will one of them fit in here, do you suppose?"

Andy had been unable to answer any questions as of yet as there was a rag stuffed in his mouth with duct tape wrapped around his head. His eyes spoke volumes, though, as he beseeched the man in front of him to not place his testicle in this clamping device that looked a bit like a cross between a wrench and a tree pruning tool.

"You must have pretty big balls to come stomping around where you don't belong," Socrates said. He opened the clamp wide with both hands, trying to position the nasty looking clamps around the man's testicle. "Stop wiggling, I can't quite get a hold of that slippery little sucker. It's like somebody greased up an oyster and attached it to a kangaroo. Hold still, dammit."

Piss spurted from Andriy's penis and Socrates stepped to the side to avoid it. "Almost had me, there, you did." He laughed uproariously. "Did they train you to piss on your assailants?"

"Lonnie," Socrates said. "Come over and help me get his greasy little oyster of a testicle in my clamps."

Lonnie edged his way forward, sweating profusely on the warm night. There were many conflicting emotions swirling in his eyes, but the fear of refusing the command overcame any other misgivings. "What do you want me to do?" he asked.

"Go ahead and squeeze his scrotum between your thumb and your pointer finger," Socrates said. "So that his testicle bulges out and then hold it steady so I can get a grip."

"I ain't grabbing his junk," Lonnie said.

Socrates looked at him. Waited a moment.

Lonnie ducked his head, reached down and held the man's penis to one side, circling the man's right testicle with his other hand, he squeezed the scrotum, popping the testicle out, an oyster ready to be shucked.

"Aha, that's the trick," Socrates said triumphantly, positioning the clamps.

"You haven't even given him a chance to tell you what you want to know," Lonnie said. "His mouth is gagged."

Socrates paused, staring at him. Lonnie held his stare for ten seconds while his hand held the man's right testicle. Then he looked away.

It made a popping sound, slippery and squelchy, like biting into a boiled pearl onion. Andy's body went rigid and he shit, the putrid smell filling the living room. A keening escaped around the rag and duct tape and the man's eyes rolled in his head. Lonnie staggered away, his face white, and his eyes in shock.

"That," Socrates said, "was fun. Let's see what he has to tell us." He ripped the duct tape from around the man's face and pulled the rag out.

He told them everything, even if Socrates wasn't satisfied for another five hours. Unfortunately for Andy, he truly didn't know much, but Socrates had to be sure. The woman had surprised him. He wouldn't make that mistake twice. There wasn't a whole lot left of Andy when he finally escaped his living hell to the comfort of death.

Chapter 19

Clay was glad that he was the first one into the office on Friday morning. Mainly because he wouldn't have wanted Baylee or Crystal to find the dead body. Especially not in the horribly mutilated state that it was. This was worse than anything he'd seen during his stint as a Boston homicide detective.

Andy Kozak was a mix of bruises and slices. He was naked, covered in congealing blood, suggesting that he'd not been dead all that long. He was sitting, or rather propped, in Crystal's chair at the reception desk. There was a piece of paper pierced to his chest with a pen that said, 'How can I help you?'. It took Clay a few minutes to be sure who it was.

A siren sounded, growing closer, and then came to a stop outside. Clay stepped to the small deck overlooking Commercial Way and scanned the sidewalks, street, and surrounding buildings. The timing of the arrival of the police suggested somebody had been watching and called it in when they saw Clay arrive.

There were two people walking dogs, a woman with a stroller, Abdar, the owner of the gift shop across the way unlocking his door, but nobody that looked out of place or suspicious at this early morning hour.

Luckily, Clay knew the two policewomen who came up the stairs, Officers Richards and Tracy. There'd been some changeover in the past couple of years with the new police chief, and the new blood seemed to follow Chief Roberts' notion that P.I.s were a nuisance to have around.

"Got an anonymous call, Clay, of a dead body, here in your office," Officer Tracy said.

"Just got here and found him," Clay said. "It's not pretty. You're going to want backup to close down the scene and get the staties and forensics and the whole nine yards."

Officer Richards stepped into the open doorway. "Jesus."

"You check his pulse?" Officer Tracy asked, stepping around her partner.

"He's dead," Clay said. "No doubt about that."

The day was a mess. Clay had a chance to call Baylee and give her a heads up, and that it'd be a good idea to get somebody to check in on Flash, Ollie, and Frank, who Clay had left fast asleep at her place when he'd left this morning. He figured they both had a long day in front of them talking with the authorities.

Dannie Cox was contacted and picked up for questioning. The state police arrived and took over the crime scene. Clay was taken down to the station for questioning before the forensics team arrived. After several hours, Baylee came into the room where Clay had been left alone after reiterating for the tenth time what he knew. She'd been getting the same treatment in a different room.

Crystal was briefly questioned and let go. Clay suspected that nobody wanted to deal with his foul mouthed and outspoken assistant. He was allowed to call her to have her stop by Baylee's house to pick up Frank. Baylee's pets were able to be left alone quite a bit longer than the puppy. A piece of his mind noted wryly that it took a community to raise a puppy.

Clay didn't say anything about the other case, being hired by Gina Yates to follow her husband for philandering, and the subsequent discovery that he was actually pursuing the same treasure that Dannie and Andy had been. This kept Westy out of the dragnet of people being scooped up by local and state law enforcement.

He did share his run-in with the four Buccaneers, but kept Murphy out of it, as well as Annette's ordeal at their hands. That was her decision to come forward or not, Clay figured, and not his to make. Besides, he didn't really think this grisly murder was really the work of the four bikers. They might be rough and tumble, they might even be criminals or killers, but he didn't peg them for this type of particularly gruesome and sadistic torture.

Ten hours after arriving at the office to find a dead body, Clay walked up the stairs to the Pelican Perch. His people were gathered, waiting for him. Baylee had been let go a couple of hours earlier than him. He touched her shoulder as he walked past to find a seat at the other end of the two tables pushed together. He sat with Murphy to his left and Cloutier to his right, across from Crystal, Baylee, and Westy. The deck was crowded with Friday summer revelers celebrating happy hour, sun, vacation, fun, and life. Their table was a bit more dismal than the others.

Silas, the bartender, wended his way through the crowd, and set a tumbler mostly full of brown liquor with just a couple of ice cubes down in front of Clay. "From the rumors, you could use this," he said. "On the house." He turned and walked back to the bar, gliding through the crowd like Moses through the Red Sea.

Murphy raised his glass. "Today was a bad dose. Let's drink to the lad, Andy, who didn't deserve to die like he did."

They raised their glasses, Westy a Budweiser, Cloutier a cosmos, Crystal a margarita, Baylee a red wine, while Clay and Murphy clinked brown liquor.

"Heard he was pretty messed up," Westy said.

"Worst I've ever seen," Clay said. "Somebody worked him over something fierce."

"You figure it for those Buccaneer fellows?" Westy asked.

Clay shook his head slowly. "I don't know. They seemed to be thugs, but this? This was sadistic. The work of a truly twisted human being."

"I spent some time researching them today," Crystal said. "The Buccaneers, that is."

"Yeah?" Clay looked at her. "What'd you find out?"

Crystal took a paper from her purse and unfolded it. "The Buccaneers, as you might suspect, originated as a motorcycle club in Tampa Bay, Florida, back in 1983. Relatively late as most of the major clubs go, but they've grown steadily through the years. They now have chapters all up and down the eastern seaboard, the closest to us being down in Boston, but they're suspected of being major players of drug smuggling across the Canadian border, most likely right into Maine.

"They have over 500 'patched' members and who knows how many prospects. Their growth has been more rapid since the ascension to the throne of their current leader, Tommy 'Grub' Boseman, back in 2012. He has patched in numerous smaller MCs to grow their ranks, attracting members through a very pro-Aryan rhetoric and hatred of Blacks, Latinos, immigrants—they fucking hate everybody that isn't white. Women are chattel to them."

Clay stared in awe at Crystal. That had been a slick and efficient report with minimal cursing. There was hope for her, after all, he thought, trying to turn his smirk into a sober nod of approval.

"They violent?" Westy asked. "I mean, fiendishly barbarous, enough to torture and kill some dude as bad as Clay says that the New Yorker got done?"

"Sure as fucking shit, they are," Crystal said. "They got several of their gang in prison. One for killing a police officer who infiltrated their gang, did him in by cutting his tongue out of his mouth and letting him bleed out. They're suspected of having set two members of the Hell's Angels on fire a few years back, not that it was ever proven. Their rise to become a one-percenter is based on vicious behavior."

"One-percenter?" Baylee asked.

"Yeah," Crystal said. "Something about ninety-nine percent of motorcyclists are law-abiding citizens, but one percent are outlaws, and wear that patch proudly to reflect their status."

"Great," Clay said. "All we need is the attention of some notorious MC in Port Essex to shake things up. Sounds like they could be good for the killing of Andy after all."

"To what purpose are they in Port Essex, do you suppose?" Cloutier asked.

"They're big drug smugglers," Crystal said. "You think they're trying to reopen that door? Coming back in through the lobster traps again?"

"Nah," Clay said. "Right after we get hired by Andy and Dannie to help them find a lost treasure, these four threaten me and Baylee. More like it has to do with that. And now Andy's murder, that, too, seems on pace with their shenanigans."

"Are we sure that Andy and Dannie hired you to find fire opals?" Cloutier asked.

"What do you mean?" Clay asked.

"Sure, I know that's what they said. Wouldn't be the first clients you've had that lied to you. Could they be looking for drugs?"

Clay sighed, looked over the railing out onto Essex Harbor. "I suppose it's possible, but they seem to have gone to elaborate lengths to concoct a historically-detailed story."

"You know, drugs are always being smuggled up the coast," Cloutier said. "Just two months ago the Coast Guard found a yacht, run aground on the Sibosek River, and abandoned. Nothing left aboard, but the drug-sniffing dogs went crazy. Perhaps they took the drugs ashore and hid them, and Andy and Dannie are here to retrieve them, but can't find them, so hired you."

"Or even a smuggler who sunk and took their stash to the bottom of the Atlantic. Like that movie, *The Deep*," Crystal said. "You know, with Nick Nolte. Fuck, he's hot as shit, spends half the movie with no shirt off. I'm telling you, I'd eat that mustache right off his face if given the chance."

The group all looked at Crystal, and there was a moment of shock and awe, and then they all laughed.

"What goes on inside your head?" Clay asked, almost glad to have the real Crystal back.

"Is Tobias lying as well?" Baylee asked. "I mean, about searching for treasure. Seems like that particular lie is getting pretty thin if he is. I can't imagine he's looking for shipwrecked drugs, being a local businessman, and it seems to be a bit of coincidence him looking for treasure and them looking for drugs. Just doesn't all fit together."

"Yeah, hard to believe that the maker of robotic sex dolls is into drugs," Crystal said.

"Whatever people are looking for," Clay said, "I suppose the point is we can't take anybody at face value. We should dig into the background of Andy and Dannie, see if they really are who they say they are."

"I got to be getting home soon," Westy said. "What's the plan moving forward?"

Clay took a haul off the brown liquor. He knew what his plan was for the night, and it included several more of what he believed to be Glenlivet. "I'll try and talk to Dannie tomorrow to see how she wants to proceed. Chances are this whole treasure hunt thing just ended with the death of her fiancé."

"Yeah, you might be right there," Westy said.

"I imagine once I let Gina Yates know her husband is not cheating on her, but rather, is looking for another kind of booty, pirate booty, then she'll no longer need our services," Baylee said.

"And then we no longer have any clients," Clay said. "Hoping to pick up some work tracking down fellows out on the golf course who've been claiming workman's comp from BIW."

"There's still fucking treasure out there," Crystal said. "And if Dannie Cox don't want any part of it, then it's all ours if we find it. I'd look good in a fire opal necklace, whatever the fuck they are."

"Treasure or lost drugs," Cloutier said.

"No amount of treasure is worth getting carved up like Andy did," Westy said. "We might want to take a breather on this."

Cloutier shuddered. "You think we're in danger?"

"Whoever killed Andy is one twisted individual," Clay said. "If Dannie Cox and Gina Yates wash their hands of this affair, I say we do as well." Secretly, he knew there was no way he was going to back out of this hunt. His motive to stay the course had more to do with finding the murderer than the opals, though, but he had no intention of endangering his friends.

"Let's not walk away until we have a further conversation with our clients," Baylee said.

"Okay, I'll try and get in touch with Dannie Cox first thing in the morning to see how she wants to proceed," Clay said. "You do the same with Gina Yates."

"Got it, boss," Baylee said. "Do I tell her everything? Rose, the treasure, and all that?"

"Tobias was supposed to go home last night and tell his wife everything, which is all we really know," Crystal said.

"It wouldn't hurt to speak with her without him around," Baylee said. "I'll give her a call first. I'm not sure if I'd be madder if my husband was cheating on me or seeking a treasure without telling me."

"Let's not forget we got a vicious murderer out there wrapped up in this thing," Cloutier said.

Clay nodded. "Sure enough. Crystal, can you keep digging away on the MC. See what you can find out about any members with the name Lonnie or Jerry."

"Where'd you come up with those names?" Crystal asked.

"I spoke with a woman who they used rather poorly," Clay said. "She gave me those two names and a general area of where they might be staying. I thought that after I spoke with Dannie, as long as she doesn't want to go out on the water treasure hunting, me and Westy might have a look around and see if we can find them."

"Used poorly?" Westy asked.

Clay gave him the look, one they'd come to know, dating back to eighth grade at least. It said, quite clearly, *I'll tell you later.*

"I got nothing to do until Monday's paper," Cloutier said. "Plus, Denise is out of town. How about you send me over everything you got on Andy Kozak and Dannie Cox, and I'll see what I can find out."

"Will do," Clay said.

"What about me?" Murphy asked. "What sort of dirty job do you have for the Irishman?"

"Have a talk with Annette," Clay said. "See if she changes her mind on going to the police. If not, tell her to keep her head low, real low, like take the kids and get out of town low. And then keep your ear to the ground. Anything about the Buccaneers, the murder, the treasure—anything—nothing is too small."

Clay looked at his group of friends. When they all kicked in together like this, it was like Wolfe & Baker was a large P.I. firm with vast resources. Investigators, techs, data analysis, and muscle—they covered all the bases. "Don't ruffle any feathers. Rather, make it quite clear that we have no interest in the treasure. Our purpose is to find the murderer and the men that violently assaulted a woman in our community."

Westy stood up. "Keep your heads low people. This is one messed up psychopath."

"Stay safe," Clay said.

"I'm out," Westy said. He fist-bumped Clay. "You need anything at all, you call."

"Flash and Ollie are wondering where their dinner is," Baylee said, standing as well. "You coming over?" she asked Clay.

"I might have another drink and spend the night at my place," Clay said.

Baylee gave him a long look. "Okay. Be careful."

"I'll walk out with you," Crystal said, standing. She looked across the tables at Clay. "You coming to get Frank?"

"I'll be along in a bit," Clay said. "If that's okay."

"Hey, Murph, you need a ride home?" Cloutier asked as she rose to her feet.

"No, thank you, lassie. I'm just a wee bit down the road, and the walk will do me good."

And then they were gone, as was his drink, and Clay was left alone with his thoughts. He moved over to the bar and claimed a seat in the corner. Silas slid another healthy double in front of him and hurried off, it being extremely busy as happy hour turned into dinner on the deck at the Pelican Perch in Port Essex.

Against his better sense, Clay thought, he'd just dragged his people back into a hunt for a sadistic killer even while possibly bypassing the monetary reward of the treasure. "Oh well," he said under his breath, "you can't tell a fish not to swim, a bird not to fly, or a bee not to sting."

Chapter 20

Dannie Cox had called Clay at seven o'clock in the morning. Saturday morning. He was a bit stiff with the events of the day before and the three large, more than doubles, Glenlivets he'd drank in an effort to erase the image of Andy Kozak's mutilated body from his mind. Thus, he might've ignored the buzzing phone, but Frank had been nipping at his ear as well.

Now, one hour later, he sat at the bench outside the diner, waiting for her to arrive. One cup of coffee while Frank had tested the boundaries of the backyard and done his business, one shower and shave, and the short walk all helping to dissolve the tendrils of booze that curled through his head.

Frank had a firm grip on his shoelace, see-sawing his head back and forth, as if in some life-or-death tug-of-war match. A gray cloud floated in front of the sun, and a light breeze wafted up the hill coming off the harbor. Downtown was partially visible through the twisting streets, delivery trucks parked with hazards flashing, restocking food and drink.

A BMW pulled into the last parking spot in the small lot of the diner, and Dannie emerged from the vehicle. She had round dark glasses on, and her hair was askew atop her head. She wore a black jumpsuit, color appropriate for a grieving woman, but also very sexy, and Clay mentally kicked himself for thinking so.

"Morning," he said, scooping Frank up as he stood.

"Thank you for meeting with me," Dannie said.

"Sorry about Andy." The words sounded incredibly lame as they hung in the air between them, but what else could one say?

"He was a good man," Dannie said, her voice cracking just the slightest bit.

The diner was full, but Clay led Dannie to the table that was kept open for him. He was a regular. Seven days a week. Truth be told, he'd missed a couple of days since he and Baylee had started sleeping together.

"How are you holding up?" Clay asked.

"Like I want to cry and punch something all at the same time," Dannie said. Her eyes, now with the sunglasses off, were indeed angry, but also, red, presumably from crying.

"Do you have any idea of who might've done that to Andy?"

"What? Tortured him? Crushed his nuts? Sliced him up like he was a fucking block of cheese?"

Clay thought it time to keep his mouth shut. Luckily, Becky, the waitress came over and poured them coffee and got their orders. Eggs Benedict for him, a fruit and yogurt cup for her.

"Will you find out who did this?" Dannie asked.

"The police are on the case."

Dannie snorted. Her voice was grating. "No chance of them tracking down the killer."

"Why's that?" Clay asked.

"They don't have the sack for something like this."

"Something like what?"

"This was a professional. There will be no fingerprints. No evidence of any kind. The police will walk around in circles for a few weeks and then quietly return to looking for missing cats or whatever the fuck it is that they do here in Maine."

Who was this woman, Clay wondered? It was as if her urban antiques dealer shell had been peeled back to reveal one rough and tough lady. "You plan on hunting down the person who killed Andy? I'd say they're pretty darn scary."

"He didn't deserve this." Dannie rubbed her hand across her face. "He had no idea what he was into."

"And what exactly was he into? What are *you* into?"

Dannie looked surprised. "We... I'm looking for an incredibly valuable cache of rare jewels hidden away in eight chests stashed by a pirate. Obviously, something worth killing over."

"You believe Andy was tortured to find out what he knew about this treasure?"

Dannie scoffed. "Don't you? What else could it be?"

"What do you want to do about the treasure?" he asked.

Dannie brushed a lock of hair from her face, her blue eyes burning into his. "Find it, of course."

"You want me searching for the killer or hunting the treasure first?" He was just trying to pin down her priorities but saw a fleeting disdain flash through her eyes.

"You do realize, don't you," Dannie said, "that the two are connected? Andy was killed by somebody trying to get information about the fire opals. I'd be willing to guess that he shared everything he knows."

"That seems to be the obvious answer," Clay said.

"When we find the opals, whoever killed Andy will come after them," she said. "And when they do, we will be waiting for them. This will make your job very easy. Like killing two birds with one stone."

Becky brought their food over, allowing Clay a reprieve from Dannie's chilling eyes. He had a feeling that finding Andy's murderer might include more than handing them over to the police. Who was this woman, he wondered? The Indiana Jones of antiques?

"Who are you, really?" Clay asked.

"You know who I am. Does it surprise you that I want my fiancé avenged?"

Clay held her gaze. People grieved in many different ways—this he knew. If it were Baylee who'd been killed, why then, there'd be no stopping him in chasing down her murderer. Why should it be any different for Dannie? Because she was an antiques dealer? A woman?

"No. You're right," he said. "I will do whatever I can to bring Andy's killer to justice."

"Tell me more about this other pair searching for my treasure," Dannie said.

"Rose Ryan and Tobias Yates," Clay said. "She is the descendant of Walter Ryan, who was a fisherman on Gorges Island, which is about six miles out, back when Black Sam Bellamy was frequenting these parts. Rose recently found his diary in which he details that twelve men from the island went to a Native American village on the mainland and found the treasure but were sunk in a storm on their return journey. Soon after, he and the other three surviving fishermen caught passage to Monhegan Island and eventually made their way back to Ireland. Tobias Yates is a local businessman. The two of them met serendipitously in Dublin and made a plan to search for the treasure."

"My treasure," Dannie said. "Do you think them capable of maiming and murdering my Andy?"

Clay gave a bit of his poached egg to Frank, then he thought on Dannie's question. He was a bit nervous about that, thinking of the incident Baylee had had with Tobias. If he *were* the killer, Baylee had been on very thin ice, as were Westy and Crystal now as well.

"I wondered about that," he said. "I've not met either of them, so it'd be hard to know for sure. But they seem to have even more information than you and Andy, so it doesn't make sense. Whoever killed Andy was trying to find something out."

"They'd be worth keeping an eye on," Dannie said.

Clay refrained from telling her that they had already been following Tobias, and that was how they'd discovered him searching for treasure. More than likely, he mused, that official capacity would be null and void once Baylee updated Gina on her husband's non-affair, but rather, that he was merely looking for long lost treasure.

"When should we resume looking for the opals?" he asked.

"As soon as you finish eating," she said.

*   *   *

Gina Yates texted Baylee back at ten in the morning to let her know that Tobias had left, and she could feel free to come by the house with whatever update she had.

Baylee had been up since the crack of dawn worrying about Clay. She'd seen the look in his eyes and knew that he was going to cope with the shit of a day yesterday through drink. And lots of it, more than likely. She'd fought the urge to call, text, or swing by to check on him. Going to chat with Gina would preoccupy her mind and then give her a reason to check in with Clay to update him on the conversation.

It was about a ten-minute drive from her house, leaving the island she lived on over a short bridge, and traversing onto Townsend Island in between two rivers over a longer bridge. It'd been just over a week ago that Baylee had been out here to tail Tobias in an effort to find proof of marital infidelity. It was hard to believe everything that happened in just eight days.

She passed the entrance of the Winnegance Nature Preserve to the left and in less than a mile, came to the gated driveway. Gina buzzed her in, the iron bars swinging inward, and she drove down the winding path. The house was more a series of houses in a U-shape, the largest in the middle in a gray-shingled cape style, and then two outbuildings attached on either side. The circular drive went around an ornate stone fountain, and Baylee was able to see the Sibosek River just on the other side of the mansion.

Gina met her wearing a floppy straw hat and flowing green dress, ushering her through the house and out the back to a patio overlooking the river. What little Baylee saw of the house was like the lobby of a museum with statues and paintings that looked quite expensive. Baylee grinned wryly, thinking that the sex doll business must be very lucrative indeed.

"Coffee or tea?" Gina asked, pausing at a serving trolley with a stainless-steel canister and a pot of hot water. There were tea bags, cream, and sugar, along with pastries and fruit.

Baylee started to decline and then caught a glimpse of the coffee cake. "Sure." She cut herself a square of the deliciousness and poured herself a cup of coffee, black, figuring the coffee cake would provide the necessary sweetness.

Gina put a strawberry and two blueberries on a plate and grabbed a Poland Springs bottled water. She motioned for Baylee to sit in one of two gray wicker chairs with plush pillows.

"Nice spot on the river," Baylee said, setting her plate and coffee down on a small table between the chairs as she sat down. She was extremely aware of the white and black dog hair on her slacks, as well the orange cat hair. "Did your husband speak with you last night about what all is going on?"

Gina sat down, elegant in her green dress, and crossed her legs. "Yes. He told me that he'd been approached by this Rose Ryan woman about a far-fetched quest for a lost treasure. He said he wasn't interested, but she offered to pay him, to be her local guide, or something like that. He thought it'd be a hoot, I believe was the word he used, and didn't think to even mention it to me as it was so improbable that anything would come of it."

"He didn't think it worth mentioning?" Baylee finished chewing a bite of the coffee cake and swallowed the delicious richness. "Even when he told you he was going to a conference out in Arizona or someplace and instead stayed at a local inn for the weekend?"

Gina popped a blueberry into her mouth. Her blue eyes blazed. "When I mentioned that, he got angry. I think it was then he realized who you were, and that I'd hired a private investigator to follow him. He called you a name that I could never repeat. He was very outraged." She sniffed, turning away from Baylee to look at the river.

"I suppose that I should just be happy that he's not cheating on me."

"My understanding is that he met Rose Ryan in Dublin, and together, they hatched this plan for a treasure hunt," Baylee said. She took a second forkful of coffee cake, its taste heavenly against the bitterness of the coffee. "He told my... lead investigator that he wanted to surprise you with the discovery."

"He told me some story about a pirate named Black Sam Bellamy and something called fire opals. That they'd sunk to the bottom of the ocean and could be anywhere."

That was mostly true, as Westy had pointed out, that the tides and movement of the ocean over several hundred years could've transported the shallop in any number of directions. "According to the diary of Rose Ryan's ancestor," she said, "the treasure had been found, but then sunk, between the mainland and Gorges Island. A distance of six miles."

"You think he believes he'll find these opals?" The blueberries had stained her shining white teeth a tint of purple. "And that they're worth a great deal?"

"I don't know," Baylee said. "But I have found no evidence of your husband having an affair. It appears that the relationship with Rose is purely business." As much as his true business of making sex dolls was purely a matter of dollars and cents, she thought, and not some perverse inclination to create a perfect woman with no mind of her own.

"There is no hanky-panky between Tobias and this woman?" Gina asked. "Nothing at all?"

Baylee pursed her lips. "They both appear to have stayed at The Port in a Storm Inn but had separate rooms. I can't be absolutely certain, but as of yet, I see no indication of anything between them other than a business relationship."

"What do you think of my husband?"

"I think he'd be crazy to have an affair," Baylee said. "You're absolutely beautiful."

"You know what his business is?"

Baylee's cheeks flushed. This was, after all, the man's wife. "Yes. Crystal told me all about it."

"He has created thirteen female models during the history of his business," Gina said. She took a swig of water. "He brings each new one home to 'try it out.' He has me watch. This is supposedly to get my input, to help make the models better, but it is humiliating to watch my husband make love to a doll. I can never be as beautiful as his own creations. He handpicks every detail, from skin color, to hair, to pubic hair, to… well, you get the point."

"That must be very disturbing for you."

"You have no idea. But then I tussle with whether it is wrong. Women have vibrators and that is acceptable. These dolls are really no more than sex toys. Would you consider what he is doing as cheating?"

This conversation had gone off the rails, Baylee thought, and needed to be steered back onto the tracks. She was not the woman's therapist or confessor. "All I can tell you is that, thus far, we have no indication of your husband having any sort of sexual affair with Rose Ryan or any other living human being."

Gina tittered, and then laughed, the sound shooting forth as if a small explosion, her eyes showing their surprise at the bellow from her own mouth. "Well, that's nice," she said.

Baylee fought to keep her face impassive and hide the grin that threatened to creep forth. "How would you like to proceed?"

"I am not convinced that that bastard of a husband is not porking this Rose Ryan, whether she is real or fake. If he can't keep his peter out of a silicon doll, well then, I doubt he can keep it out of some hussy who is telling him what he wants to hear."

"You'd like us to continue our surveillance of your husband?"

"Yes. I know that he screws around. Bring me proof. With this Rose Ryan or somebody else, it doesn't matter. But bring me verification of his philandering. And I'd also like to know how his little treasure hunt goes, as well, because half of anything he finds is going to be mine."

Baylee stuffed the last bit of coffee cake into her mouth. She wondered if this was a conflict of interest, working for two separate clients searching for the same treasure. Chances are, once Clay got an opportunity to speak with Dannie Cox, they would be down to just the one patron in search of treasure, making the conflict a moot point.

Baylee wanted so badly to say, Very well, Gina, I'll find out and let you know if your husband gets any booty, of any kind, but she managed to keep her mouth shut. With a wave, she walked off around the house to her car.

Chapter 21

Clay thought Baylee would've been into the office by now. It was going on eleven o'clock in the morning. He was just about to call her when he heard footsteps on the stairs, and then the key turned in the lock.

Baylee came through the door wearing white capris and a white cotton shirt with red vertical stripes, a look that made Clay question why he'd not gone to her house last night. Frank went yipping out the door and tumbled into her feet as she leaned down and picked up the pup, kissing him on the nose.

"I didn't expect you to be up and about much before noontime," Baylee said as she carried Frank into the inner office.

"Had to get up to make the donuts," Clay said. "And Dannie Cox woke me with an early phone call wanting to get together."

"Yeah? Thought she might take a few days to recover from the death of her fiancé."

"She was far from the grieving widow," Clay said. "Or whatever you call it when the one you're engaged to dies."

"Do tell."

"The grief stage seemed to have come and gone very quick. She is onto angry. And vengeful. I do believe that a layer or two of veneer has been stripped away from the façade of mild and meek antique dealer."

"Bereavement works in many ways," Baylee said. "There is no right or wrong way."

"Yeah, well, she wants to get right back on the horse looking for the treasure. We're meeting at noontime down to Knox Wharf with Westy and Murphy to go scuba diving for treasure in the Atlantic."

"That is quick," Baylee said. "Murphy?"

"To be aboard ship while we dive. I called him a couple hours ago, and he actually answered his phone. Hopefully I got him before he was too far into his cups."

"Wouldn't know what that Irishman looked like sober."

"Yeah, well, it was him or Crystal. Don't think we'd be getting Cloutier out alone on a boat while we were down below. And both of them are hopefully digging deep, researching who these people are and what they're really doing here."

"What about me?"

"Got to thinking about that Native American woman you spoke with," Clay said. "What was her name?"

"Niben. Niben Glenn of the Chbo So Clan."

"Niben." Clay filed the name away for safe keeping in the future. "She seemed to know the history about all of this pretty well. I remember, you seem to have some doubts after your visit, like maybe there was more to the story. I was thinking you should go back and talk to her, see what she knows about the fishermen from Gorges Island coming ashore and finding jewels around their encampment, if it truly was the... Chbo So on the Sibosek River where Black Sam hid the stuff. Ask her what she knows about Rose Ryan's story, as it is so different from what she told you."

"Makes sense," Baylee said.

"I know we're grasping at straws here, but what if the fishermen never came and took the jewels?"

"Then the diary of Rose Ryan's ancestor was a fake?"

"Could be." Clay shrugged. "Maybe they came and took them. Didn't want to share with the four men left behind, so they staged the shipwreck. Hitched a canoe ride from the Chbo So, either overland, up the river, or along the coast."

"Leave no stone unturned," Baylee said. "And Dannie is a licensed diver?"

Clay shook his head, not in negation, but in wonder. "She assures me she that she is."

"That woman is not who she says she is."

"There is definitely a few more layers to her then I thought."

"Well, we might have a conflict," Baylee said.

"Yeah? What's that?"

"I just stopped by the Yates' chalet to speak with Gina. She wants us to continue to keep an eye on Tobias, certain that he is most likely having an affair of some sort, but also, wanting to keep tabs on how his treasure hunting goes."

"Why does she believe he's having an affair? You told him that the relationship with Rose Ryan appears to be platonic."

Baylee grimaced, wrinkling her nose up and baring her teeth. "She shared some... interesting stories of Tobias and his sex dolls with me." Baylee went on to fill Clay in on Tobias trying out his new models while his wife watched.

Clay nodded his head slightly, his lips twisted in a wry grin. "That is pretty effed up."

"Anyway," Baylee said, "he hasn't put her through that ordeal for a few months now, which makes her believe he's got something else going on the side."

"I can see why she might be angry."

Baylee shook her head. "Whereas your Dannie Cox appears angry, I'd say that Gina Yates has entered a more practical, albeit, jaded, stage."

"When did you start throwing words like albeit around?" Clay asked. "Is that because you started hanging out with the upper crust of society? You and Gina making plans to have a soirée at the yacht club?"

Baylee smiled coyly. "I'm not just some bimbo arm candy for Clay Wolfe. I know things."

Clay chuckled. "Yes. Yes, you do."

"I'm thinking Gina would be awarded half of everything in a divorce, including the fire opals, if Tobias can find them, and she can prove his philandering." She paused and cleared her throat. "Before, ahem, Dannie Cox finds the treasure."

"Yes, it seems like a moral and ethical dilemma, all right." Clay sighed. "We should probably drop one of them."

"Which one?"

"Dannie, and Andy, were the first to hire us to help them in their search for the treasure."

"And Gina was the first to hire us, period. To find out what her husband was doing, which turns out, is looking for the treasure."

"Could be, there's enough to go around," Clay said.

Baylee snorted. "I don't see either one of them sharing the jewels with the other, even if they find them."

"No, that I doubt very much."

"Did you and Dannie discuss... how Andy was killed? Like, maybe, who did it?"

"Not a bit," Clay said. "Which was surprising. She had me off balance from the get-go, and it wasn't until after she'd sailed out of the diner that I realized we'd barely talked about the Andy's death. Dannie seems to think we can avenge Andy by finding the opals first and using them as bait to lure in the killer to be punished."

"Avenge? How so?"

"She didn't say. But my guess would be that it doesn't involve the police or jail. She sounded like it was more of an eye-for-an-eye thing."

*   *   *

It soon became apparent to Clay that he was the least-experienced diver of the three of them. With Westy, this came as no surprise, as he'd been a SEAL for eight years. But Dannie was an antiques dealer. When did antique dealers find time to plumb the depths of the ocean blue with oxygen tanks on their backs?

While Murphy navigated them out of Essex Harbor, Westy laid out a map. On it he'd made an isosceles triangle in pencil. It was four miles from the tip of Spruce Island to the tip of East Essex, passing through Brimstone Island and Hogs Head Island, two tiny crags in the ocean. From East Essex it was four miles to Gorges Island. From Gorges Island, it was just under three miles to Spruce Island, passing through Squirrel Island.

This, Westy had said, motioning at open ocean in the middle of his triangle, *is where we'll sneak and peek.*

It seemed like quite a bit of area to cover. They decided to start out just past Brimstone Island. This is where the protection of the peninsulas gave way to the open ocean. Clay should've begun donning his gear before arriving at their destination, as now Westy and Dannie were waiting for him.

Westy had driven to Portland to purchase underwater metal detectors as soon as Clay had contacted him this morning. This was why they hadn't started right after breakfast, as Dannie wanted, but hadn't left the Knox Wharf until almost 1:00 PM. Westy had grumbled that the right way to do it would be by dragging sonar 'fish', or a magnetometer, through the water that would alert them to shipwreck below.

"Like looking for a needle in a haystack," Westy said.

"More like the Quest for the Holy Grail," Clay said, pulling his flippers on. *"Are you suggesting coconuts migrate?"*

Westy glared at him. "What the hell you talking about coconuts? You mean the cup that Jesus drank out of after the Last Supper?"

Clay realized that he'd become a Monty Python fan in college, while Westy was off somewhere in the Middle East doing other things. He shook his head. *"You make me sad. So be it. Come, Patsy."* He slid into the water before Westy could express his irritability at another silly movie quote he didn't understand, this one from when Arthur leaves the armless Black Night behind.

The strategy was for the three of them to work in a grid pattern. The deepest depth here was only 100 feet. The underwater metal detectors were waterproof up to 200 feet, but at this depth, their dives would be limited to twenty minutes for safety. The three of them kept a distance of about ten yards between them as they peered and probed a thousand feet forward, and then back, at which point they'd take a break and move to a new spot.

As Clay suspected from the way Dannie had donned her gear, she was much more proficient in the water than him, and he struggled to keep pace. About halfway out, Westy found an anchor, rusted and brittle, but there seemed to be nothing else, and they continued.

Up ahead, Westy raised his hand and came to a stop, halting Clay a few feet back, and Dannie doing the same thing on the far side. Clay watched as a great white shark came out of the murk, swimming above and past them in a nonchalant fashion. Shark sightings in Maine had become more prevalent as of late. Just two years ago off Mackerel Cove in Harpswell, a woman swimming with her daughter had been killed, but this great white didn't look like he was looking for food.

When they came up to move to a new location, Murphy pointed out the *Coronado* about a mile to their east. Tobias and Rose were busy searching as well.

*   *   *

Baylee found Niben in her rocking chair under the rickety awning in front of her trailer. Same blanket over her lap, faded scarf on her head, and denim dress. Baylee wondered if the old lady had even moved since her visit a few days earlier.

"Real People," Niben said by way of greeting as Baylee sat down in the broken chair at her side.

"Good afternoon."

"Have you been thinking about your people since we talked?"

Baylee had been thinking of little else when she was alone and not with Clay. Last night had been a time of deep introspection. "Yes. What do you know of the Abenaki who lived at Winnegance?"

"The *Winnegansis*," Niben said. "Meaning portage. They lived on Barlow Pond, giving them access to the ocean, but also to carry their canoes across the spit of land to the Dunbar River, and from there, connect to the Sibosek to travel inland for hunting expeditions and visiting. My clan, the Chbo So, lived on Townsend Island, the land between two rivers, and would often see them putting their canoes in the water. They were friendly, and would wave, and sometimes stop to speak. Over time, the Abenaki enveloped my people, and we became one."

"But trouble brewed with the Europeans?" Baylee asked.

Niben spit a stream of tobacco juice into a ceramic flowerpot. "Not at first. Not when they were just here to fish. But then their hunger grew. White hunger. They shared that hunger so that my people became hungry as well, hungry for the guns they brought, and then they said no more. We drove them out time and again, but they always came back."

"Do you know of the men who lived on Gorges Island and fished, back in the early 1700s?"

"The men who lived on Gorges Island?"

"White men. From Ireland, I believe."

Niben rubbed her eyes with her hand. "What of them?"

Baylee felt a shifting in the air between them. It seemed as if she was suddenly evasive. "I've heard that they came to the mainland in the spring of 1717 searching for treasure. Treasure hidden by the pirate, Black Sam Bellamy, with the knowledge of the Native Americans, although it is not quite clear if it was the Abenaki living at Winnegance or the Chbo So Clan who lived on Townsend Island."

"Is it this treasure that you are seeking?" Niben looked up in the sky, steadily rocking in her chair. "Who determines the value of what a treasure is?"

"We've been hired to search for this missing treasure," Baylee said, neglecting to mention by two separate clients. "And we heard that a dozen of these fishermen came to the mainland looking for the treasure in late April or early May of 1717."

"Gold and gems and paper money are little more than a curse. What value do they bring to the holder? Pain and suffering."

"Have you heard any stories about these men? Anything passed down through the generations?"

Niben sighed. Spit. Wiped her lips with her hand. "I do not know the year, but there was a story similar to what you speak of. How twelve white men came ashore aboard a large canoe to the people of the Chbo So."

"Looking for hidden treasure?"

"They came looking for the orange-red gemstones. They said that Bellamy, who was a friend to the Chbo So, had hidden them and that they knew where these gems were hidden."

"And did they?"

"A young man took them to find what they wanted."

"And did they find it?"

"The story goes that eight chests were carried from the rocks to their large canoe and then they rowed themselves back down the river and toward their home. The legend says my people tried to get them to stay the night, as a storm was blowing in, but they were in too much of a hurry, and went anyway. Sometime later, it was heard that they never made it back to their island with the treasure. This is why I say that riches are nothing more than a curse. What did these gemstones bring these men other than death? And how many other men died fighting over them?"

Both good questions, Baylee thought, but almost a distraction. She sensed the woman was lying to her, or withholding something, but she couldn't be sure. Not now, certainly, as Niben had again fallen asleep, her snores like the rattling of a snare drum.

Chapter 22

Clay woke with a grin plastered on his face. It'd been a perfect evening of nothing with the same planned for today. He'd barbecued steak and asparagus on Baylee's charcoal grill the night before. They'd eaten outside until the mosquitos descended, and they had to move inside for a dessert of apple pie that Baylee had made. They'd watched a Netflix movie called *Money Heist*, or half of it, anyway, before other things developed. Maybe finishing the flick today would be on the agenda, especially if it proved again to lead to other developments.

The digital clock on the headboard said that it was just after six. Light seeped through the white curtains and bathed the room in a soft glow as birds chirped away outside. Baylee slept with her bare back to him, the sheet having slid down to her waist. Clay traced the curve of her shoulders down to the small of her back, caressing the skin gently with his eyes. He restrained from touching, not wanting to wake her.

"You just going to stare?" Baylee asked, seemingly feeling his eyes touching her skin. "Are you the kind of guy who won't cuddle his woman after a lustful night?"

Clay's grin got bigger, and he slid in behind her, one arm around her, hand on her stomach, the other massaging her neck lazily. "Morning," he whispered, his lips canoodling her ear.

"Mm." Baylee wiggled her way tighter into his spoon. "Don't wake Frank." The puppy lay at the end of the bed in the corner, small snores rippling his tiny body.

It wasn't until they went to get out of bed almost an hour later that Frank was roused from his slumber. Clay got his food while Baylee fed Flash and Ollie, and then they took cups of coffee and walked down to the water and sat on the bench swing while Ollie hunted birds, Flash lay in the rising sun, and Frank played at getting his paws wet.

"I'm glad that Dannie had to cancel the treasure search today," Baylee said. "And that she didn't want you going out without her."

"I think she doesn't trust us," Clay said with a chuckle. "That we might find the opals and keep them for ourselves. She quite clearly said not to go out looking for them."

"Something to do with Andy's death?"

"I don't think so," Clay said. "She was supposed to go down to the station for another interview with the police when we got off the water yesterday, but she said something about going out of town."

"Didn't say where?"

"No. She is a mysterious woman, that's for sure."

"Bet she looks awesome in a bikini," Baylee said as a sailboat went past. "Did you follow her around in the water yesterday appreciating her firm swim strokes?"

"Yep. Kept bumping into her butt."

Baylee hit him on the arm, spilling his coffee. "She is a good-looking woman, don't you think?"

"First of all, we dove in dry suits, not bathing suits, and second of all, yes, she is quite a looker. But there's something about her eyes that's a little bit scary, have you noticed?"

"I've only really seen her in passing," Baylee said. "She seems to have latched onto you."

"What do you think Niben Glenn was lying to you about?" Clay asked, thinking changing the topic from Dannie's charms was his wisest move.

Baylee stared out across the harbor to the town without replying, then took a small sip of coffee. "How do we know that the twelve men from Gorges Island found the treasure and then sunk in a storm?"

"The diary of Rose Ryan's ancestor," Clay said. "One of the four men left behind."

"They weren't there, though, were they?"

"What do you mean?"

"What if the men never left the village of the Chbo So?"

It was Clay's turn to stare across the water at Port Essex. Then he turned his gaze to Baylee, lost for a moment in her caramel eyes. "They'd brought guns, knives, hatchets, and other tools to trade for the treasure. You're suggesting that maybe the Chbo So killed them and took their barter as well as the fire opals?"

"Just a thought I had," Baylee said. "Probably nothing."

"According to Yates and Ryan, three of the men washed up on shore as well as some other debris from the shallop."

Baylee got up and walked down the few steps to the water, giving Frank a nudge into the water. The puppy was not too pleased with her as he rushed back up over the rocks. "Like I said, probably nothing. But the Chbo So could've dumped the bodies and debris at night so that they'd be found by the survivors on Gorges."

"And then told those same survivors that the others had come, collected the treasure, and left just before the storm hit. From what I've read, they were a peaceful people. I can't see them killing twelve people for some gemstones they most likely didn't care about."

"Like I said, probably nothing."

* * *

Westy was standing on the dock at the Knox Wharf drinking a cup of coffee when Tobias Yates arrived. He'd been up with the sun this morning, nettled that they weren't going out to search for the treasure, which turned to wondering whether their opposition would be out on the water today. It was only a couple of miles from his house, so he'd taken a drive down, noting as he passed Baylee's house that

Clay's Jeep was in the driveway. He saw Adam Dube on the *Coronado* getting the boat ready, so he'd waited. He could be incredibly patient when required, but this morning, he only had fifteen minutes to wait.

"You again," Tobias said.

"Yep."

"What do you want? Are you here to board my boat again?"

"Not your boat."

"What?"

"The boat is Dube's. Not yours."

"Saw you out on the water yesterday looking for my treasure," Tobias said. "You going back out today?"

"Maybe we found it."

Tobias scoffed. "It'd be a zoo out there right now if you came across anything."

"Did see a great white trolling," Westy said. "You should be careful out there."

Tobias looked a bit miffed at that.

"You again," Rose Ryan said, walking up behind the two men.

"You're like two peas in a pod, the two of you, aren't you?" Westy said. "You sure you're not sleeping together?"

Rose's eyes glinted maliciously. "Maybe we are."

"The word on the street is that you're not," Westy said. "Why, I wonder? You're a pretty young lady, and Tobias likes women more beautiful than him. Of course, you are a real human being, and not a fuck doll, so that may be the problem. Are you not impressed with his weight, age, and bulbous nose? Does the idea of screwing a wildly successful sex doll maker not appeal to you?"

"I am faithful to my wife," Tobias said, his face flushed in anger.

"I hear different, but then again, we might have two different definitions of faithful."

"What are you talking about?" Rose asked.

"How come you didn't tell your wife about the treasure?" Westy said. "Are you planning on cutting her out somehow? Running off with Rose and the fire opals? *Rose and the Fire Opals.* Sounds like the name of a movie."

"My wife is not the woman everybody thinks she is," Tobias said. "If anybody was going to run off with my money, it'd be her, and not me."

"What's that supposed to mean?" Westy asked.

"Exactly as it sounds, Mr. Beck. Yes, I have looked into who you are. Perhaps your time would be better spent fishing and not treasure hunting. Good day to you." Tobias stepped around Westy and went down to a skiff at the end of the dock.

Rose eyed Westy carefully. "What was that talk of sex dolls?"

"Good question. Might be that you're too smart to be screwing Tobias. Just using him, would be my bet."

Rose looked over where Tobias was in the skiff waving her to come. "I have to go, now, Weston, but maybe later on today we can get a drink together and talk about this?"

*   *   *

Socrates had told her he planned on cleaning up his mess tonight. She thought it might be interesting to see how he went about that. So, as soon as it got dark, she found herself outside of a double wide at Botany Village. The trailer was for sale and empty of contents, so there was no chance of anybody coming home and surprising her. It was a cloudy night and somebody walking by on the road would be hard pressed to make her out in the dark. And it had a good view of Annette Williams Ward's front door.

She'd hired the man who went by the name Socrates off a site on the dark web. He didn't come cheap. But he'd slid seamlessly into the fabric of Port Essex and had his finger on the pulse of the town, most importantly, including the progress of the hunt for Black Sam's fire opals. Unfortunately, the men he hired to be the muscle if and when the time came, well, their behavior was less than professional.

Whereas Socrates was like a polished international operator, a modern-day James Bond, suave and debonair, the four Buccaneers were just the opposite, Austin Powers buffoons who'd not yet grown into men.

Their first strike came when they threatened Wolfe and Baker. She wasn't sure where the fools had gotten the cutlasses. Perhaps the entire motorcycle club had them, as they were Buccaneers. It was that sort of behavior that made people sit up and take notice. She put it down as strike one, had Socrates move them to an isolated house, and tell them they weren't allowed to leave until called upon.

She understood they wanted a girl to entertain their boyish natures. Socrates had suggested that one was less likely to talk than four, and that they wouldn't mind taking turns. He found Annette through barroom gossip, reached out to her, hired her, and brought her to the Buccaneers blindfolded. When he went back to pick her up at 2:00 a.m., she was gone.

She didn't believe for a minute that she'd run off without provocation, as the bikers claimed, and could only imagine what they might've done to her. Strike two. If the Buccaneers messed up again, they'd be done. She'd very much like to have Socrates kill them if that happened, but bringing down the wrath of a MC with upwards over five-hundred members seemed to be a bad idea when trying to keep a low profile. So, they'd just get their walking papers.

The Buccaneers had to be moved to another house, a hassle, and to be honest, she was running low on funds. It was time for the treasure to be found, either by her people, or stolen, also by her people. That was what she was paying them for, after all.

Socrates came walking down the dimly lit street at just past ten. There were very few lights on in any of the trailers at that time on a Sunday night. He didn't see her but went up to the door and knocked. After a bit, it opened, and he pushed his way in. She got up, crossed the street, and went to the back where she, luckily, found an open window leading to the kitchen table where Socrates and Annette sat.

"I am sorry about what happened the other night," Socrates said.

"Who are you?" Annette asked.

"Somebody trying to right a wrong."

"What exactly are you referring to?"

"The four men whose house you went to the other night."

Even outside, she could see Annette's blue eyes turn cold and angry. The woman was quite pretty, not exactly what came to mind when you thought of someone selling her body for money, but in a way, she thought, don't we all sell sex for some kind of payment.

"You are the man who called me. Blindfolded me. Drove me to…"

"I would like to compensate you for any damage, emotional or physical, that may've been caused by the drunken actions of these men."

Socrates spoke in a low and comforting voice, but his approach was clumsy, she thought. Even whores like a bit of tact when being paid off for their services being abused.

"Men? You mean filthy pigs is what you mean."

"Nevertheless, I'd like to compensate you for your duress and put this matter behind us."

"They should be in jail is what they should be. Or worse."

"How does a thousand dollars sound?"

Mistake number two, she thought, starting out too low was more of an insult than an offer.

"How about I call the police and send you all to jail where what happened to me happens to you? See how much that's worth to you then."

"Calling the police would not be a very good idea."

Annette stood up, cell phone in hand. "Fuck you."

Socrates rose like a snake uncoiling, taking the phone from her hand and grabbing her by the straw-colored hair. "Please keep your voice down."

"Why? What the hell are you going to do to me that those pigs didn't already?"

A boy of about thirteen came into the room. "Mom? What's going on?" He held a pistol up in two shaking hands, pointed at Socrates.

Socrates looked surprised by the intrusion. Certainly, she thought, he'd done his homework enough to know that Annette had three boys, eight, eleven, and thirteen.

"Is this the man who hurt you the other night?"

Annette's eyes shifted from anger to fear in less than a heartbeat. "Go back to bed, sweetie."

"You should be worried about the safety of your children, don't you think?" Socrates asked in a low purr. He positioned Annette between him and the boy as a shield.

"Put the gun away, sweetie," Annette said. "Lay it down on the floor and go back to your room."

"Not until he walks out the door," the boy said, showing some mettle.

"You will keep your mouth shut?" Socrates whispered into Annette's ear.

"Yes. Yes. I will do whatever. Just don't hurt my boys."

As if on cue, two younger boys, eleven and eight years old, appeared down the short hallway, the younger one rubbing his eyes sleepily.

"I will be leaving now," Socrates said. "Don't make me come back." One hand firmly clutching Annette's hair, another at her waist, he moved sideways to the front door.

"Easy, sweetie," Annette said. "The bad man is leaving. Just be easy."

As she watched from outside, she suddenly realized that Socrates was about to make another mistake and escalate the situation, but there was nothing to be done, it was too late. As he and Annette sidled past the boy with the pistol held up in shaking hands, Socrates suddenly sidestepped with the speed of a snake, reaching out for the gun, but he misjudged ever so slightly, and knocked the weapon upward instead of grasping it.

As if in slow motion, the pistol swung upward, underneath the boy's chin, and there was a bang, the bullet traveling through his throat and blowing particles of his skull and contents onto the low ceiling of the trailer.

She cursed under her breath, thinking how hard it was to get good help these days, as she pulled the pistol with silencer from her bag and went through the front door. Annette had just started to scream, having fallen to her knees, when she put the bullet through her ear, stopping the noise. The two younger boys stood frozen in shock and were making no noise. They barely reacted as she shot both of them. She then shot all four of them again making sure there'd be no miraculous survivals who could possibly become witnesses. She then turned off the lights.

"I didn't mean for the boy to get shot," Socrates said. "I don't kill children."

"Shh," she said.

They stood in the dark house with the four corpses for several minutes waiting to see if any curious neighbors would snoop their way over or call the police. One gunshot late at night and a scream cut short could easily be written away as the backfire of a car or a Netflix show on a flatscreen with the sound up to anyone roused and half-asleep.

"Okay," she finally said. "Clean this up. Make them disappear. No family of four will ever be found murdered in Port Essex." She walked out the front door and left.

Chapter 23

Dannie called Sunday to say she'd be ready to resume the treasure hunt at noon on Monday. Thus, Clay and Westy were out roaming the roads early that morning looking for the house where the Buccaneers had brought Annette a few nights earlier. Mentally, Clay was kicking himself because this should've been done days ago, but truth be told, it'd been quite an eventful time, the most significant event being the brutal slaying of Andy Kozak.

The only real time to go searching for the bikers would've been Sunday, but Clay had needed a day to refresh. The reality was, there was nothing to be done even if they found the Buccaneers. If Annette was not going to press charges over their abusive behavior, well then, it might be nice to find their location. Maybe the thing to do would be to quietly watch them, for they were certainly involved in some way, he wasn't sure how.

It was the third house that matched the area and the description Annette had shared that hit pay dirt, so to speak. The owner was there with a carpenter and a cleaning crew, pissed off at the abuse his house had taken. The man who rented the place, he said, was smooth, cultured, and suave. The neighbors had told him, too late, that there were four bikers on Harleys staying there, and not the single and cultured man he'd met.

The owner's name was Gary. He was a short, spare man, with a baseball hat and a thin mustache. "These fellows broke a table, a door, and two lamps, not to mention the mess of beer bottles and food left lying around," he said.

"How about the guy who rented it?" Clay asked. "He do that online? Got his credit card, I hope."

"I got the place on a rental site, you know, but the guy called me, wanted to meet." Gary spit, shuffled his feet, shrugged his shoulders. "Said he didn't want to put it on his credit card 'cause his wife didn't know he was here. Offered me double the price, cash, and a security deposit on a check. Just talked to the bank, and that check ain't no good. Serves me right, I suppose."

"He met with you?" Clay asked. "What'd he look like?"

Gary sighed. "Average. Brown hair, beard, black glasses. His hair was, ah, swept back, styled a bit more than people around here would do, if you know what I mean."

"Any tattoos? Marks? Anything at all stand out?"

"Only, just, that he moved like a cat, and his eyes were pretty intense."

"What color?"

"Dark."

"What was the name he gave you? The one on the check?"

"Robert Gordon. Bank said the fellow been dead for six months."

"They leave anything behind?"

"Yeah. There was some woman's clothing. Dress, heels, panties, and bra. And a pocketbook, mostly empty." Gary picked up a trash bag on the ground. "Kept them separate from the other garbage. Didn't quite feel right just throwing them out."

"You mind if I take those?" Clay asked. "I think I may know who they belong to."

"What's this all about?" Gary asked. "I was gonna go to the police, but seems like it's my own damn fault. Course if I see them, that's gonna be a different story, now that sure is."

"Can't be sure, but I think the people might be real bad people," Clay said. "Not the kind you want to mess with. Wouldn't hurt to report what you know to the police."

Gary's eyes widened suddenly. "They didn't have nothing to do with that fellow that got murdered the other day, now do they?"

"Don't know about that, not for sure," Clay said. "But steer clear of them. You give me a call if you think of anything you forgot or run into them again." He handed the man a business card.

As they climbed back into Clay's Jeep, Westy said, "I'd sure like to go pay that woman a visit. Annette. Annette Williams. Weren't you sweet on her back in high school?"

"I wasn't sweet on her," Clay said. "But we got along."

"Got along? Ha. You were all googly-eyed over her, kinda like that new puppy of yours, Frank."

"We got time before we have to meet up with Dannie at the boat," Clay said. "Might as well go see if she's had a change of heart. Murphy got her address for me. We can use the excuse of returning her clothes."

"Change of heart about you?" Westy asked.

"You can be a real dumbass," Clay said. "It'd be helpful if she'd come forward and finger those bikers for what they did. Then we could get the cops involved looking for them."

"Yep. Best those fellows be behind bars," Westy said. "Even temporarily."

Clay took a left of Route 29. "Not that Chief Roberts is going to take kindly to working with us in any capacity."

"He sure don't like you much," Westy said. "Annette lives in Botany Village? Where Crystal used to?"

"Yep. Couple of spots down, actually."

Botany Village consisted of an inner and outer circle road, trailers dotting both sides, tucked up close to each other. Annette's home was on the outer circle. There was no car in the driveway. No answer when they knocked.

"You said she got three boys?" Westy asked.

"Yep."

"And none of 'em home?"

Clay's phone buzzed with a text from Crystal. Coppers are here looking for you. They're back in the office with Baylee now.

Westy reached down, rolled up his jean pant leg, and pulled his SEAL Ka-bar blade from a sheath there. "Somethings not right here," he said.

A car rolled by, a man with grizzled facial hair and a cigarette hanging from his mouth, staring at them. As soon as it rounded the corner, Westy stepped up and popped the lock, opening the door almost as if he'd used a key. They stepped inside.

"Annette," Clay called out. The name disappeared into the silence of the double wide.

Clay pulled his Glock. Westy still had his Ka-bar in hand. They moved down the hallway. There were three bedrooms. All empty.

"Clothes on the bed like they packed up," Westy said.

Clay checked the closets. Things did appear to be missing. "See any suitcases?"

"Nope."

"Maybe they followed advice and got out of town for a few days," Clay said.

Westy paused in the hallway. "Smells like they gave the place a good cleaning before they left."

Clay became aware of the strong smell of disinfectant. "That's a bit odd." There was a small discoloration on the carpet, and he knelt to look at it. He had a sinking feeling that the spot was blood. Clay's phone buzzed. It was a number he didn't recognize. He ignored it.

Westy looked at it, then at the walls, his eyes scanning for marks, before coming to rest on the ceiling. He reached up and ran his fingers along the wood, grunted, and moved to a wall, and did the same thing.

"What do you got?" Clay asked.

"Gouges in the paneling," Westy said. "The kind that might be made when somebody digs a bullet out so that it won't be found."

His phone buzzed with a text from Baylee. Police are hot to talk to us. I'm on my way down to the station. Wouldn't say why.

"Might be time to turn this over to the police," Clay said. "I feel in my bones that something isn't right here."

Chapter 24

Clay sat in the conference room at the police station. To the left, going around the table, were Baylee, Chief Roberts at the head, Tobias, Gina, Rose, the new head of state police Major Crime Unit at the far end in a bad suit, and then Dannie, next to Clay. The last time Clay had been in this room, Grandpops had come and freed him. That wouldn't be happening today, not that he was being held for anything. Though, he certainly would've liked the presence of a lawyer like Grandpops right now.

Clay had missed the suit's name, the replacement for Jackson Brooks, but it didn't seem to matter, because Chief Roberts was running the show. Clay thought it amusing that Gina and Rose had been seated next to each other, the tension radiating from their bodies as they studiously ignored the other.

"We've spoken individually with all of you and gotten your statements regarding the death of Andriy Kozak," Chief Roberts said, looking around the room and pinning each of them with his piercing eyes. He was a tall, angular man, slightly stooped forward at the shoulders, with a curved nose like a hawk. "But I thought it best to bring everybody together and make sure we're on the same page."

Clay looked at the head of the MCU for the state police and wondered about the deferential role he was playing in this proceeding.

"Mr. Wolfe, it does appear that wherever you poke your nose, someone turns up dead," Chief Roberts continued. "My understanding is that Mr. Kozak and Miss Cox hired you to search for a long-lost treasure. Balderdash if you ask me. Pirate loot in Port Essex? Ridiculous. How do you justify your actions, Mr. Wolfe?"

Clay looked at the chief, a bit confused as to what the question was. "I am a private investigator who has been retained by a client for a task, Chief Roberts."

Chief Roberts slammed his hand down on the table. "Which has in turn led to the death of Mr. Kozak."

"I don't think that is quite fair to say," Clay said.

"And Mr. and Mrs. Yates, the two of you and Miss Ryan are searching for this same leprechaun pot of gold?"

"I just recently became aware of the notion of lost treasure," Gina said. "My husband, as I told you, has been hunting for this pirate loot with the hussy to my left."

"Better a hussy than an uptight bitch," Rose said.

"Unless the two of you want to be sharing a cell for the next forty-eight hours," the chief said, "shut your goddamn mouths."

Gina's face colored. "For what?"

Rose glared at the chief but didn't say a word.

"As a goddamn suspect in the murder of Andriy Kozak," the chief said slamming his hand on the table.

"You have no proof of any such thing," Gina said. "And I provided you with an alibi."

"I can hold you up to four days without charging you, Mrs. Yates, in a murder investigation, so don't tempt me."

"I'd like to call my lawyer," Gina said.

"Here's the thing," Chief Roberts said, ignoring her request. "We're in the middle of a murder investigation here, one that seems to be connected to this farcical pirate treasure hunt of you all. Until we have found and arrested the killer, you will desist from any further childish games."

"Childish games?" Baylee asked.

"You will cease and desist from searching for pirate treasure," Chief Roberts said. "Until the murderer is brought to justice."

"You can't stop us," Rose said. "We're not doing anything wrong."

"All of you can be held, if necessary, in connection to the murder," Chief Roberts said. "If you don't refrain from this pirate treasure hunt, we will bring you in, and believe me, we are watching you. Miss Ryan, your travel visa is already being reviewed. As is the license of Mr. Wolfe and Miss Baker. And as a local businessman, Mr. Yates, I don't think you want to get on my bad side. Do I make myself clear?"

* * *

Clay walked out of the police station seething. It wouldn't do any good to confront the man as he seemed to thrive on confrontation. Better to just listen quietly and then do what he wanted. No need to poke the bear.

Once in the parking lot, Clay's phone buzzed with a text from Cloutier. Got some interesting info on your client Dannie and her murdered boyfriend.

Clay tapped into his phone. Do you want to share?

I'm going on break. Over lunch at Kurt's. You owe me.

5 minutes.

K.

Clay turned to Dannie, who'd walked out with him and Baylee. "Hey, I have to run an errand. Can we get together in an hour?"

"Sounds good," Dannie said. "Your office." She walked off, either having come on foot or parked down the road.

"Why don't you check in with your client, if you can get her separated from her husband," Clay said to Baylee. "See where Gina stands in regard to the dictum passed down by the chief."

"Sure thing, boss," Baylee said, saluting. "But any lawyer worth his salt would shred the chief. What's your errand?"

"Cloutier has some information on Dannie she thought I should hear. Going to buy her lunch at Kurt's."

"Bring me a meatball sub back to the office. Pick up something for

Crystal, too, why dontcha?"

"Gotcha. Don't spend too much time with Gina or that Cajun who works for us will eat it," Clay said.

"She's a ragin' Cajun, lunatic from Brunswick," Baylee sang. "You think ole Jason Aldean was singing about Crystal?"

Clay chuckled and got in the Jeep. "Could've been," he said through the open window as he pulled out into traffic. He wended his way through the busy streets of Port Essex and up the hill to Kurt's Deli next to the *Daily Register* offices. Cloutier came out the front door as he parked in the newspaper lot, the small deli lot full.

"Hey, buddy, this lot is for newspaper business only," she said.

"I'm a subscriber," Clay said. "Gives me full privileges."

There was an open table out back with an umbrella that provided a bit of shade and a breeze that supplied just enough coolness. Cloutier sat while Clay went inside to order them sandwiches, get a beer for her, and a lemonade for himself. It was bustling inside but Tony took Clay's order off to the side, pouring him the beer and handing him a lemonade.

"Thought I'd hear from you before now," Clay said to Cloutier as he settled into the chair across from her. "Weekend off and Denise out of town."

"Texted you yesterday," she said. "You never replied."

Clay sheepishly remembered getting the message. You got a minute? He'd been distracted at the time and had filed it away to get back to her, but the pleasurable day off with Baylee had erased it from his mind.

"Sorry," he said. "Got a lot going on."

"Not to worry. I don't know how much of this you already know, but first of all, Andriy Kozak and Daniela Cox are both Ukrainian. Not sure if that means anything. Andriy, Andy, emigrated to the United States about twelve years ago. Daniela, Dannie, was born here. Her mother was a mail order bride, if that's what it's called, for the billionaire playboy John Cox."

"And her mother was from Ukraine?" Clay asked, and when Cloutier nodded, he shrugged. "I guess it makes sense for two people with the same cultural background to seek each other out."

"They make an annual trip to Ukraine to visit Andy's family in Kyiv." Cloutier looked at the notebook in front of her. "And they own an antique business in the Gravesend neighborhood of Brooklyn."

"Which is close to the large Russian community of Brighton Beach," Clay said.

"Yes," Cloutier said, "I also learned that their annual income from that business is only about twenty-grand a year."

"Of course, her father is the billionaire, John Cox. They don't really need the money. Probably just a hobby to them. Why so intent on finding this buried treasure, then?"

"John Cox divorced Dannie's mother when Dannie was five. Brought proof that she'd broken the prenup and tossed her out without a dime. They lived in the East Village, and her mom raised her as a single parent until she remarried when Dannie was twelve."

"So, born with a silver spoon in her mouth, had it pulled violently away, and wants to replace it," Clay said. "Was stepdad wealthy?"

Cloutier shook her head no as Tony brought their sandwiches out as well as a second beer for her without having been asked. She was a creature of habit, which he knew well. Lunch meant two beers.

"Hey, Tony, you hear anything about that guy who was killed?" Clay asked.

"You mean the one found in *your* office?" Tony asked.

"Yeah, that'd be the one. He was a client. Wonder if you've heard any rumors?"

"Everybody's got a guess, far as I can tell, of what it was all about, but just the regular loud mouths wanting to be validated for knowing nothing, far as I can tell."

Tony was a tall guy with red hair, probably Irish, which led Clay to his next question. "You know a woman named Rose Ryan? Gal over visiting from Ireland with a thick accent and red hair?"

"Thin as a wisp?" Tony asked.

"Yeah, that'd be her."

"She was in a couple days back with Annette Ward. They were deep in conversation, about mid-afternoon it was, but I didn't catch any of what they were talking about."

"Annette Williams... Ward?" Clay caught himself, remembering that the Annette Williams he knew had a married name, and that, it was, in fact, Ward. "Annette was with Rose?"

"I know Annette well enough," Tony said. "And the woman she was with is the spitting image of the one you just described to me. Right down to the brogue."

"And you didn't hear any of what they talked about?" Clay asked.

"No, sorry, I'll ask around and see if anybody else did." Tony walked off.

"What's that all about?" Cloutier asked.

Clay shook his head slowly. "Don't know. You were talking about Dannie's childhood?"

"Stepdad was a rug salesman. Mom took off with some hustler when Dannie was fifteen and left her behind with her stepdad. Guy did right by her, or so it seems, but died a few years back. Don't seem to be any money in the coffers, though. Certainly not to own a business with little to no income."

"And Andy didn't have money either?"

"Not that I can track down. His parents live in an apartment in Kyiv. Had one sister but she might've been killed in the war. Been missing since March, right after Russia invaded."

*   *   *

"Who are you?" Clay asked Dannie, who sat across from him in his office. Baylee was not yet back, and Crystal was out front.

"What do you mean?" Dannie sat easily in the leather chair, her blonde hair tousled on her head and full lips in a pout. "I'm your client. Dannie Cox."

Clay saw the smoldering good looks, likely inherited from a mother who'd lured the attention of a billionaire. But he also saw a keen intelligence in her eyes and a fit body that did not believe in indolence.

"Tell me about your childhood." he said and watched a flash of angst slide quickly over her beautiful features.

"There is not much to tell you," she said, "and it sounds like you already know. My father kicked us out when I was young, my mother left me at fifteen, and I left my stepdad's when I was eighteen to make my own way in the world."

"Does your father give you money to live on?"

Dannie glared at him. "No. I haven't seen him for twenty years. Not that it's any of your damn business."

"Is there much money in the antiques business?"

"Enough. But not a whole lot."

Hmm, Clay thought. Nobody living in Brooklyn would ever make the claim that $20,000 a year was enough money. Especially not for two people. "How is it that you became an antiques dealer?"

"When I met Andy. He taught me everything, and then we fell in love." Dannie tossed her hair. "And now he is dead." A tear crept down her cheek.

Clay stared at her, biting back inquiries on her income, respecting her anguish. "There are no words that are right for this type of thing," Clay said. "It sucks, and I'm sorry for you."

"What is, is. All we can do is keep moving."

"One step at a time." He knew that all too well. Felt her pain.

"What'd you think about what that small-town cop with the big-city britches said about ceasing and desisting in looking for the treasure?"

Clay shrugged. "He certainly revels in his power. I'd not put it past him to throw us in jail if he catches us. He'll claim we're interfering with a murder investigation."

"Any lawyer worth his salt would get us out. I've made inquiries."

"Probably take at least twenty-four hours."

Dannie stood and walked behind Clay to the window overlooking the harbor. "It would behoove us to take precautions, then."

Clay didn't like the sound of *behoove us to take precautions*. "How would you like to proceed?"

"Can we dive at night?" she asked.

*   *   *

Westy was at the bar of the Pelican Perch when Rose Ryan sat down beside him. It was lucky she was slim, or she wouldn't have fit next to his broad torso, most likely the reason that the seat was open. He was halfway through a haddock sandwich.

"Weston, how opportune to run into you," she said.

He looked at her with a smirk that didn't reach his face. "Miss Ryan."

"Oh, please call me Rose, now that you've boarded my boat and all."

Westy wasn't sure what the 'all' was, so he just nodded. Rose ordered a Guinness and a house salad.

"Guess you were lucky you didn't get called into the *Garda Síochána* along with the rest of us," Rose said. "That one fellow who looks like a stork, Chief Roberts, was eating the head right off us, now he was."

"What do you want, Rose?" Westy asked.

"Just making some polite conversation and getting a pint of the black stuff, is all."

"Any progress on Black Sam's treasure?"

"Not so much." Rose took a gulp of her beer, the froth clinging to her lips. "I'm not sure that Mr. Tobias Yates' heart is in it anymore. Trouble on the home front, you know, ever since his wife found out what he was doing."

"At least she knows he isn't having an affair with you," Westy said. He stuffed the last bite of his sandwich into his mouth. "He's not, is he, having an affair with you?"

Rose scoffed. "I'm not attracted to overweight older men who think masturbating with a sex doll is love." She took another drink, the Guinness now two-thirds gone. "I like my men younger. Vibrant. Powerful. Strong." She put her hand on Westy's arm, a wicked glint flickering in her eyes.

Chapter 25

After Dannie left, Crystal came into Clay's office. "Thanks for the sandwich, boss. What'd Nikita want?"

"Nikita?" Clay said.

"Yeah, you know, that 90s movie, French or something, *La Femme Nikita*? Where she's recruited to be a government assassin after she kills some cops."

Clay started to reply, paused, and thought, *hmm, government operative*. Was Dannie Cox a government operative? Abandoned, effectively orphaned, by her parents. Stunningly beautiful. Ripe for the picking. Ukrainian? Possibly Russian. Could even be American. But this wasn't a movie.

"Ground Control to Major Tom."

Clay shook his head. "She wants to dive at night and keep looking for the treasure even though Chief Roberts has threatened to bring her in on suspicion of murder and revoke my P.I. license if we do."

Crystal whistled, a keening noise that grated through the air like #80 coarse grit sandpaper. "Seems to me she wants to find those fire opals some bad. How much you think they're worth?"

"No idea. Only that Black Sam was willing to give away all the gold, silver, and other treasure to the pirates on his ship and just keep the gems some three hundred plus years ago."

"People seem to think it's worth something," Crystal said. "That's for sure. You got La Femme Nikita, that wispy Irish lass, the sex doll guy, and the Buccaneers all looking for a piece."

"You find out any more on that particular motorcycle gang?"

"Probably nothing helpful, but the leader who transformed them from your local mom and pop variety club into a force to be reckoned with is an interesting fellow. Not that anybody knows who he is."

"Nobody knows who he is?" Clay asked, his attention gathered.

"Well, he used to be Tommy 'Grub' Boseman." Crystal sat down across from him. "But, yeah, about seven years back, he was implicated in a murder. Feds had eyewitnesses that saw him torch this guy. And he disappeared. Disappeared from the scene for almost a year. This guy, Jack Weber, has been running things, but the rumor is that he's just a lackey for Boseman. You get out on the message boards, and there's whispers of a new name, a new face, a whole new guy."

"A ghost who might just be interested in a pirate treasure from years ago," Clay said.

"Or just a rumor of creative imagination," Crystal said.

The outer door opened, and a second later Baylee breezed into the office. "Hope you didn't forget my meatball sub," she said. "I'm famished."

"In the fridge," Clay said. "What'd Gina have to say?"

"I'll get back to digging into the Buccaneers MC," Crystal said as Baylee went to the half-fridge and pulled out her sandwich, looked at the microwave, shrugged, and came to sit down next to Clay at her desk.

"Gina stood me up," Baylee said. "She told me to stop by the house and that Tobias would be at work. Not only was she a no-show, but that creepy husband came rolling up the driveway behind me and blocked me in."

Clay chuckled. "Didn't you already teach him who was boss once?"

Baylee snickered back. "He wasn't getting too close, that's for sure. Got out of his fancy car and stood about ten feet from my window."

"What'd he have to say?"

"Wanted to know what I was doing there. If I'd been hired to find out whether he was having an affair, it was now quite obvious that he was not. Case closed. If it was about the treasure, well, he wasn't looking for that anymore, not after the murder and police warning."

"Guess he's got a point, of sorts," Clay said.

"Told him I just stopped by to tie up loose ends with his wife," Baylee said. "He laughed, rather coarsely, I might add, and said something about I was just trying to get paid, like all the other bitches out there. He asked me how much I was owed and pulled out his wallet and fanned hundred-dollar bills at me."

"Yeah? What'd you do?" Clay grinned.

"Told him he owed me one Buck."

Clay furrowed his brows. "One buck?"

Baylee laughed, the chimes spilling through the air in a delicious melody. "He knew what I was talking about, after a second to process, that is. Buck is the name of the male sex doll that he produces and markets."

Clay shook his head and said with a straight face, "So, did you drop Buck off at home before coming back in?"

"Judging by the redness of his face, he was not receptive to the idea. I'd guess the man's going to die of a heart attack within the year if I was a betting gal." Baylee took a large bite of the sandwich, getting marinara sauce on her cheek. "How'd it go with Dannie? Same thing?"

Clay reached out with his thumb and cleaned the sauce from her cheek. "No, quite on the contrary. She asked what I thought about night diving."

"That's more dedication than Tobias seems—"

"Jesus fucking Christ on a popsicle stick," Crystal said loudly from the next room.

Clay and Baylee waited for more, then heard the printer, and a second later Crystal appeared in the doorway. "Ain't this the fucking bartender at the Pelican Perch?" She crossed the room holding out a printed picture, setting it on Clay's desk with a flourish.

It was of seven or eight men, seated in row seating, out front of a glassed-in booth. "What is this?" Clay asked.

"That one," Crystal said, tapping the picture of one of the men. "Right there. They're at the Daytona 500 a few years back."

Baylee leaned on Clay's arm to look, her scent and touch excruciating. "Looks like him, sure enough. So what?"

"I found it on a forum in which an anonymous person claimed that, yes, he, is the mysterious Grub Boseman. He claims to know the doctor who did his facial reconstruction surgery and was angry about a hit Grub ordered by some of his buddies."

Wow, Clay thought. Could it be possible that Silas the bartender was the head of the Buccaneers Motorcycle Club, a man wanted for murder. He looked closer as the outer door opened and shut.

"Anybody here?" a faint voice said, followed by a sob.

Clay and Baylee stood as Crystal turned. Gina Yates trembled her way into the doorway. Her face was covered in blood, her expensive blouse ripped, and one eye was puffed up and an angry red.

Baylee rushed around the desk, passing Crystal by, and grabbed the woman by the arm. "What happened?" she asked, guiding Gina back to a seat.

"I'll get the first aid kit and some ice," Crystal said.

"Do you need a doctor?" Clay asked.

Gina sniffled. "No, I'm okay. Just scared. They grabbed me right in broad daylight. Pulled me into a van. I thought they were going to kill me."

Crystal came back and handed the medical kit to Baylee who took out several gauze pads and went to the bathroom to wet them while Crystal broke open the ice pack. Clay studied Gina as the two women cleaned the blood from her face, applying a few small Band-Aids, and then holding the icepack to her swollen face.

Gina was shaken, but there was a resolve in the set of her chin that showed her strength. She was not a woman to be trifled with, he judged, and it most likely hadn't been the first time she'd been physically attacked.

"Can you tell us what happened?" Baylee said gently.

"It was a white van," Gina said. "I stopped at the convenience store on my way home out on Route 29, not the quickest way home, but I needed… I needed cigarettes after the police station and all that's going on. Oh God, I haven't smoked in seven years, not until about two weeks ago, but—"

"Just tell us what happened, Gina," Baylee said.

"I parked on the side and got out just as this white van pulled up next to me, blocking my view of the road, and a man stepped out, punched me in the face, grabbed me, and threw me into the back. There were two more men back there who grabbed me, threw me on the floor face down, tied my hands then put a gag in my mouth." She stopped, wiping the back of one hand across her lips. "Water?" she croaked. After she'd taken a few sips from the bottle Baylee offered, she started to speak. "They blindfolded me and then we drove off before I had any idea what was going on. Oh, God, I thought they were going to kill me."

"You're okay now," Clay said gently. "You're safe."

"Safe? Didn't the police chief just get done saying they were going to be watching all of us so that we stopped searching for that fucking treasure and then this happens? Goddammit."

"Go on," Baylee said. "What happened next?"

"They drove me somewhere and led me inside a house where they strapped me to a chair and started asking me questions. They wanted to know where the treasure was. They seemed to think I knew. But I didn't. I mean, I don't. I don't know where it is, and I don't care. I just want my life back."

"How'd you get away?"

"I must've convinced them I didn't know anything, so after a bit, they brought me back to my car and dumped me in the bushes. I managed to get my hands free," Gina held up her hands to show two raw wrists, "and pulled the blindfold off, and the gag, and got in my car and came straight here."

"Why not the police?" Clay asked.

"After this morning, I don't trust them," Gina said. "I trust Baylee and Crystal, no offense Mr. Wolfe, but I don't really know you. So I came straight here."

"Did you see any of them?" Baylee asked.

Gina sobbed, collected herself. "I just saw a tattoo on the man who grabbed me at the beginning. I think it was an octopus. And the man had a beard. Denim vest. That's all."

"And you had no idea where they took you?" Baylee asked.

"That's the thing," Gina said. "I was blindfolded the whole time but... have you ever been out toward East Essex where the guy has the alpacas? I went out there once to buy some of their farm produce, and they make the noise, sort of like a low horn, you know, blowing on a trumpet poorly or something. Well, I think I heard those alpacas. I must've been right out by them, unless somebody else has alpacas in the area."

Chapter 26

"I'm going to go home," Gina said. "Clean myself up before I have to sit down with the police again, today."

"Do you want somebody to go with you?" Baylee asked.

Gina scoffed. "I think the worst has most likely already happened to me. Can't imagine what else could go down except more trouble from Chief Dickhead. But my lawyer knows to answer the phone if I call. I'll be fine. Let me know about the men who took me, when you get something, that is."

Gina stood up and walked out the door. Her stride was firm and decisive, and she didn't linger.

"Wow," Baylee said.

"I always wanted to go check out those alpacas," Clay said.

"Not too many places close enough to hear them," Crystal said. "Maybe two or three at most."

"What's the play?" Baylee asked.

"Let me give Westy a jingle," Clay said.

Westy answered on the third ring. "What?"

"Where you at?" Clay asked.

"Pelican."

Events were happening fast, but that one clicked in with Clay. "Silas the bartender there?"

"He just left. Why?"

"Tell you later. We got a lead on where those bikers might be. Can we pick you up?"

"We?"

"Me and Baylee."

"We need... tools?" Westy asked.

"You still packing your Sig?"

"Police wanted to keep it but had no reason."

"That should do. We'll be out front in ten minutes."

Westy hung up.

"What was that all about?" Rose asked.

"Friend needs help with a broken-down car," Westy said. "I gotta scram. Maybe tell me more about the treasure and how you got caught up in all this another time."

*   *   *

Tobias Yates was still seething from his encounter with that woman P.I. in his own driveway, the one who'd punched him in the throat before, and lied to him. What business did that femoid have working as a private investigator, anyway, he wondered? It was a gray time in history for sure, what with women thinking they were the equal of men. Hell, they weren't nearly as strong nor as smart as men and certainly not suited for business, physical labor, or most jobs that required intelligence or strength.

It was early in the day, but Tobias dropped three cubes in a glass and poured himself a vodka, Jewel of Russia Ultra Black Label. Women, he thought, enough to drive you to drink. His wife Gina, who'd been so loving at first, and then they'd been married, and the divide between them had been like that of the Western Front in WWII. He'd dreamed of the day that he would spring upon her his discovery of the fire opals, wealth beyond their wildest dreams, and the reigniting of her passions that would stir.

And then there was that Irish sprite, Rose Ryan. He was starting to think that she might not be the innocent and naïve young waif he'd thought on first running into her at a conference in Ireland. It was even possible that she'd sought him out and had been pulling his strings. He probably should've plowed her when offered, shown her who was boss, but Tobias loved his wife, even with all the problems they were having. Gina was a woman who knew her place in the home and at her man's side. That was all too rare these days, even if they were having some problems connecting in the bedroom.

Gina. Rose. Baylee Baker. Goddammit, he thought, I've got myself a skirt problem. He laughed loudly, realized he'd slugged down his cocktail, and poured another. Maybe he should pursue the treasure. That'd show that P.I. bitch. He could just picture her face as she realized his superiority. And Rose, when she realized she'd be going back to the Emerald Isle minus any jewels, would be flummoxed at how she'd been outfoxed. And then there was the reward that he'd get from his wife, Gina, and how they'd live the life of luxury they were meant for.

A shadow fell across where he stood looking out the kitchen window over the Sibosek River. Tobias turned and saw her in the doorway. "What are you doing here?" he asked.

The figure stepped closer without answering. His eyes were glued to the knife in the gloved hand. It looked to be their cake knife. He looked back up at the face as the figure stepped closer, and too late, realized the knife was moving upward in an arc, and then the blade with the rounded tip plunged into his eye with a sickening noise.

* * *

"That'd be them," Clay said.

He handed the binoculars to Westy. Baylee and the two men were hunkered down in a copse of pine trees about 200 yards from a house off the back property of the alpaca farm. There was a large shed in the rear. The door had been left open, and the front wheel of a motorcycle was visible. Through the window into a living room Clay had glimpsed three men, drinking beer, and apparently watching television. One of them was Octopus Arm.

"What's the play?" Baylee asked for the second time in an hour.

"They threatened us with cutlasses and a blunderbuss," Clay said.

"Stomped on your face a bit, as well," Westy said.

"Were abusive to Annette," Clay said.

"Hopefully they didn't go back and finish the job," Westy said.

Clay drew his breath in slowly, trying to think through this clearly. Rationally.

"A couple of hours ago they kidnapped Gina Yates," Baylee said. "Beat her, threatened her, and now they're sitting around watching fucking television and drinking beer."

"That's the only thing that might stick with the police," Clay said. "Waved some steel at us. Annette won't bring charges, even if she can be found. Just some rednecks hanging around for no apparent reason."

"Will Gina be reporting this to the police?" Westy asked.

"She planned on it," Baylee said. "Was going home to clean herself up to speak to them."

"Probably been better to go in torn and beaten," Westy said.

"Women like Gina don't go in torn and beaten," Baylee said. "Best appearances at all times."

A fourth man came into the living room where the other three were sitting. He waved his arms and was saying something.

"We got to do something before they disappear on us again," Westy said.

"We brace them, they're going to fight back," Clay said. "That won't sit well with Chief Roberts. Probably throw us in jail and bring charges."

"Let's call it in," Baylee said. "Have the police pick them up."

"Call Gina," Clay said. "Have her report them to the police, and they can come pick them up."

Baylee dialed and held the phone to her ear, shook her head, left a message for Gina to call back.

One of the men came out of the house and went to the shed. He wheeled his bike out, grabbed the saddlebags off the back, and went back inside.

"They're getting ready to go," Clay said, looking through the binoculars. "It looks like they're packing up."

"I'll call Officer Tracy," Baylee said. "Get the police to pick them up on threatening charges and by then we'll get Gina in to identify them and share her ordeal."

"Do it," Clay said.

"I best go slow them down," Westy said.

Before Clay could argue, the man had walked away. He crossed the small field to the tree line leading to the back of the shed.

Baylee called Officer Tracy, who was a lone friendly face on the Port Essex PD. There weren't many since Chief Roberts had assumed command and soured the force on the local P.I. firm. Clay half-listened as Baylee shared details while watching Westy work his way to the back of the shed. When Westy reached the back, Clay's phone buzzed.

Good to go? Text from Westy.

Clay was already checking the house. He had sights on three of the men stuffing items in bags. Then the fourth one went in the kitchen to the fridge.

Go. He texted.

Westy slid around the shed, inside, and was back out in thirty seconds. As he came out the door, the man in the kitchen came out the backdoor, too late for Clay to give a warning. Westy froze, and the man turned without seeing him, saying something over his shoulder, and then turning and going back inside. Westy stepped to the bike outside the shed, steel flashed in the sunlight, and he was back behind the shed and out of sight.

"Holy cow," Baylee said.

"That was close," Clay said.

"What? No. Officer Tracy just told me that Tobias Yates was killed."

"What?" Clay turned to look at her in astonishment.

"Yep. Gina called it in half an hour ago. Luckily the staties are already in town and are heading things up so she thinks they can get a couple of cars out to pick up our friends down there, especially when I shared what'd happened to Gina at the hands of those goons."

Down below, the bikers came out. Even at 200 yards the cursing was clear as they discovered the puddles of gasoline underneath their bikes. They all pulled out pistols, not cutlasses, and scoured the area, looking for whoever had done the dirty deed. Westy was long gone, and Clay and Baylee ducked their heads.

"Somebody murdered Tobias?" Clay whispered.

"Apparently. All Tracy knew was that Gina called up in hysterics. Got home and found him in the middle of the kitchen in a pool of blood."

"What's it been? Three hours since you were out there talking with him?" Clay asked.

"Not even," Baylee said.

Westy slid in beside them. "That should slow them down. You got the boys in blue coming?"

"Girl in blue," Baylee said.

"Tobias Yates is dead," Clay said.

Westy whistled. "The plot thickens. How?"

"Gina found him when she got home," Baylee said. "No details as of yet."

Clay poked his head up a tad and put the binoculars to his eyes. Down below, one biker was keeping watch, while the others were wrapping duct tape around the severed fuel lines. In the distance, sirens could be heard.

"Shoot," Baylee said. "I told her no sirens."

The bikers looked up, one of them going to the corner of the house to look out toward the road some hundred yards. The sirens grew closer, and then the first of two police cars pulled into the driveway. The man at the corner of the house called a warning to his buddies and then snapped a shot at the patrol car, more a warning than anything else.

The cruisers skidded to a stop at the end of the driveway, the officers piling out, as the bikers begin refilling their gas tanks with a can from the shed.

"We can't have that," Westy said. He took out his Sig Sauer, resting it easily in front of him, drawing a bead, and then shot the gas can out of the man's hand.

The four bikers looked up in their direction in bewilderment. Westy shot one of the bikes. The four men broke for the house, tumbling through the back door frantically jostling each other out of the way as they went.

"Holy shit. Not bad from this distance with a pistol," Clay said drily.

When the police told them to come out with their hands up, the four bikers ignored them. Or not quite, as one of them shot out the windshield of the patrol car.

"What say we get out of here," Clay said. There was no argument.

Chapter 27

Clay and Baylee dropped Westy at his truck, swung by the office, grabbed Frank, and sent Crystal home, before going to Baylee's house. There, they walked the dog, puppy, and cat down to the water and had a drink. It was a few minutes of solace before heading back out into the storm.

Not five miles away, around the curve of the peninsula, the police were investigating the murder of a man the P.I.s had been tailing for his wife, a man who'd been secretly looking for a lost treasure with an Irish woman named Rose. Across the way, also about five miles, the Port Essex PD was in a stand-off with a motorcycle club out of Florida. Just offshore, maybe five miles as well, the sunken treasure of Black Sam Bellamy rested on the ocean floor. Or not.

The cupboards were bare, so to speak, so they decided to go out to eat. As they walked out the front door, a BMW pulled into the driveway. The man who Clay had tussled with at the Pelican and since learned was named Roderick something or other got out of the car. What now, Clay wondered? Who was this guy?

"What are you doing here?" Baylee asked.

Clay looked sideways at her in surprise.

Roderick strode forward angrily. He had dark glasses on that gave his long face a wolfish look. "What do you mean what am I doing here?"

"Whoa, buddy, take it easy," Clay said, stepping in front of him.

"Is this why you won't answer my calls or reply to my text

messages?" Roderick asked, stopping inches from Clay, looking over his shoulder at Baylee. "Now you're fucking your partner?"

"This isn't a good time, Rod," Baylee said.

"What's going on here?" Clay asked. "You know this guy?"

"That's what I want to know," Roderick said. He moved, if possible, closer to Clay, bumping him slightly, all up in his space.

"Back your wagon up," Clay said. "Last time I kicked your ass I was blind drunk. How do you think it's going to go for you when I'm sober?"

Roderick took a half-step backward. "Are you dumping me for this chump?" he asked, again looking at Baylee.

"Let's take a breath here," Baylee said.

"Dumping him?" Clay said.

"I was seeing Rod on occasion before we... got together," Baylee said.

"Ha," Roderick said. "By that, she means we were screwing. Doing the nasty. The—"

Clay cold-cocked him in the chin, his glasses flying off his head as he went over backward. Roderick lay flat on his back for several seconds before sitting up, rubbing his chin. "I oughta file charges for assault," he said, spitting blood to the side.

"Get in line," Clay said. He was hoping, praying, that the man got up and fought back. He wanted to rip his head off and beat him senseless, erase his words from his mind, start over. "But right now, this moment, if you're not in your car driving away in ten seconds, I'm going to kick the living shit out of you."

Roderick rose to his feet, looked at Baylee, looked at Clay, and went to his car and drove away.

"It was before we got together," Baylee said.

"Let's go to dinner." Clay went to the Jeep and got in.

Baylee climbed in next to him. "I'm sorry I didn't tell you about it."

"How about we go out 29 to Old Salt's," Clay said. He didn't really want to visit any of the usual haunts. "Have you and Roderick ever been there?"

"No. It was nothing, really. Just a couple of months."

"Just to be clear, I have to ask, I'm sorry, but it's going to eat at me," Clay said. "When was the last time the two of you had sex?"

"The Wednesday before last," Baylee said. "July 6th."

Could that be true, Clay thought, that he and Baylee had only started their whirlwind romance just over a week earlier? It seemed that they'd been together forever, and in many ways, they had, ever since she walked into his office a few years back looking for a job. But the carnal part to their affair had only existed for eight days now.

That explained the irritating presence of Roderick in Port Essex, Clay thought, and possibly eliminated him as a suspect in the horrific murder of Andy Kozak and the man behind the Buccaneer MC. Or not? The two things didn't have to be mutually exclusive, he figured.

They rode for several minutes in silence. As they started out of Port Essex on Route 29, a vibration filled the air, shook the road, trembled the trees. "What the?" Clay said.

Around the corner toward them came the first motorcycle riders, and then the road was filled with a horde of them. Clay counted upwards of fifty bikers, riding Harleys, dressed in leather and denim, vests and chaps, all with Buccaneers displayed.

"Boston chapter," Baylee said reading a smaller logo of one of the men as the steel beasts rumbled past.

"Wow," Clay said. "You might give Officer Tracy a heads up."

Baylee dialed, held the phone up to her ear. "Voice mail," she said.

"How about the front desk of the PD," Clay said. "If those jamokies are going out to spring their brethren from their police stand-off in East Essex, things could get real weird."

Baylee called, spoke for a moment, hung up. "They are well aware of the situation," she said to Clay.

That didn't really answer the question of what they might do if the MC was set on freeing their brothers from captivity. "Suppose if they need to, they could call in the National Guard," Clay said.

"Not much we can do," Baylee said.

Clay pulled the Jeep into Old Salt's. "Might as well have some dinner," he said.

They ate and spoke, not once mentioning Roderick, Black Sam Bellamy, Buccaneers, the murdered Tobias Yates, the widowed Gina, the Irish treasure hunting lass, or even Silas, the motorcycle club's president posing as a bartender. It was a blissful hour, the eye of the storm, in which they were friends, partners, lovers—and nothing else mattered.

Then Baylee's phone buzzed. She looked at it. "Tracy," she said.

"Gotta answer," Clay said. It looked like the eye had passed, he thought, and they were about to head straight back into the storm.

Baylee answered the phone, exchanged a few comments, including their present location, and hung up. "Tracy is coming here," she said to Clay.

"She say what for?"

"Not really," Baylee said. "Only that she had some things to share. I said we'd meet her out in the parking lot."

The bill was already on the table, signed and paid for. As they reached the Jeep, Officer Tracy pulled into the parking lot in her cruiser. She couldn't have been far away, Clay thought, as the policewoman got out of her car. She seemed to be flying solo. Tracy was a bit over medium height with black hair pulled into a tight bun at the back and a plain face.

"Clay," she said.

"Tracy," he replied. It'd taken some time, but Clay had figured out that Tracy was her last name, but he'd never heard her called by any other name. "What's going on?"

"Let's step over in the shade," Tracy said, leading them underneath an oak tree that provided both shade and cover from prying eyes and ears.

"What happened with the bikers?" Baylee asked. "That's why I called you, 'cause we saw what looked to be the Buccaneers Boston chapter roll into town. Some fifty strong."

Tracy removed her sunglasses, revealing her powder blue eyes. "They came out to the house. Once they got there, the guys inside surrendered. Came out with their hands up. Then, the Boston Buccaneers escorted us and our arrestees down to station. Said they'd come up to make sure their brothers got a fair shake."

"Seems to be a lot of trouble for assault," Clay said. "I mean, how'd they even know that Gina had partially ID'd one of them? And their location? Why'd they open fire? The smart play would've been to just surrender, one would think."

"Kidnapping and assault," Tracy said.

"And now they've added resisting arrest and attempted murder of cops," Baylee said. "Not the brightest bulbs on the planet."

"Unless they had something more to hide," Tracy said.

"Like what?" Clay asked. "What'd they have on them? Drugs?"

Tracy looked around, stepping closer to the two of them. "This is not for the ears of that editor friend of yours, you hear me? Not from me, anyway. Got it?"

Clay and Baylee nodded their assent.

Tracy's eyes went hard and her jaw tightened. "Four bodies were found down in the basement. A woman and three boys. Young boys."

"Shit," Clay said. "You know who?"

"No identification on any of them."

Clay breathed out in a whoosh. "You know Annette... Ward?"

Tracy pursed her lips. "There was gossip of that name around the station. That she might be prostituting herself."

"Yeah, well I guess the rumors are true. She was hired to have sex with what she thought was a single gentleman who wanted to retain his anonymity." Clay shifted his feet. "But in reality, it was the four guys you just arrested. They treated her badly, threatened to keep her as their sex slave, and she was forced to flee naked through the woods in the middle of the night."

"And you're just telling me this now?" Tracy said, an edge to her tone.

"She didn't want it to get out. Refused to press charges. Didn't want her boys to know what their mom did for extra money."

"Boys?" Tracy said.

"She had three boys," Clay said. "Young boys."

"Fuck," Tracy said. She turned to go, stopped, turned back around. "I got to git but there's more bad news."

"Yeah," Baylee said. "Of course there is. What else you got?"

"You need to turn yourself in," Tracy said.

"Me?" Baylee said.

"Neighbor saw you leaving the Yates house," Tracy said. "She was walking her dog. Recognized you from the newspaper, she said, and wondered what a snoop, her words, not mine, was doing with the Yateses. Officers canvassing the neighbors, not that there's many of them out that way, got her statement."

"And an hour later or so, Gina finds her husband dead." Baylee sighed.

"Pretty slim," Clay said. "How was Tobias killed?"

"Somebody stuck a knife in his eye and on into his brain. Pretty quick more than likely."

"A knife? It still there?" Baylee asked. "Or did the killer take it with them?"

"Believe it was still in his eye," Tracy said. "J.D. told me that he got a peek at it, before the staties and forensics ushered him out of the room and said that it looked like it was a cake knife, you know, one of those long blades with a rounded end."

"Gruesome," Baylee said. But her mind was abuzz. She thought back to stopping by to visit with Gina and cutting herself a piece of coffee cake. With a long-bladed knife with a rounded edge.

"No motive. No link to the weapon," Clay said. "I don't believe there could be an arrest warrant out for Baylee."

"As of now, she is only wanted as a person of interest," Tracy said. "But the chief sure doesn't like the two of you very much and has been feeding the new head of MCU a bucket of venom about you both. I got to go before somebody that shouldn't spots me talking to the two of you. And pass on what you told me about Annette Ward. Two fucking murder scenes at the same time. And the two of you all wrapped up in both of them. Shit."

Chapter 28

Clay woke up in the morning with adrenalin coursing through his veins. He could only surmise that his blood contained an odd mixture of sexual desire and repression with dabs of murder, mayhem, and menace thrown in from everything that had happened in the last days. It was that time of first light, near 5:00 a.m., and there were birds chirping outside, but inside, everything was swirling and full of angst.

He'd brought Baylee to the police station, walked in with her, and watched as they marched her back to a conference room, not the large comfortable one of the morning, but a smaller one with one-way mirrors and recording devices. An interrogation space squarely in the middle of the building intended to sweat the inhabitants into confession. Clay knew the room she'd be going to.

The man at the desk told him it'd probably be quite some time because they were also housing four bikers who were prime suspects in a murder case. Clay wended his way through the mass of bikers filling the sidewalk and parking spaces around the police station. Their presence was heavy, a mixture of supporting one of their own and intimidation of the police and town of Port Essex.

Clay shook his head and went back to Baylee's house to let the dogs out. It seemed time to get a lawyer, he thought, sighing. Grandpops had always been there watching their backs when they muddled into troubles like this, but not anymore. He'd been retired from his practice for a few years before his murder the previous year, but Clay still knew several of the lawyers at his old practice. He put a call into one of them, sharing what he knew, and setting up a meeting for the following week. He hung up assured that, if legal troubles blossomed before that, he'd be taken care of.

After finishing the call, he went back to sitting aimlessly, his mind a black hole of thoughts. Annette and her three boys dead. If he had reported the incident to the police, Clay thought, perhaps her reputation would've been sullied, but she and her children would still be alive. Her safety had crossed his mind, but the fact that she wasn't going to the police seemed to have allayed his fears that the bikers would come looking for her to make sure she kept her mouth shut. It was unlikely that they'd even have been charged with anything, as in the eyes of the courts, she was not a person, but a whore.

He also couldn't keep the image of Baylee and Roderick having sex out of his mind, like the tongue returning to the sore tooth. Both he and Baylee had had many partners before each other through the years, this he understood. But there was something about her and Roderick that hit him deep. Maybe it was how recent it had been, just days before he and Baylee tumbled into bed for the first time, or perhaps it was the man himself who grated on Clay's nerves. Or the fact that she'd kept him secret from Clay. Whatever the case, it gnawed at his very being and twisted his insides into tight little knots.

Just past midnight, Baylee had called, saying that they were done with her for now, and could he pick her up? There wasn't much to talk about, as Baylee told them of being stood up by Gina, who she now knew had been abducted. While waiting in the driveway, Tobias had come along, they'd conversed, and Baylee had left. The police tried to pick holes in that simple story, and may've continued to do so, but their resources were thin with all that was going on in town, and they kicked her out to the streets with orders to stay close to Port Essex for further questioning.

They'd climbed quietly into bed, Baylee in a T-shirt and panties and Clay in his boxers, lying next to each other but not touching. It'd been some time before either of them fell asleep, and now, at first light, he was wide awake again with a potent cocktail of lust and anger swimming through his body and mind like an insidious virus. Roderick. Baylee. Annette. Three boys. At the base of the entire mess was a pirate treasure that seemed to curse everybody it touched.

"You want to talk about it?" Baylee said.

"I want to find the treasure and use it to lure the baddies out of the water where we can get our hands on them," Clay said.

"I told the police about the bartender at the Pelican possibly being a match for the president of the Buccaneers," Baylee said. "I don't think they put much stock in it."

"It's a bit of a stretch," he said, "that we plucked a picture off some forum of a guy who might be the secret Grub Boseman and happens to look like a fellow named Silas who pours drinks at a local bar."

"It'd be a good idea to at least disprove the theory, so it doesn't cloud things up, don't you think?"

Clay swung his feet to the floor. He couldn't lie in bed any longer without touching Baylee, but he couldn't quite bring himself to bridge that distance. "Sounds like a job for Westy. He fits in with the biker crowd a bit better than the rest of us."

"If, and I know it's a mighty big if..." Baylee said. "If Silas the bartender is really the president of the Buccaneers MC, he knows all of us. More than likely, that's why he's working there, to keep an eye on us."

"I'm thinking that if it really is him, he's in the wind," Clay said.

"What do you want to do?" Baylee asked, standing up, looking incredibly sexy in her large T-shirt and tangled hair with sleepy eyes.

"Well, it certainly looks like the four Buccaneers murdered Annette and her boys," Clay said. "But on whose say so? It could be this mysterious Grub Boseman hiding out in Port Essex searching for pirate treasure. Although, why kill her and her children? That doesn't make sense. They may be brutes who brawl, but that doesn't put them up there with psychos who kill women and children."

"It makes sense that there is a higher up who ordered the kill," Baylee said. "Grub Boseman is my suspect number one. Who else?"

"I find it odd that both of our clients have had their male partners killed," Clay said. "Which doesn't seem to fit in with the killing of Annette and her boys."

"Okay," Baylee said. "Let's take them separately for now, and if they come back together at the end, so be it. I got Grub as my number one in ordering the killing of Annette and her boys. Who do you like for the other two murders? Assuming they're connected."

They went out to the kitchen. Clay had made the coffee the night before and put the timer on for early, knowing he wouldn't sleep. He put the gourmet creamer they both liked in two cups, poured, and handed Baylee one of them. The animals all had to go out, and the morning routine was to go down to the water and drink a cup of joe while they took care of business.

"Rose Ryan," Clay said as they walked. "I'd have put Tobias Yates at the top of the list but now he's dead."

"Dannie Cox is not who she says she is," Baylee said. "I'd be willing to lay odds she's not merely a failed antique dealer."

"Guess we might as well add Gina to that list," Clay said. "She did hire us to follow her husband, who is now dead."

They sat down on the rope swing, the distance between them small and gaping at the same time. The sun was rising to the east, pretty much over the house by the alpaca farm where a team of investigators was most likely still searching the scene of the grisly murders of that family.

"As for Annette, we're thinking those four Buccaneer idiots offed them." Baylee set her coffee cup between them and stretched her arms over her head. "So, if we're going on the premise that somebody was pulling the strings of those bikers, the most likely person would be Silas, that is, if he is really Grub Boseman."

"And he, they, very well may have done the other two murders," Clay said. "But we can't dismiss the women. Rose, Dannie, and Gina."

"Two of whom are our clients."

"That's a fact."

"You're thinking finding the treasure will draw the puppeteer from hiding," Baylee said. "But how do we find it?"

"Not sure," Clay said.

"Here's an idea,' Baylee said, "I been tumbling around in my mind. I think Niben Glenn was lying to me about something. What if those fishermen from Gorges Island came to the mainland and the village of the Chbo So, but never left with the treasure? What if it stayed right there, where it was originally?"

Clay snuck a peek sideways at Baylee. "That'd certainly be easier than searching all of Davie Jones's Locker."

"How about we go pay Niben a visit and see what we can dig out of her."

"Sounds like a plan to me."

"A bit early yet," Baylee said. "I could use a shower and then maybe some breakfast at the diner?"

*　*　*

Niben sat rocking in front of her home as usual when they pulled into her driveway. It was the first time Clay was meeting the elderly woman, but he could tell from how Baylee spoke of her, that she'd made an impression. There was a quiet calm and wisdom to her eyes as they approached her.

"Real People," Niben said by way of greeting. "This is him?"

"This is my partner, Clay Wolfe," Baylee said. She flushed slightly. "He wanted to meet you. Clay, this is Niben Glen."

"Good to meet you, Niben," Clay said. Baylee had coached him to not refer to her as Mrs. Glenn.

Niben patted the rickety chair next to her, looking at Baylee. "Sit," she said. She looked at Clay. "There is another chair on the side over there."

Clay followed the direction of her nod around the corner of the trailer and found a wooden chair with the slats broken out and only three legs. This he brought back, leaning it firmly against the trailer wall before sitting down tentatively.

"You come looking for the treasure, don't you," Niben said. "It is not worth the trouble. A curse follows it and devours all who search for it."

"You might be right," Baylee said. "Have you heard what's been going on around here?"

Niben looked up at the sky where a lazy white cloud barely drifted along. "I listen to the radio. Neighbors stop by to gossip. They say there was a woman and her boys killed at the hands of pirates," she said.

"A motorcycle gang called the Buccaneers," Clay said. "Or so it appears."

"They did not do it," Niben said.

Clay looked at her, looked at Baylee, and held his tongue.

"You mean the four men arrested for the murders are not the actual killers?" Baylee asked.

"Sometimes the pirates are the innocents," Niben said. "Just like sometimes the Native American people are not the villains. It is not always a cowboy and Indian movie."

"Do you know who did kill the woman and her children?" Baylee asked.

"There was another murder," Niben said. "A man was killed on Townsend Island. Close to where the village of the Chbo So was some 300 years ago before being absorbed into the Abenaki, who in turn were wiped out by the weapons, disease, and greed of the white men."

Baylee cast her eyes down. "Not quite entirely erased." She put her hand on the woman's knee and touched her own chest and then head.

"Some of us live on, here and here."

"The Abenaki is strong within you," Niben said. "But has been lost for some time."

"What do you know of this other murder?" Baylee asked.

"He was not a good man. But not a bad man either. He merely lusted after the fire opals, and they came to collect their due."

"They?" Baylee asked.

"The fire opals. Long hidden. Dormant. Safe. But the door has been thrown open, and their curse lives among us again."

"The men from Gorges Island never took the opals from where Black Sam Bellamy hid them, did they?" Baylee said, her hand still on the woman's knee.

Niben spit a string of tobacco juice into the pot at her feet. "No."

"Will you tell us about it?" Baylee asked.

"The men came from the sea in a long boat with many oars," Niben said. "My people, the Chbo So, knew these men, and had always gotten along with them. When they came looking for what Sam Bellamy had hidden in the cliffs, though, my people were very nervous. Sam Bellamy had always been a friend to the Chbo So, but they knew he could be fierce, as could the many sailors aboard his ship. My people didn't want to anger Sam Bellamy. But when the white fishermen explained that he'd been in a shipwreck, and that he and all of his men had drowned, my people decided to show them where Sam Bellamy had hidden the eight chests of treasure.

It was as I told you earlier, they were guided to the spot by one of my people, a young man who hoped to be rewarded for his troubles. There was no way down the cliffs where the treasure was to the water, so they took it back to the village overland. By the time they got back, the wind had picked up, and black clouds were rolling in from the northeast. My people convinced the fishermen that it wouldn't be safe, and that they should spend the night, and journey back after the storm had blown through.

It was good until the men pulled out a bottle of firewater, and then another. They started to make crude comments, especially to one young girl of the Chbo So, a girl too young for a husband, but her body already womanly. It is possible that she liked the attention of these strange white devils at first. But when they became bolder, she said no. When they refused to listen, her brother said no with a stick to the head of one of the men. They fell upon the young man and beat him, and when others tried to interfere, threatened them with their muskets. By this time, the girl had been hidden away, but her brother was killed that day in trying to defend her honor.

"After what seemed forever, as the storm raged around, the wind howling, and the rain thundering down like a waterfall, the sailors fell asleep."

"And the Chbo So killed them all," Baylee said.

"That they did," Niben said fiercely, her eyes burning hot. "They did what they had to. But they knew that there would be retaliation, so before first light, as the storm lessened, they took the boat along with the bodies of the sailors and some of the fire opals and sunk it off Gorges Island."

"The remnants of which the remaining men found washed up the next day," Clay said. The men from Gorges Island who'd come looking for the fire opals, threatened to rape a girl, and killed her brother. These are the men you speak of?"

"Yes."

"You said some of the stones?" Baylee aid.

Niben smiled, the wrinkles of her face making her look like an apple doll. "My people sacrificed some of the gems to the gods to placate them and then returned the bulk of them to where Sam Bellamy had originally hidden them."

"Above the village of the Chbo So on the Sibosek River," Clay said.

"On Townsend Island," Baylee said.

Niben spit in the pot. "If you look closely, just below where the man was killed yesterday, you will find the remains of the Chbo So village, although very, very faint. Between those archaeological remains, and the house of Tobias Yates, you will find the fire opals. But I warn you, they kill all who touch them or search for them."

Chapter 29

Westy visited his weapons locker at his house and retrieved a few valuable items before slipping out before his wife and son could wake up. No sense in alarming them. Clay had texted asking if he was awake, a bit after five, knowing full well that Westy always rose before the sun. He'd stepped outside to call him back. Clay had given him the mission of finding the man who called himself Silas to find out if he really was the president of the Buccaneers Motorcycle Club, Grub Boseman.

With various rifles in a gun bag behind his truck seat, Westy drove off Spruce Island, noting that Clay and Baylee had not yet left her house for the day. Clay had said that they planned on visiting the Native American woman, Niben, but thought they best wait until at least eight in the morning before showing up unannounced. Westy did not believe in such courtesies when life and death were on the line.

Chris Kenny was the daytime manager of the Pelican, which required him to be in by six to serve breakfast to the early risers. The top bar was not yet open, but the restaurant on the first floor was, serving the fishermen before they headed out on the water for the day. Kenny also liked to fish, and Westy had taken him out a handful of times on his boat.

It did not take much to convince Kenny to share that Silas the bartender had gone AWOL the day before, disappearing from his shift without so much as a word. Kenny was happy to oblige Westy and gave him the man's job application and materials, cursing him all the while. The middle of July was not the best time to be down a bartender, especially one as capable and pulling as many hours as Silas Laskin had, which was the name on the paperwork.

Westy wrote down the man's address, which was a P.O. Box in Essex, his social security number, and several other pertinent pieces of information. The next stop was the coffee shop about four doors down called Joe Cuppa. As he knew, Officer Dan Sterling of the Port Essex PD was in there hard at work on a huge breakfast, the sports pages of the newspaper spread out across the table. Sterling was a twenty-year veteran of the Navy. He, also, was more than happy to help out, telling Westy that the Buccaneers up from Boston had taken up residence in a campground the other side of Essex that hadn't survived the pandemic. The police had thought about rousting them to move along, but knowing their whereabouts seemed to be more important than dispersing them to God knows where.

The campground was quiet this morning, other than the snoring of passed out bikers. Westy parked his truck on the road and walked in through the woods. He was now within a distance to hear the rumble of white males sawing logs as they lay scattered about, some in bedrolls, some just on the ground. There was a scattering of cabins. Westy figured that if Silas had indeed joined the bikers, he'd be in one of them.

It was at the third cabin, as Westy peered in the window, that the voice came from behind him.

"Looking for somebody?"

He turned to face Silas Laskin, aka, Grub Boseman, standing behind him holding a Beretta in his hand, the pistol casually pointed at Westy. Silas had lost the black-rimmed glasses and beard. He wore a white tank top that revealed previously hidden body art curling around his shoulders and arms. But it was him. The bartender.

"Was hoping to get a Budweiser, if you're on duty," Westy said.

Silas laughed in merriment. "You and your friends were all quite helpful talking about the case up on the Perch."

Westy nodded his head toward the snoring men scattered around the campground. "They all know that you're actually Grub Boseman, president of the MC?"

"I wondered how much you knew," Silas said. "How'd you get on to me?"

"I had a problem with grubs in my lawn a couple years back," Westy said. "Had quite a time with those little white worms, but I finally got rid of them. One day I was looking at you, and I said to myself that man is one little white worm. He must be Grub. Grub Boseman."

Silas laughed, but this time it was more brittle. "They know me only as the hand of the president. The red right hand."

"The one he masturbates with," Westy said.

"I don't believe I've ever killed a SEAL, Mr. Weston Beck. This will be a pleasure."

Westy nodded his head behind Silas. "And now he knows who you really are."

It was just the waver of the head, the slight nod to the right, the eyes flickering—all that Westy needed to dive for the corner of the cabin. He felt the angry buzz of the bullets cut the air above him, embedding in the wooden logs, and then he rolled around the corner. He heard cursing behind him, and then he was in the bushes, bullets plowing into the shrubbery like irritated bees.

With the gunshots, Westy could hear Silas calling out behind him. "Intruder. We have an intruder."

He crawled until he came to a stream, wading through and running up on the other side. He heard men crashing into the thicket behind him. He took his Sig Sauer out and wished for the assault rifle in his truck.

The rumble of awakening motorcycles kicked into life, and he could hear the steel horses fanning out, traversing the pathways of the campground. He was cut off from going back toward the road, back to his truck, and was forced to go deeper into the woods behind the campground. Westy came to a path and heard the sound of a Harley coming toward him.

Westy put his back to the tree and waited. The roar came closer, the bike vibrating in low gear as the man astride navigated the narrow path. When the Buccaneer drew abreast of Westy, he stepped out, and smacked the man with his pistol solidly in the nose. Westy followed the man to the ground, his hands cutting off the man's air until he stopped flailing, unconscious.

Westy climbed aboard the Harley and pointed it back toward the road. He passed several other Buccaneers, but not close enough for them to realize he wasn't one of them, swinging onto Route 29 and opening the bike up. He'd have to come back later for his truck.

*   *   *

Murphy knew if you wanted the real dirt going down in the town of Port Essex, the place to hear it was the Side Bar. Thus, at just past nine in the morning, there he was, ensconced at the bar, which was no more than a piece of plywood over four empty kegs sitting on cinder blocks. There was seating for four and the spaces were all filled, one of them being Murphy. There were also five or six dingy tables in the room, only half of which were taken.

The liquor was cheap and the amenities sparse. The bartender had only one eye and no patch, the cavity a gruesome road map of scarring. Murphy knew two of the others at the bar with him, a woman named Tricia who worked nights at the 7-11 and came here after her shift, and a fellow with the nickname Cro-TO who dug blood worms until he had enough money for a bender, after which he was back to forking through the mud for fish bait.

The fourth person was a stranger. He was less than five feet tall and almost as round, his eyes recessed into his cheeks, so they were barely visible.

"Name's Murphy," he said to the man, who sat on his left.

The man turned his thick jowls to the right. "Albert Hutch. But people call me Jabba."

"Pretty crazy doings in town yesterday, huh?" Murphy said.

"Effed up about them boys," Jabba said.

"You know them or their mother?"

Jabba shook his head, the stretched skin of his face rippling like the tide. "Nope. Heard she was a whore, though. Fellow in here said he had a buddy who paid her for a knobber."

"Dug clams for fifty years," Murphy said. "Had to be worse than giving the occasional knobber."

Jabba looked sideways at him, shock on his face, and then he laughed, a rippling sound like a growing volcano erupting from his mouth. "Might be right, there. I drove a school bus for thirty years. That job really sucked." He laughed again, slapping the bar top with a meaty hand.

"Any way you look at it, those bikers from away should go away for a long time for what they did," Murphy said.

"Got that right. Heard they was up from Boston. Damn city-folk."

"Some of their gang came in here yesterday," the bartender said, setting a fresh Jameson in a dirty glass in front of Murphy. "I told them to git the hell out. They didn't like it much, but then I went in back and got my shotgun. They gitted, all right."

Murphy eyed the drink. What could it hurt. He turned the glass to a relatively clean spot and took a sip of the brown liquor. "How about that other thing, over to Townsend Island," he said.

"Where the feller got stabbed in the eye with a cake knife?" Jabba said.

"Huh," Murphy said. "I didn't know how he got killed, only that somebody murdered him."

Jabba leaned closer to Murphy, his body oozing in waves as it moved. "That's what Adam Dube told me. He was taking the feller out on his boat looking for pirate treasure."

"Pirate treasure?" Murphy said. He took another slug of Jameson to cover his lack of surprise.

"Yep, sure thing," Jabba said. "Dube said that this guy and some hot tamale redhead been out toward Gorges Island looking for sunken treasure. And now somebody up and killed him."

"It was that Baylee Baker who done it," the bartender said. "I'd bet ten dollars on it. You know she killed her husband a few years back?"

The man on the other side of Murphy, Cro-TO, leaned in and said, "Heard she was seen leaving the murder scene. Once a killer, always a killer. She just don't like men, would be my guess. So she kills 'em."

"Couple of them fine-looking state police came in last night," the woman named Tricia said from the far corner of the bar, a distance of no more than four feet. "Heard one of them say something about having evidence tying her to the scene, I mean, other than that she was seen there. Something about finding something with her name on it. Didn't hear what, but they seemed to think it was a pretty big deal. They was hoping to get something done about getting fingerprints from the weapon. Expedited, they said."

"You don't even know what expedited means," Jabba said.

Tricia scoffed. "I watch 'CSI'. I know that means they want the results right now."

*   *   *

Cloutier came through the front door of the P.I. office to find Crystal sitting behind her desk wearing a shocking pink tube top and with a corn cob pipe in her mouth.

"What's with the pipe?" Cloutier asked. She made no mention of the top, but had often wondered if Crystal had to go back to the 70s to find her outfits.

"Found it at the flea market," Crystal said. "Gives my mouth something to do when nobody's around to talk to."

Cloutier knew that Crystal had given up a heroin and smoking cigarettes. A corn cob pipe was certainly harmless in comparison.

"The Clay man here?" she asked.

"Nope. Him and Baylee should be back soon. They went out to see that Native American woman."

"What's the latest?" Cloutier asked.

"They didn't say. Just that they were on their way into the office." Crystal leaned back in her chair and snapped her gum. It appeared she was chewing gum *and* had an unlit pipe in her mouth. "You find out anything new about the Slavic lady we been working for?"

"Maybe," Cloutier said. "Just maybe."

"Yeah?" Snap went the gum. "What'd you get?"

"Her bank account gets a monthly payment of twenty grand from an off-shore account."

"How'd you find that out?"

Cloutier looked slyly at Crystal. "Us journalists have our sources," she said.

"So she is getting money from her daddy," Crystal said. "I knew that broad had dough. You can just tell. Try as you might, you can't hide the effects of a fucking silver spoon in your mouth."

"That's what I thought at first," Cloutier said. "But it turns out that the money comes from an office in Kyiv that is attached to the SZR."

"Kyiv is the capital of Ukraine, right?"

"You got it."

"And this SZR thing?"

"It's what us westerners call the foreign intelligence agency of Ukraine. The real name you couldn't pronounce in a month of Sundays."

Crystal took the pipe out of her mouth, snapped her gum, and cursed. "You're telling me that Dannie fucking Cox is a spy for the government of Ukraine? Shit fire and save matches. That there is something. An international spy in Port Essex. Hired us. Well, I'll be."

Chapter 30

"Let me see if I got this straight," Clay said. The gang was sitting at the Pelican Perch, figuring that a public venue was the safest place for them right now. "The fellow that just a couple of days ago was slinging drinks here, Silas, is actually Grub Boseman, president of the Buccaneers motorcycle club."

Westy nodded. "The club thinks he's just the right hand of Boseman and that he speaks for the man, but in reality, he is Grub, just with a reconstructed face and a new identity, Silas Laskin."

"I might've been a little loose with some of the things going on," Clay said. "Especially when I had the brown water in me."

"Isn't a bartender like a fucking priest?" Crystal said. "I thought that anything you told them was in the strictest of confidences?"

They all looked at her, not sure if she was joking or not. Finally, she smirked, and they all laughed.

"Meaning he had something to do with the deaths of Annette Ward and her boys," Clay said. "I know I never mentioned her name to him, so why kill her?"

"No loose ends," Westy said.

"Maybe," Clay said. "I don't see those four buffoons they got in jail being the killers, though. Far more likely it was Silas or Grub or whatever his name is, and he stashed the bodies there until they could dispose of them. And it was just their bad luck that Gina turned us on to where they were at."

"Don't much believe in bad or good luck," Westy said.

"That's because you're Sottish and not Irish, and a Presbyterian to boot." Murphy said. "Luck is all around us."

"Whatever," Westy said. "Let's suppose that it wasn't bad luck, but that somebody wanted them to take a fall for killing the woman and children."

"You're talking Gina?" Baylee said.

"Exactly."

"Why would Gina Yates… how would she even know the bodies were there?" Cloutier asked.

"Can we assume that Silas Grub is after the pirate treasure, same as the rest of us?" Westy asked.

"Don't like to assume," Clay said. "But it sure looks like it'd be a good bet."

"And now that Gina knows of the treasure, maybe she's working on whittling down the competition," Westy said. "That could be the why, but I don't have a theory on the how."

"Seems a bit of a stretch," Cloutier said. "But worth keeping tucked away."

"Okay," Clay said. "Let's not forget that the same day the bodies are found, thanks to Gina and the alpacas, her husband is murdered."

"And the suspicion was cast on me," Baylee said.

"Who is also looking for the treasure, albeit for your clients," Murphy said.

"Eliminating Tobias in the process," Cloutier said.

"Okay, okay, okay," Clay said a bit sarcastically. "Let's go on the premise that Gina is *not* a criminal mastermind who through murder has hampered the efforts of the bikers, her husband, and us in finding the treasure. Who does that leave?"

"Rose Ryan," Crystal said. "That red-haired bitch."

"What do we know of Rose?" Clay asked.

They all looked around the table at each other, and as one, reached for their drinks.

"We need to know more about this Rose Ryan," Clay said. "She claims that she ran into Tobias at a conference in Ireland, and they got to talking? Seems pretty slim to me."

"Thinner than her bony ass," Crystal said, adding with a snort, "And what was it, a sex doll manufacturers annual trade show?"

"And, of course, then there's our client, Dannie Cox," Clay said.

"An operative of the Ukrainian Secret Intelligence Agency," Cloutier said. She'd already briefed the table on how she drew a substantial monthly stipend from this agency, or so it appeared.

"What is an operative of the Ukrainian government doing in Port Essex, Maine?" Cloutier asked.

"You should ask her," Murphy said. "Seeing as she's your client, and all."

"She's not replying to my messages," Clay said. "You mentioned some gossip that the police might have an important piece of information about Tobias' murder?"

"Trish down to the Side Bar said she overheard a couple of the state police talking. That they found something at the crime scene with Baylee's name on it and that they thought there might be a good print off the murder weapon. They're trying to get the crime lab to expedite the results."

"Gina hired us to tail her husband who she thought was having an affair," Clay said. "I'm sure there are several documents in the house with Baylee's name on it. I would hope the police are looking closely at Gina as the prime suspect. I'd say nine times out of ten in this situation, the spouse is the murderer."

"I'll reach out to Officer Tracy and see if she knows anything she's willing to share," Baylee said.

"What'd you and Baylee find out from the Native American woman?" Westy asked.

"Nothing much," Clay said. "Just that I think we now know where the fire opals are hidden."

*   *   *

Clay smirked to himself. Nothing like putting off the hunt for pirate treasure and murderers—likely biker gangs and foreign operatives among them—so that you can go let the dogs out. Now he chuckled. That song had come out his first year in high school and had become very popular, sung before sports games and on victorious bus trips home.

"Who, who, who, who," he said under his breath.

"What's that?" Baylee asked.

"Remember that song, 'Who Let the Dogs Out?'" he asked.

Baylee snickered. "I suppose somebody's gotta let them out."

They were in his Jeep crossing the short bridge over to Spruce Island. Crystal was taking Westy to retrieve his truck and then they would meet at Knox Wharf to take Westy's fishing boat out hunting pirate treasure. Cloutier was doing further research on Rose and Gina. Murphy was doing what he did best, namely trolling the local bars for information.

"About the thing with Roderick," Clay said. "I'm sorry to be a jerk about it. It just kinda got sprung on me, and I'm having a hard time processing it."

"It was just some guy to pass the time before me and you got together," Baylee said. "He means nothing to me. As a matter of fact, I always thought he was a bit of a pretty boy dink, but then again, I don't think I was looking for somebody I liked. Just somebody to pass a few lonely nights with."

"Like I said, my issue, not yours. I just need some time for it to slide off, if you know what I mean?"

"Gotcha."

Clay drove past the driveway and then pulled a U-turn and parked on a pull-off just about a hundred yards past Baylee's house. "Seems to be a lot of people getting hurt lately," he said. "Most likely related to Black Sam's treasure. Almost enough to make you believe Niben when she says they're cursed. And now, we know where they are."

"*About* where they are," Baylee said. "We can cut through the woods. This parking space is for a trail connected to the back of my house by another, fainter, trail."

There were no baddies at the house, just a very excited Lab puppy, a yowling basset hound, and a loudly purring cat.

*   *   *

They motored up the Sibosek River as far as the Yates house before turning back. The buzz of activity surrounding an active murder scene had died down, but Clay didn't figure that Gina had been let back in to get anything but a few belongings. Much like Dannie, Gina wasn't returning messages. Maybe it was because her husband had been killed and the P.I. she'd hired was a main suspect in that murder. Maybe it was something else.

It was about a mile back to where there was a small cove in the river, about where they figured the village of the Chbo So had been located, according to Niben Glenn's instructions for how to find the village. It was in the Winnegance Preserve, and the first clue would be the remnants of shell middens, oyster shells accumulated in piles over thousands of years. The garbage dumps of shells had been drastically reduced over the years to be ground into chicken food and for the building of roads, but several small middens, or piles, remained.

The second clue was not so easily picked up from the river but was no less important a clue that the Chbo So had lived there. On a large granite rock was a plaque that in faded letters said that this spot had been the home of the Chbo So People of the Etchemin Tribe until 1730 when they had been absorbed into the Abenaki village of Winnegance. Baylee found the memorial, and the four of them gathered around it, in silent tribute, and then looked up the river toward where the Yates house stood. It was less than a mile, but the terrain was rugged, overgrown with pine trees and strewn with granite rocks and boulders.

Clay suggested that Westy and Crystal take the boat and work their way upriver looking closely for the granite rock shaped like a church bell while he and Baylee worked their way along the shoreline on foot. The walking was difficult as they scrambled up and over rocks, roots, and struggled through thickets of prickers pulling at them. Clay wished he'd brought a machete to chop his way through some of the brush. After an hour, they'd only traversed about a quarter of a mile.

Clay's phone buzzed with a call from Crystal. "What do you got?" he said by way of an answer.

"Think we got it," Crystal said. "Rock right where the river bends to the right. You should be about right on it now. There's a place to tie up just ahead, and we'll meet you there."

A half hour later, Clay and Baylee were joined by Crystal and Westy.

"I don't see any rock shaped liked a church bell," Clay said.

"That one right behind you," Westy said.

Clay turned around. There were seven or eight granite boulders scattered about. None of them looked much like a church bell to him. He'd never been all that good in seeing shapes in clouds, now that he thought about it, and wondered if he lacked imagination. He turned to Baylee. "You see a rock shaped like a church bell?"

"Nope."

Westy laughed. "I'm sure it's that one, but from here, it sure don't look like no bell. Let's take a gander from the other side."

The four of them walked to the edge of a cliff that fell forty feet down into the river. It still didn't look much like a church bell.

"I guess you got to see it from the water down below," Westy said. "But that's the one. What's the next step?"

Baylee took a crumpled sheet of paper from her back pocket and opened it up. "Their village was situated on the Sibosek River. Just past is a rock outcropping in the formation of a church bell. At the base of the outcropping there should be a place to go ashore. Climb to the top. You will see a pine tree taller than the rest back toward the village a hundred steps. At the base of the tree, face the river, and walk twenty steps. There will be a granite boulder shaped like a heart. Underneath that will be the entrance to catacombs, within which lay the fire opals."

"How far back did you walk just now from where you moored?" Clay asked.

"About a hundred steps," Westy said.

"If this tree and the bell-shaped rock are in the same spot, why didn't he just write, at the church bell, turn and face the river?" Baylee asked.

"Maybe because once you get up here, the rock doesn't look anything like a bell," Crystal said. "So he gave another landmark that would be obvious from up here."

They all looked up at the treetops. None stood out as particularly taller than any other.

"Look, we got to be roughly in the right place," Clay said. "How about we put ten yards between each of us, step off twenty paces, and then search for a heart-shaped rock?"

They spread out in a skirmish line and went the twenty paces, bringing them but ten steps from the edge. It took another hour and several false heart-shaped rocks before Westy pried one such boulder free with a crowbar and a yawning chasm stared them in the face.

"Eureka," Clay said.

"Holy fucking black hole," Crystal said.

Westy took his pack off his back and removed two flashlights and a length of rope. "Let's see what we got," he said.

Crystal eyeballed the hole with apprehension. "I'll stay up here and stand watch."

"I'm going down with Westy," Baylee said.

Clay knew that she'd rushed this declaration out to stop him from suggesting she stay atop with Crystal. Just like he also knew that suggesting Baylee stay out of harm's way was asking for a fight. "You two go down," he said. "Me and Crystal will keep watch and help pull you back up."

Five feet down, Westy's voice drifted back up, "It opens up down here." After a bit more, "We're on the ground."

Clay went to the edge of the cliff. There was a small skiff with an outboard motor going down the far side of the river. He looked up the shoreline trying to see the Yates house. It was ironic, he thought, that Tobias had been looking for sunken treasure out to sea when it was practically in his own backyard. And now the man was dead.

The Maine laws were tricky as far as lost treasure was concerned. If Tobias had found the Fire Opals on his own land, then he most likely would've been allowed to keep them all. Just off his property, on state-owned land, there was a good chance that the bulk of the cache would go to the state of Maine. A find on the ocean floor was much more in favor of the finder, as there was no real owner. If the treasure was indeed down below, it was unlikely that anybody had a legal claim other than the state.

A muffled yell came from down the hole, and the ropes tightened. Clay and Crystal pulled Baylee up, not before Westy emerged from the opening and clambered up next to them.

"Well?" Clay asked as soon as the four of them had caught their breath.

"After about five feet down it opens up, maybe about fifty feet wide. We reached bottom after another thirty feet or so. It was dry enough, but there was water stains, probably when the river runs high in the spring—"

"Did you find the treasure or not?" Clay interrupted impatiently.

"Eight chests down there," Westy said. "Maybe a bit bigger than a sea chest."

"Treasure fucking chests," Crystal said.

"What's in them?" Clay asked. "Come on!"

"I pried one open," Westy said. "It was filled with these."

He flipped an object the size of a ping-pong ball to Clay. Clay's first thought was that it was bright as it flashed through the sunlight. His second was that it was heavy. It was a gemstone, roughly polished, revealing all the colors of the rainbow, the primary one being red. It glowed as if there was an inner light inside trying to shine out into the world.

"Fire opals," Clay breathed.

"What do we do?" Baylee asked. "Can we get them out of there?"

"Not without help," Westy said. "They're not very light."

"Well, then, my fine friend. Today is your lucky day." Rose Ryan stood there with a short and ugly assault rifle pointed at them. Fanned out behind her were Adam Dube, captain of the *Coronado*, and three other men, all holding various weapons. "We are here to help."

Chapter 31

"Weapons and phones on the ground, please," Rose said. "I wouldn't want to have to kill half our labor force."

Clay stared at the woman he knew so little of. She seemed comfortable with a semi-automatic rifle in her hands, the strap around her pixie-thin shoulder. Her face and body were that of a teenager, but in her eyes, there was a much older woman. There was none of the nervousness that one would normally associate with an armed stand-off over the entrance to catacombs leading to immense wealth.

"I'm not a murderer," Rose said. "Do as I say, and you'll live."

Clay looked at Westy, who shrugged slightly. Clay agreed with the assessment, they didn't really have a choice. At this range, Rose could kill them all with one touch of her finger. They'd be tumbling to the ground dead before Dube and the other goons could pull their triggers, and long before Clay and company could bring a weapon to bear.

Westy carefully removed his Sig from the holster at his waist and laid it on the ground along with his phone. Clay followed suit with his Glock and phone. Baylee looked at both of them, reached inside her blouse, and pulled out her Smith & Wesson MP Shield and laid it on the ground.

"Phone, Miss Baker," Rose said.

Baylee pulled her phone out of her back pocket and set it down next to the Shield.

"Fucking wienies," Crystal said and removed a pistol that looked more like a cannon and placed it on the ground. "I didn't bring my fucking phone, okay? It's in the fucking boat."

Rose looked at her, nodded. "Miss Baylee Baker," she said. "I haven't had the pleasure of officially meeting you as of yet. I, of course, saw you in the lobby of the inn, but that doesn't really count, now, does it. I'm Rose Ryan, the true owner of this treasure. Will you step over here, please. And the rest of you, please take a few steps backwards from your weapons."

Baylee hesitated, and then took a few tentative steps forward.

"Turn around, Miss Baker, and put your hands behind you." Rose stepped forward with the assault rifle leveled at the rest of them. "Move back," she said.

Clay, Westy, and Crystal shuffled backward a few steps. Rose reached into her pocket and pulled something out. "Adam, be a dear, and zip-tie Miss Baker's hands behind her back. And blindfold her. You," she looked at another of the men," gather up those weapons on the ground and bring them back behind us here."

Clay looked at his pistol on the ground, Baylee being restrained, the gaping hole down to the treasure—and was frustrated with no move to make, certainly not until he had a better idea of what this woman's intentions were.

"Is it down there?" Rose asked. "The treasure? The fire opals my ancestor wrote about? Are they down there?"

She was met by a stony silence. Even Crystal kept her mouth shut.

"Look," Rose said. "This is how this is going to go down. You will answer my questions, or I will put a hole in the head of Miss Baker. There's no time to play around. Is the treasure down in that there hole."

"Yes," Westy said.

"Tell me about the treasure and the cavern it is in."

"There are eight chests," Westy said. "I opened one and it was filled with gemstones. Fire opals, I imagine, is what they were."

Rose made little chirping noises that might've indicated she was excited. "And the cave. How far down? How big?"

"After about five feet it opens to a space maybe twenty feet wide by fifty feet long. It's about thirty feet down."

Clay figured Westy still had his Ka-Bar on him, the blade often sheathed at his ankle. He didn't recognize any of the goons with Rose other than Adam Dube. He wasn't sure if anybody had the stomach for killing. The trick now was not the treasure, but getting himself and those he cared for out of this situation alive.

"You can have the treasure," Clay said. "Just let us go."

Rose cackled. "I believe we might need your brawn, Mr. Wolfe. Good thing we don't need your brains, because that part of you seems to be significantly lacking. Here's how it's going to play out," Rose added. She waved the rifle off to the side. "Me and Miss Baker are going to go sit over here in the shade and drink Mint Juleps. If anybody gets any funny ideas, I'm going to put a bullet in her head. That is for you, Mr. Weston Beck. Mama knows you could kill these men with your bare hands if given half a chance. Just know that Baker is dead if you make so much of a wrong twitch. Meanwhile, you men and granny there will be transporting my opals to the *Coronado* down below. And make sure those chests don't get *banjaxed.*"

"Banjaxed?" Crystal said.

"Broken. Smashed."

They ran heavy rigging lines from the boat down below up the side of the cliff, across to the cavern, and up and over the limb of large pine. One of the men went back down below to work the winch. Another man and Crystal went down below to put netting attached to a sling around each chest and then attach it to the steel cable via a hook and latch. Dube stood at the top of the cliff yelling instructions to the man working the winch down in the boat. The last man stood off to the side with his gun pointed at Clay and Westy as they guided the chests up to the top, maneuvered them to the side, and sent the cable back down the hole.

The first couple of chests took some time as they figured out the angles to lift them without banging the sides, the hole at the top being just big enough for them to fit through, and fear that the limb above would break. The chests were old and rotting, mostly held together by the netting, but it wouldn't take much for them to crumble to nothing tumbling the opals back into the catacombs below.

Up above, they could hear Crystal cursing a blue streak, insulting the man with her, Rose who had called her a granny, and everyone and everything in between. The sun slowly dropped over the cliff, and then the horizon to the west as the last chest emerged from the cavern and was positioned next to the other seven.

They lowered the cable and pulled Crystal up, and then the man from the cavern, as the moon, not quite full, rose in the sky to bathe them in a soft light.

"Perfect," Rose said. "Mother Nature has provided lighting for the next stage, not so bright that others will see what we're doing, but enough for us to accomplish our task. First, let's move these chests to the edge. Then, Adam, grab one man to help you, and leave the other two up here with Wolfe, Beck, and Granny. We'll set up the pulley there," she pointed to a rock outcropping at the edge, "and lower the chests to the Coronado."

They wrestled the chests from the cavern to the edge of the cliff, near the designated rock outcropping. Clay wondered about pushing one of them over the side to cause a distraction, but the tip of Rose's rifle barrel didn't waver from the back of Baylee's head. Whatever he did, Baylee would die, and that he couldn't face. Not even the possibility.

"Adam, please go down to the boat to help ensure the safe delivery of my opals. Mr. Wolfe, can you see that white rock over there? I will be there where I can keep an eye on you and Weston. If you so much as think of doing something off script, I will put a bullet in the back of Miss Baker's head. Do you understand me?"

Dube and one of the men started to pick their way back down the river to a spot where they could climb down to the boat below. Rose prodded Baylee along in front of her until they reached the white rock, just about fifteen feet above the waterline, and with a view of the men on the top. The last two goons fanned out facing Clay, Baylee, and Crystal.

"Be easy enough to take these two out," Westy said under his breath.

"Then what?" Clay asked. "I don't think that Rose was bluffing. She has the eyes of a killer. She'll shoot Baylee first and worry about the rest later."

"Let's go, you two," Rose yelled out. "Stop acting the maggots. Let's get that first chest attached and on its way down."

The process was slower going down than it had been coming up. The angle forced the chest to bump its way down the side of the rock wall. Dube was smart enough to know that, after 300 plus years, those chests wouldn't be all that sturdy, and that a pile of Fire Opals on the bottom of the Sibosek River wasn't going to earn him any brownie points with Rose, Queen of the Fire Opals.

It took three hours, but finally they were lowering the final chest onto the deck of the boat below.

"You lads catching anything over there?" The voice wafted out of the darkness below.

Clay looked over at Baylee. "Murphy," he whispered to Westy.

"Buzz off," Dube yelled back.

"What's that you got on the winch?" Murphy said.

Clay could see him in his skiff emerging from the darkness, only about twenty feet from the *Coronado* now.

"What's his plan?" Westy asked.

"I told you to buzz off," Dube yelled.

"Hey, lad, take it easy. I'm supposed to meet up with a buddy, but I got a late start and now it's dark," Murphy said. "You ain't seen anybody around, have you?"

The two goons watching Clay and Westy came their way to see

what was going on. Westy nudged Clay, nodded at the one on the left. Below, Dube had a gun in his hand, aimed at Murphy. The treasure chest had paused in its descent. Clay looked over where Rose and Baylee were. Rose's rifle had followed her eyes in looking at Murphy approaching in his skiff.

The tree next to Rose spit splinters as a shot rang out through the gloom. Baylee hooked her foot around Rose's ankle and tripped the woman and then tried to kick the rifle off the edge as Rose grabbed the barrel.

Clay went low and hard at the man on the left, reliving his days as a safety for the Port Essex football team, zeroing in on the receiver, except instead of a ball, the man had a gun. The man grunted and started to turn, bringing his shotgun to bear as more shots rang out from all over. Clay went in just under the rifle barrel and struck the man hard, driving the wind from him in a whoosh as he went over on his back, Clay on top of him.

Westy was a step slower and his man a step faster. He got off one shot that stung the top of Westy's shoulder like an angry bee and then Westy slammed him off the cliff. The man bounced off the treasure chest halfway down, snapping the net attached to the cable and plummeting, chest and man, to the boat below.

Dube took two shots at Murphy as the Irishman dove off the back of his skiff.

Rose drove the butt of the assault rifle into Baylee's chin, knocking her over backward, stunned.

Clay saw this and watched in horror as she brought the rifle to bear. He stood up and yelled, trying to distract her. Below him, the man gasping for breath, brought the shotgun up.

Baylee rolled as Rose pulled the trigger, *bap-bap-bap*. Three quick shots that puffed dirt where Baylee had been.

Crystal yelled for Clay to look out.

Clay looked down into the gaping end of the shotgun barrel as the man's body jerked, two red circles appearing on his chest, which then gushed forth blood.

Baylee dove at Rose's legs, upending the woman and sending the assault rifle out of her hands and clattering over the side, only about fifteen feet from where they were, to the water's edge. Rose grabbed her by the hair and flung her over the side following the rifle.

A bullet whistled through the air next to Rose's ear, and she jumped down following Baylee who was crawling toward the assault rifle.

Clay pulled the shotgun from the dead man's hands and pointed it at Rose but now the Irish woman was too close to Baylee.

Dube came off the boat and kicked Baylee in the ass, knocking her flat on her face. Rose kicked her in the side of the head, and she went limp. Dube picked up Baylee, Rose grabbed up the rifle, and they climbed aboard the Coronado. A man lay splayed on the deck, his limbs at odd angles, and fire opals glittered in the moonlight from the broken chest.

Clay took three steps and jumped off the side of the cliff. The wind whistled, and it seemed to take a long time, and then all of a sudden, he landed on the deck of the salvage boat and rolled, the shock vibrating up through his legs and his spine and jarring his brain.

Dube kicked him in the side and then picked him up and threw him overboard. The other goon was already steering the boat out into the river. The shock of the cold water cleared Clay's mind as he stood up in the shallow water, but it was too late. The *Coronado* was chugging away down the Sibosek River.

Chapter 32

Clay watched the *Coronado* disappear into the darkness, the last glimmer of moonlight giving out, and then it was gone. There was a splashing just down the river and he realized Murphy was staggering ashore about fifty feet downriver. He turned to follow suit, Westy arriving to give him a hand for the last step, having taken the longer journey down.

"That was pretty badass," Westy said. "But you let them get away."

"They took Baylee," Clay said.

"We'll get her back," Westy said.

"You lads okay?" Murphy stumbled up to them. At the best of times, he looked like Dobby, the wrinkled house-elf from the Harry Potter books, but now appeared even more emaciated and worn in his dripping clothes.

"Where's your skiff at?" Westy asked.

Murphy waved his hand downriver. "Gone."

"Who was that shooting from up above?" Clay asked.

"That'd be me," Dannie Cox said as she and Crystal arrived at the same time.

Westy looked at her, the way they'd come, then looked upriver. "We need a boat sooner than later," he said and dove in the water and struck out upriver to where he'd moored his fishing boat.

"What the hell?" Dannie said.

"That freak of nature swims faster than most people can run," Crystal said. "His boat is up around the bend. Hey, here's the bag of phones and guns those goons took from us." She held up the sack. "It was up top there where that bitch was holding Baylee."

"What are you doing here?" Clay asked, looking at Dannie.

Dannie snorted. "It seems that you were leaving your client out in the cold. Didn't I hire you to help *me* find the treasure and not find it for yourself?"

Clay opened his mouth, shut it again. That was the facts, he thought. "You were unavailable, and we were acting on quickly emerging intel," he said.

"Oh, look, going all secret agent on me. What you appear to have been doing was helping my competition," Dannie said with a grin.

"At gunpoint," Clay said, taken aback at her banter.

"Yeah, I caught on to that."

Clay shook his head, water flying from his hair, fog from his mind. "You saved my life," he said. "You shot that goon who was about to pump a shotgun round into me at point blank range."

"Yeah," Dannie said. "Thought about not doing it so that I wouldn't have to give you your cut of the treasure, but then figured I might still need you to help track it down. Found only to be lost again."

"More stolen than lost," Clay said.

A boat motor churned into life from the darkness upriver and a few seconds later, Westy was sidling up to them and they were clambering aboard.

"They're gone," Clay said. "Long gone."

"No reason to hurt Baylee," Westy said.

"There was no reason to kill Annette and her three boys, but somebody sure as heck did, and I don't think it was those redneck bikers," Clay said.

"You think it was Rose?" Westy asked as he opened up the throttle perhaps a little faster than was safe in the dark.

"We need to get to the office," Crystal said. "And my computer."

Clay shivered in his wet clothes out in the cool night air. Murphy was wrapped in a blanket up front keeping lookout for objects in the water.

"What for?" Clay asked, his mind elsewhere, trying to grapple with the task of how to rescue Baylee before Rose decided she was no longer needed and slit her throat and fed her to the fishes.

"I got the phone tracker app on it," Crystal said.

"So?" Westy asked, reaching into the bag to grab his phone and pistol. He handed Clay his Glock and phone as well, and then Crystal her gun.

"My phone's not in there," Crystal said.

"Yeah, you left it on the boat," Westy said.

"That's what I told that red-headed bitch," she replied.

Clay snapped into the present and turned to his foul-mouthed receptionist. "Where is your phone, really?" he asked.

"Well, I did have it hanging between my tits in a neck pouch," Crystal said with a leer. "But when I went down below, I took it off and slid it into one of those treasure chests, must've been the one that Westy opened up."

* * *

Rose took a deep breath. There was a dead man with a broken neck on the deck. An unconscious woman lay next to him with her hands zip-tied behind her back. She had splinters in her face from bullets that had just missed hitting her. Dube was at the wheel, and another man was up front keeping watch. Fire opals glittered on the deck like some obscene fireworks display. And there were seven more chests filled with those precious gemstones. She had done it. Rose Ryan was rich beyond her wildest dreams.

She found a roll of trash bags and a broom and began sweeping the loose gems into bags as they left the river and began to go around Spruce Island. For a moment, she considered telling Adam to just keep going. They could go up the coast to Canada and nobody would ever find them. No, she told herself, stick to the plan.

Rose gathered the last of the opals as they rounded the tip of Spruce Point, and Baylee Baker began groaning and twitching, her eyes fluttering around the blindfold. Rose stuck another rolled up handkerchief into her mouth. What to do with her, Rose wondered? Probably just turn her loose once they'd made their escape. Rose wasn't a murderer. She'd talked a good game back there, but she'd never ever actually killed another human being and wasn't sure she could do it if necessary. That was why Baker was still alive, Rose thought, thinking back to her finger hesitating on the trigger. And then it'd been too late.

They weren't returning to the Knox Wharf. Too many prying eyes, even at this time of the night. Adam had suggested another dock over by the Point. It had once been a marina but had been out of business for some years now. That was where the truck was parked. Adam steered around the numerous moored boats in the harbor with the moonlight guiding his way.

Baker rolled over and tried to sit up. Rose gently pushed her back down with her foot. She looped a rope through her zip-tied wrists and secured her to a cleat. What to do with the dead man on the deck, Rose wondered? They probably should've just tossed him over the side back on the river and let him wash out to sea to be found later, if at all. Adam eased the boat into the dock, and the man up front jumped out of the boat and tied up. The marina building had boarded-up windows, and weeds had taken over the parking area.

"What about him?" Rose asked, nodding at the dead man, as Adam turned away from the wheel to look at her.

"We'll toss him in the bushes after we load the truck," Adam said.

"And her?"

Adam didn't reply. Rose sighed and stepped out of the boat, went down the dock, and around the side of the building where the rental truck was parked. She backed it down to the dock, and Adam and the other man whose name she didn't even know, opened the back and took the flat trolley out and lowered the ramp.

While the men loaded the truck with the treasure, Rose went back and pulled the gag from Baylee's mouth after holding a finger to her lips.

"What do you want from me?" Baylee's words were slurred and blurry.

"I want to know if you can keep your mouth shut, so I don't have to kill you," Rose said.

"About what?'

"Very good," Rose said. "I think you understand. We'll leave you tied up and gagged in the building here while we crack on. If you haven't been found in three days, I'll call in an anonymous tip. Okay?"

"Three days?"

"Better than having your throat slit and your carcass dumped into the harbor."

"Okay," Adam said. "We're all loaded up."

Rose stood and stepped up onto the dock. "We're going to leave her tied, gagged, and blindfolded in the building," she said.

"Whatever you say," Adam said. "Tom, come give me a hand."

Rose passed the man who she now knew as Tom as she walked to the truck. A shadow flitted its way onto the dock and then a dark figure stepped around the truck. Rose's eyes widened as she saw that the woman held a pistol in her hand.

"Thank you for finding my treasure," Gina Yates said, taking a step further, so that her face was illuminated in the moonlight.

"Your treasure?" Rose asked.

Gina smiled, a glint of teeth in the moonlight. The pistol in her hand was very long, and then Rose realized that it had a silencer on the end. Had Gina seen Adam and Tom, Rose wondered. If she could keep her distracted, it should be easy enough to gain the upper hand.

"I deserve this treasure," Gina said. "I was the one having sex with that pig of a husband. Rumor has it that you didn't have to put up with that particular horror."

Rose had tried to seduce Tobias, thinking that would facilitate the treasure hunt. He'd turned her down, claiming marital loyalty and love for his wife. "How about we split it, fifty-fifty?" she asked.

Adam and Tom pulled Baylee up on the dock next to Rose.

"She has a gun," Rose said. Was the man blind, she wondered?

"Ah, Miss Baylee Baker has joined the party," Gina said. "What are you doing with her, sweetheart?"

Rose furrowed her sparse eyebrows. Sweetheart? She looked sideways at Adam, and then back to Gina.

"There's a dead man in the boat," Adam said.

"What's going on?" Rose asked.

Gina took a few steps closer, now fully in the moonlight, just about ten feet away. "Didn't you tell her yet, sweetheart?" she asked.

"What?"

"Adam and I are lovers," Gina said. "And now we are very, very wealthy."

Rose was left speechless. Gina snickered and shot her twice in the head. Rose stood very still for several long seconds and then toppled forward and fell on her face.

"What about Baker?" Adam asked.

Gina turned the pistol toward Baylee, She took another few steps until she was two feet away. She pressed the tip of the silencer against Baylee's head.

"What about Wolfe?" Gina asked.

"He knows about me," Adam said. "Him and that fucking Westy."

Gina nodded. "It might be a good idea to keep her for a little while as insurance. Put her in the back of the truck." She looked at Tom. "Ride back there with her."

"What about the body in the boat?" Adam asked.

Gina's eyes blazed at him. "Not my boat," she said.

"I'll come back later and clean it up," Adam said.

* * *

Westy pulled the boat right up to the back of the P.I. office. The five of them hustled up the stairs and inside. Crystal went straight to the computer, still fuming, because Dannie had suggested that Crystal just log in using one of their smart phones and track her phone that way. When Crystal admitted that she didn't know her password, Dannie asked how that was possible and muttered something derogatory under her breath.

"How'd you and Murphy join forces?" Clay asked Dannie as they waited for Crystal.

"When you didn't check in," Murphy said, "I came over here to check on you, and she was banging on the door. I didn't tell her at first where you was, but when another hour went by, I figured we had to do something. So I told her all about it. Figured she knew her way around a gun."

"Fair enough," Clay said. "I guess bringing a foreign spy to our aid was a good call."

Dannie's face remained impassive.

"How long have you been working for the Ukrainian government?" Clay asked.

"What does it matter who I work for?" Dannie asked.

"Well, slice my fucking wanker with a butter knife," Crystal said. She looked up from the screen at their staring faces. "They're right across the harbor."

Clay led the way into his office and the picture window overlooking Essex Harbor. Across the way to the left was the footbridge leading to a hotel and restaurant with lights of several different establishments illuminating the surrounding area. To the right the light was sparser, but still glowed with activity. Directly across it was dark except for two glowing red lights.

"The old marina dock," Westy said. "That's where they are."

"Boat or car?" Murphy asked.

"Did you get your password so we can use a phone to track your phone?" Dannie asked.

"No, I didn't get my fucking password," Crystal said.

"You mean you don't have it written down somewhere? Or on your computer?" Dannie asked.

"Do you not understand English, you fucking Ukrainian spy?" Crystal said.

"Okay, here's what we'll do," Clay said. "Murphy goes with Westy in the boat. Dannie comes with me in my Jeep. Crystal stays here and tracks them if they move. Let's go."

Chapter 33

Commercial Way, the main street of town, was still buzzing on this Tuesday night as Clay tried to get around the harbor to save Baylee and recover the opals. Drunk tourists weaved their way off the sidewalks and into the road and cars were almost at a standstill as he lay on the horn and yelled for them to move.

"The others will beat us there," Dannie said.

"Are you really an antiques dealer?" Clay asked.

"Sure," Dannie said, and then laughed. "Just not a very good one."

"Was Andy a spy as well?"

Dannie's face grew somber. "No. He had no idea."

"Just a cover for you?"

Dannie shook her head. "No. I loved him. He was a very good man. Not much of an antiques dealer, but a very good man."

Clay assumed that spies were well versed in lying, but her words had a ring of sincerity that he believed. "Who killed him?"

"I don't know."

"Come on. Somebody who knew that you were a spy and probably suspected that he was as well."

"Nobody knows that I'm a spy. Not until you."

"Was it the CIA do you think?" Clay asked. "I mean, if we caught on to you, I can only imagine that the Feds know about you. Did they take him out? Am I getting myself on a federal watch list?"

"It's not really like that," Dannie said. "I'm not here stealing state secrets. The U.S. and Ukraine are allies. I'm here to keep tabs on the Russians in Brighton Beach. Many of them have very strong connections to their motherland. Some of them are gangsters, arms dealers."

They reached the tip of the harbor and the road opened up, many of the cars going to the left, as Clay went to the right and out the Point. His phone buzzed. It was Crystal.

"What?" he answered.

"They're on the move," Crystal said. "Coming back toward town."

"Where?"

"They just left the old marina traveling north toward town."

And there it was. A large yellow moving truck went past going the other way. "That's gotta be them," Clay said, cutting the wheel. The turning radius of the Jeep was not great, and he had to make a three-point turn, cars honking at them. "The truck."

There were three cars between them and the van. Clay wondered about just following the moving van to wherever Rose and Dube were going and confront them there. But a little piece of him worried that he might be wrong and that this might be just some married couple in the middle of moving late on a Tuesday night.

Clay picked the phone up from where he dropped it. "You still there?" he asked.

"Sure thing, boss," Crystal said.

"Are they heading up toward Route 29?" he asked.

"Yep. Just about there. Okay, call Westy and—"

The phone beeped. Call waiting from Westy. "I got Westy on the line. I'll call you back." Clay hit end and accept. "Westy," he said.

"I got two dead bodies at the boat," Westy said.

Clay's insides melted. "Two?"

"The fellow I threw off the cliff and our very own Rose Ryan. Two bullet holes in her forehead."

"Wow. Sounds like maybe Dube didn't want to share the treasure after all."

"Dube's not that smart. He's a follower, not a leader. Somebody else is leading the way."

"I'm following a yellow moving truck that appears to have Crystal's phone in it, so one would assume it has Baylee and the opals in it as well. We just got on Route 29."

"Me and Murphy will go get my truck and be right behind you," Westy said. "Keep us updated."

"Did I hear that Rose Ryan is dead?" Dannie asked.

"Yep. Somebody shot her."

"This is getting pretty nasty."

"Yep." Clay saw a small gap and passed one of the cars between him and the truck. "Are you after the treasure for Dannie Cox or for the country of the Ukraine?"

"Ukraine could use all the help they can get right about now," Dannie said. "Those gems will buy quite a few missiles to use in their war with Russia."

The truck turned left ahead of them on the crosscut toward the top of Townsend Island. Clay followed suit. There were now no cars in between them. He floored the accelerator, rocketing the Jeep up the left side of the truck. He stole a glance sideways as he pulled abreast of the driver's side door of the truck. Gina Yates was driving. This jolted him, but not as much as her cutting the wheel and slamming into the side of his Jeep did. He was shoved toward the edge of the road that fell off into a deep ditch as the truck inched him further and further over.

With a curse, Clay hit the brakes and the moving truck shot forward, opening a gap of about fifty feet between them. Dannie fired her pistol at the tires of the truck as Clay gunned the engine again. The bullets splatted off the asphalt. He gained ground as Dannie took two more shots at the tires.

And then he heard the motorcycles coming up behind them. There were at least twelve Harleys riding right up his ass, he judged from a quick glance in the rearview mirror. As they rounded a corner, the Jeep just inches behind the bumper of the truck, a dozen bikers on his tail, the long bridge to Townshend Island came into view, all lit up in the black of the night.

"Shoot the tire," he said. "What kind of poor excuse for a spy are you?"

Dannie took a pistol from a side holster and racked the slide. She leaned out the window, drawing a careful bead. A biker pulled up next to Clay's window with a gun pointed at his head. He swerved the Jeep. The windshield exploded in fragments and Dannie's shot went wide, the biker cackling as he braked to avoid being hit.

The truck slowed going around the curve to the bridge, and Clay drove the Jeep into the corner of the bumper trying to hook it off the road but the truck, weighted down with treasure, weighed too much and broke free from contact. A biker with a tire iron in hand pulled up on the passenger side as Dannie leaned out to take another shot and clobbered her shoulder.

Clay heard a gunshot, and the Jeep spun out of control, a rear tire having been shot out, and then, as if in slow motion, it hit the rocks on the side of the road and flipped, tumbling down the rocks to the very edge of the Dunbar River where it came to rest upside down.

"You okay?" Clay asked.

"I think that lug broke my shoulder," Dannie said. "So the seatbelt locking up hurt like hell, but it's probably good I still had it on."

Clay clicked his belt and tumbled to the rocks as a gunshot rang out, and the rock next to him spit fragments into the air. He reached over and undid Dannie's seat belt, and she fell into his arms with a grunt of pain. It was no time to be gentle as bullets began to zing around them. He dragged her from the Jeep and behind a boulder.

His phone was gone, somewhere back in the Jeep. Dannie's pistol was lying back in the road somewhere. Clay pulled his Glock out. He peeked out from the side to see two men climbing down the rocks toward them. He snapped off a shot, and the two men went to ground. Several bullets whapped into the boulder as he ducked back behind it for cover. Dannie had slid to the far side and was looking up the slope to the road.

"I only count six of them," she said. "Weren't there about a dozen back on the road?"

"The others must've gone on with the truck," Clay said. "You got your phone still?"

Dannie handed her phone over, and Clay called Westy. Murphy answered.

*   *   *

Gina punched the code to open the gate of her house just as the rumble of approaching motorcycles swept up behind her. She continued through and up the driveway without acknowledging they were there. Adam sat next to her looking quite shaken. She thought that he may have pissed himself by the smell but didn't want to look at his lap to see. They'd seen the Jeep go down over the bank toward the river just as they got on the bridge.

She pulled around the side of the house so that the truck would be out of sight. She put a smile on her face and stepped out of the truck. "*Socrates. Silas. Grub.* Whoever you are today. I'm glad you made it."

Silas slid off his Harley and smiled back at her. "You are, are you? It looks to me like you might be trying to cut me out on the treasure."

"Not at all," Gina said with a coy smile. "I just saw my opportunity, and I took it. I planned on calling you as soon as I got to the house, but no need, as here you are."

"Isn't your house a murder scene?" Silas asked looking at the dark mansion.

"They finished up last night and let me back in this morning," Gina said.

"Is it the fire opals?" Silas nodded at the truck. "Like you said?"

"Adam, be a dear and open the back up," Gina said.

Dube got out of the truck. There was indeed a wet stain on the front of his jeans. He seemed to not notice as he walked woodenly to the rear of the truck, undid the latch, and slid the door up.

"What the hell, man?' Tom said, crawling through smashed chests. His nose was bleeding and there was a gash on his cheekbone.

Fire opals glittered across the floor like the burning embers of a campfire.

Silas stepped up next to Dube and whistled as he looked at the bounty of gemstones. "Did you piss yourself, mate?" he asked.

"What?" Dube said in a halting tone.

"Is that Baylee Baker I see?" Silas asked.

Tom half climbed and half fell out of the back of the truck. "Who are you?" he asked as he stood up.

"In a moment it won't matter to you a whit who I am," Silas said.

"Why's that?" Tom asked.

Silas pulled a pistol from the back of his jeans and shot Tom in the face, and then Dube in the ear. "Do you care who I am now?" he asked the two inert bodies on the ground.

Baylee staggered to her feet. She no longer had the blindfold on, but the gag was still in her mouth and her hands restrained behind her back. There was a cut on her forehead and blood trickled down her face.

"And why do we have this beautiful young lady?" Silas asked Gina who was staring at the two bodies on the ground.

Gina looked at him, looked at Baylee, and then the semi-circle of five men behind them. "Insurance," she said.

Silas pointed his pistol at Baylee. Paused. Nodded. "Not a bad idea. And maybe for a tad bit of pleasure when it's all done and told."

He put the pistol back into the waistband of his jeans and hopped nimbly up into the truck. Silas pulled the gag from her mouth, grasped Baylee under the armpit, and swung her legs out and sat her on the back of the truck. He turned back, picked up a single opal, looked around, and whistled again.

"You got your treasure," Baylee said. "Let me go."

Gina laughed harshly.

"What's the escape plan?" Silas asked, jumping from the back of the truck.

"I have a sailboat out back on the river," Gina said.

"Perfect," Silas said. "Me and you sailing off into the... moonlight? Sunrise? Either way, with a boatload of gemstones."

"What about us?" one of the bikers asked.

Silas looked at him. "First, you load the treasure onto the sailboat. Then you get the hell out of here. Go back to Boston. I'll contact you where to meet once things cool down."

"What about them two?" the biker asked, nodding at the dead bodies.

Silas looked down at them. "Leave 'em. We disappear into the sunrise, and you go lay low in Boston. They'll be looking for Gina, but I know how to disappear. In a week, Gina Yates will no longer exist."

"What about her?" the biker looked at Baylee who had stood up, still dazed, blood on her face, her blouse ripped open to reveal her bra underneath.

"I regrettably don't think I will be doing with her as I wanted. Once we sail off, kill her," Silas said. "Until then, we keep her in case that fucking Clay Wolfe shows up with the cavalry."

"She's a mighty fine-looking woman," the biker said.

Silas looked at Baylee and then back to the man. He shrugged. "Once you get the opals on the boat, you can have your fun. But make sure she's dead before you leave here."

Chapter 34

Crystal looked at the computer screen. Then she looked at her pistol sitting on the desk. She had a choice to make. Murphy had called to let Crystal know they were on the way to rescuing Clay and Dannie from a bunch of bikers just short of the big bridge to Townsend Island. And that Gina Yates had been driving a moving truck across that very bridge escorted by Silas Laskin and cronies, most likely to her house. It was also fairly certain that Baylee was also in that truck, either dead or alive, they didn't know.

It seemed that the showdown was going down at the Yates house. That is, if Westy and Murphy could free Clay and Dannie from the trap they were in. But that might take some time. Crystal could cross over the short bridge from this end of town and be at the Yates mansion on Townsend Island in ten minutes. Likely, before the others could arrive, perhaps in time to save Baylee.

But if Gina and Silas didn't hole up at her house… well, Crystal didn't want to think about that, because she'd been tasked with tracking her phone from this computer. They were at the Yates house now. But what if they were switching trucks or picking something up or realized that in lieu of being chased by Clay and Dannie that it'd be a good idea to keep moving. To get out of Dodge. "Escape from fucking New York," Crystal said aloud.

Crystal cursed, stood up, stuck the pistol in the waistband of her skirt, unplugged the computer, and carried it out the door. If she could save Baylee's life, she had to try. If Gina and Silas were in the wind, she'd just hook the damn thing up at the Yates house and track them from there. It seemed a fair enough compromise.

*   *   *

"You know, I always thought the moon was pretty," Dannie said. "But I sure wish it'd go away now so we can sneak out of here."

They were sitting with their backs to the boulder, facing the river, peeking every so often to make sure the bikers weren't descending upon them. Clay had called Westy, who said he was just ten minutes out. At this witching hour of 2:00 a.m., not a single car had come by.

"Westy and Murphy will be here any minute," Clay said.

"Meanwhile, our treasure disappears into the night," Dannie said.

Clay pointed across the river. "That's Townsend Island. Where Gina Yates lives. Who happens to have been the one driving the truck. No, she's holing up for the night, I'd say."

"It doesn't make sense," Dannie said. "Maybe before we gave chase, they thought they'd be safe. That nobody would know. But now? They gotta figure we'd call in the police. Why haven't we called in the police?"

"Chief doesn't like me much," Clay said. "Plus, we got a better chance of saving Baylee if we don't go in all sirens blaring and whatnot."

"We are doing a pretty crackerjack job of saving your partner," Dannie said.

Clay took a peek and saw two shadowy forms approaching down the rocks. "We got company," he said. He drew a bead just as headlights came around the corner. The two men froze, illuminated, but Clay held his fire.

The headlights materialized into Westy's truck as it pulled up on the road next to the motorcycles. The other men must've been hiding behind the rocks there, because Murphy's voice came drifting out of the driver's side window. "You lads all okay here?"

"Get the fuck out of here."

"You have an accident?" Murphy asked.

Clay squeezed the trigger, one, two, *bap-bap*. Westy stood up in the back of the truck like a Greek God and fired a burst of bullets into the rocks above.

"You two okay?" Murphy called.

"Yep," Clay said. "Coming up."

* * *

Baylee was chained to an oak tree in the backyard, but at least her hands were now tied in front, and she'd managed to wipe the blood from her eyes. She'd been left alone while the bikers went about moving the opals into large, green duffel bags that Gina brought out. It seems that she'd thought of everything. The men scooped up the gems and then emptied the unbroken chests into fourteen bags and carried them to the sailboat, a Pearson 34, stowing them away below deck.

Gina came over with concern etched on her face. "I'm sorry about this," she said.

Baylee eyeballed the woman. She was a strikingly beautiful woman, her long blonde hair tumbling around her face, currently in disarray, but if anything, even sexier. Her body was extremely fit, what Baylee had originally thought from yoga or Pilates, but now had an inkling her physical conditioning regime might be a bit more intense than that.

"Help me get free," Baylee said. "You can sail away, and I'll walk out of here and keep my mouth shut."

"I can't take that chance," Gina said. "You go blabbing to the Coast Guard, and we get picked up before we make it to the end of the river."

"I'm sure Clay has already called them."

Gina shook her head. "No. I don't think so. Not until he finds you safe."

"Or dead."

"I think then he will come after us on his own. But I have enough money stashed away to stay hidden until we can sell the gems, and then, nobody will find us."

"You don't actually trust Silas, do you?" Baylee said. "You know his real name is Grub Boseman, don't you? And that he's the president of the Buccaneers motorcycle club?"

"Of course, I do. That's one reason why I chose him. Because he knows how to disappear off the face of the earth and be reborn as somebody else."

"But you were with Adam Dube," Baylee said. "Who double crossed Rose for you. And you were going to double cross Silas, weren't you?"

"Double cross is a vague term," Gina said.

"How did you get Dube to turn on Rose?"

Gina smiled wickedly. "Sex, my dear girl. One romp in the hay and that big oaf would've… well, I guess he did die for me."

"You shot Rose," Baylee said slowly. She'd been blindfolded and dazed earlier at the forsaken marina dock, but now the pieces were clicking back into place. "Two shots. And your voice didn't change before or after you did it."

"Of course, I shot that bitch," Gina said. "Who'd you think did it? Adam?" She laughed harshly.

"It was you that killed Annette Ward and her boys, wasn't it? So she wouldn't finger those four Buccaneers for what they did to her. Because that might lead back to you."

"Lead back to me? Those redneck bikers had no clue I existed. Silas handled them. Brought them in. That was a major fuck-up on his part. I sent Silas to fix their mess, but then he added to the shambles, and I had to clean it up. All of it."

"You killed them? Three little boys?"

"Everybody dies, honey," Gina said. "Young or old, it doesn't matter. When your time comes, your time comes."

"You weren't abducted and beaten by them." Baylee took a deep breath. "But your face was black and blue. Still is."

Gina sneered. "I had Silas do that to me. I think he may've enjoyed it."

"Why'd you turn us on to them?"

"Because they were useless and a distraction," Gina said. "And so that the police wouldn't be paying too close attention to other things."

"Like the fact that you then went home and killed your husband."

"Oh, they did their job, lifted prints, interviewed the neighbors, but they were stretched pretty thin, and the media scrutiny was on four bikers from Boston who killed a mother and her three children. Nobody really cares about some pervert who makes sex dolls for a living. Of course, if they arrest anybody for that, it's going to be you. I orchestrated that little meeting between you and Tobias at the house. It was just fortuitous that nosy Jeanine Jenkins saw the two of you together. But what the police are going to find, I trust, is your prints on the murder weapon."

"The knife I used to cut the coffee cake when I was over talking about the case. You were planning the murder and setting me up even then."

Gina scoffed. "He was a pig. And you were easy."

"You never really believed that Tobias was having an affair, did you?" Baylee said. "You just wanted us keeping an eye on him to see if he got any leads on the treasure."

"Couldn't have worked out better." Gina sniggered. "And you being hired by that other couple who were also searching for the treasure. It allowed me to keep tabs on both my husband and them at the same time, courtesy of you."

Baylee shook her head. Looked bleakly down the yard where the men were returning from delivering the last of the bags to the boat under Silas' supervision. "Not a chance you're going to help me, I suppose," she said. "I thought there might be a hint of compassion in you, but you're cold as fucking ice. You know the saying, money doesn't buy you happiness, don't you?"

Gina laughed. "But it bought me a boat. And soon, I'll have everything I want."

"You're going to kill Silas after he helps you disappear, aren't you?" Baylee said.

"You're not really disappeared if somebody knows where you are," Gina said. "But you're wrong. I do have a shred of empathy in me. I don't really care for sexual violence. Men are pigs."

"You'll help me?"

Gina took Baylee's hand and placed a pill in it. "This is a poison pill I carry in case I was ever caught. Take it. You need it more than me." She turned and walked up toward the house.

Chapter 35

Baylee sat in the living room of the mansion. Her hands were still tied in front, attached to the chain that had bound her to the tree outside, but now served as a leash. Silas held the other end, a sneer on his face. The five Buccaneers were drawing straws to see who would get to go first with her. Gina was off gathering some things prior to boarding and disappearing on the sailboat.

"That's the long one, boys," a biker said. "First dibs goes to me."

"You might be first, but I got the long one," another man said, and they all laughed loudly.

The man with the long straw came over and grabbed the chain from Silas. "You're in for a treat," he said.

"You hear from the others?" Silas asked. "They aren't answering their phones."

"Little bit back, Terry texted me, said they had Wolfe and that broad pinned down behind some rocks. Said they were going to come around the side of 'em. I'm betting you'll hear right soon that they're dead."

"You hear back from him, you tell them to kill those two, and then get on the road for Boston. This place is going to be hot pretty soon and for quite some time."

"They wouldn't want to miss the pleasure of this little dish," the man said.

"What part of putting Port Essex in the rearview mirror don't you understand?" Silas asked. "You're lucky I'm letting you have your jollies. You tell Terry to get scarce."

"Got you," the man said. "I'll reach out as soon as I'm done my business."

"Do what you will, then kill her, and get out of here." Silas stood up. "As soon as Gina gets some things together, we're out of here."

"Come on, honey, there's a bedroom right over here that we can go play in," the man said. He pulled Baylee up and tugged her along behind him.

"Hurry up," another biker yelled. "I done drawed the short straw. I don't want to be sitting out here twiddling my thumbs for goddamn ever."

"What's your name?" Baylee asked as he shut the bedroom door behind them.

"Ace," the man said.

"You're the best looking one of the lot," Baylee said. "I'm glad you got the long straw."

Ace's face lit up. "I'll show you the long straw, alright." He yanked her chain, pulling her to the bed, bending her over at the waist onto the mattress.

"If I'm going to die, I might as well have some fun, don't you think," Baylee said. "I want to see your face. I want you on top of me, not behind me."

"You're a feisty one, ain't you?" Ace said. He flipped her over onto her back and tore her blouse, already ripped, all the way open.

"Slow, Ace, slow," Baylee said. "Kiss me."

Ace leaned over her on his forearms. Baylee put her zip-tied hands around his back. He leaned in, smelling of stale beer and chewing tobacco. There was no other choice, Baylee thought, trying not to vomit as his lips clamped onto hers, his tongue thrusting greedily into her mouth. She could feel his excitement, his erection, pushing into her thigh through his jeans.

It wasn't the first time she'd been kissed by somebody who repulsed her, Baylee reminded herself, gathering her will. She pushed back on his tongue, forcing her tongue deep into his mouth, the poison pill on the tip. She brought her tied hands to his neck, pressing his face into hers, his mouth trapped by hers. Ace's eyes widened, and he tried to pull back. Baylee kept her mouth on his and rolled over on top of him, pressing down, devouring him.

Ace finally managed to jerk his head sideways, taking a huge gulp of air. Baylee couldn't tell if he'd swallowed the poison pill gifted to her by Gina or not. She reached forward and bit into his cheek, her teeth sawing at the tender flesh. Ace wrenched her arms from behind his head, standing up, Baylee attached to the front of him, legs wrapped around him, teeth clenched on his cheek, anger giving her superhuman strength, or so she thought.

He grasped both sides of her head and pulled her mouth free of his cheek, skin and flesh tearing away, and then ran her into the wall, all of the breath whooshing from her lungs in a huge belch. Ace released her as she crumpled to the floor. He grabbed her hair and her ass and threw her face down on the bed, cursing and calling her names as he tried to yank her pants down. Baylee twisted and turned, kicking backward she felt her foot connect with his groin and he grunted.

Rolling over, Baylee saw Ace, standing a few feet back, his hands over his genitals, his face ashen. As she watched, his body started to convulse, spasms wracking him from head to foot, and then he vomited a mouthful of saliva and blood as he fell face down in his own puke.

Somebody banged on the door. "What's going on in there? Don't be ruining her for the rest of us, Ace, you motherfucker."

* * *

Crystal passed the Winnegance Nature Preserve and pulled to the side when she came to the fence of the Yates estate. She left the computer, took the pistol, and climbed over it, if not easily. It was wrought iron bars with pointed tops, one of which scraped her shin good. It reminded her that she wasn't a young whippersnapper anymore. Just not a fucking granny.

Aging was easier when you had people you cared about. Crystal had given up trying to be in the lives of her children and grandchildren. She'd fucked that up royally, yes, she had. "Nobody to blame but yourself," she said under her breath.

But now, later in life, she'd made friends. Good people. More a family than friends. And one of the most important pieces of that new family was being held hostage by some high society trophy wife and the president of a motorcycle club. If they hadn't already killed her. She'd tried to call Clay, Westy, and Murphy before she left the office, but they didn't answer, and her cellphone was in a chest of jewels in the back of a moving truck. If it was still there.

Too many ifs, Crystal thought as she made her way through the pine trees. She came to the edge of the yard, and while the house was lit up, it looked quiet. Too quiet. What if they'd already gone, she worried. What if Clay was trying to call her at the office to see which way they were going and couldn't reach her because her cellphone was with the treasure.

Then Crystal realized there was a man sitting on the front porch smoking a cigarette. Somebody was still here, at least. She moved down to the side of the house so that she was out of his view as she crossed over the lawn to the house. Just after she was halfway across the fifty-foot-long yard, there was a banging and crashing followed by cursing. She froze, thinking she'd been spotted, but realized it had nothing to do with her. As she reached the house, the noise stopped.

Crystal peered through the window into the lit room and saw a man standing there, swaying, his face bloody, and then he vomited, before falling face first into his puke. A woman sat up on the bed, her hands bound in front of her, her blouse ripped open. It was Baylee.

Then there was a banging on the door and a voice rang out. "What's going on in there? Don't be ruining her for the rest of us, Ace, you motherfucker."

Baylee stood, spit on the floor, and got down on her knees, her hands searching the pockets of the man lying in his own puke.

"Ace. You okay, man?"

Crystal realized she'd drawn the pistol and was pointing it at the door through the window.

"Ace, I'm coming in." The door rattled, and then burst open and a man with a bushy mustache stepped through it with a gun in hand.

Crystal put two bullets an inch apart into that bushy mustache just as a truck came racing up the driveway and smashed into the front of the house.

Chapter 36

Clay was lying prone in the back of Westy's pickup truck holding on as tight as he could. Across the truck bed Westy was doing the same thing. Murphy was driving, Dannie riding shotgun, actually carrying a shotgun from Westy's arsenal. They crashed through the front gate, Murphy flooring the accelerator up the driveway, stomping it all the way to the floor as they came around the bend and leveled out for the mansion. The target was the large plate glass windows to the right of the front porch.

Two gunshots rang out. There was a man smoking a cigarette on the front porch who leapt from the porch in the opposite direction from the truck. And then they mashed into the house, up and over the shrubberies out front, the truck grinding and tearing through the wall until the front wheels came to rest just short of a glass-topped coffee table.

Westy came up on his knees and sent a burst of bullets at the man who'd leapt from the porch, a gun now in his hand, shaking in fear and confusion soon turned to nothing at all as he dropped dead.

Clay went up over the cab of the truck and into the empty room as Murphy and Dannie exited the truck on either side. Silas stepped into the arched doorway and opened fire, bullets buzzing through the air, smashing glass, hitting the truck, whistling by Clay's ears. He slid off the front hood and rolled behind a sofa. The barrage of lead paused, and he came to his knee and snapped a shot at Silas as the man dove to the side.

Murphy was sitting with his back to the wall pressing something that was slowly turning red against his right hand. He nodded at Clay and waved his hand that he was okay and to go get the bastard. As Clay came to his feet, Dannie did as well, shotgun extended in front of her. They crept to the doorway that appeared to lead into a hallway. Across the way was a kitchen and to the right, the dining room.

Clay pointed for Dannie to cross the hallway into the kitchen. She nodded, He rolled into the hallway with his Glock in front of him as she hopped over him. A man was catty-corner down the hallway in a doorway with a pistol in hand. Clay pumped two bullets into the door frame by his face, splinters spitting at the man as he tumbled backward into the room.

Clay stood just as Silas stepped from the other side of the hallway, his semi-automatic rifle blazing, and Clay lunged back into the first room as the world above exploded in a cacophonic jumble of bullets and destruction. There was a doorway to another room behind him, and he reached up to open it and crawled through. There were no lights on, but even in the gloom, he could tell it was filled with people.

Clay swung his Glock to bear, realizing in the dim light that they were all naked. There was a light switch by the door and he flicked it on. There were twelve to fourteen people in the room, all frozen in place, the collection of sex dolls that Tobias Yates had created. A bevy of nude females and one male in all sorts of positions of repose. If this was Scooby Doo, Clay thought, he'd take off his clothes and hide out amongst these sex dolls until Silas came searching, and he could surprise him and get the drop on him.

* * *

Gina was at the backdoor, leading from the kitchen onto the patio, trying to ignore the noise coming from the bedroom at the front corner of the house. Baylee must've decided to not take the poison pill, Gina thought with a shake of her head, and now was paying the price with her life. It'd be a long few hours before her death, as Ace was only the first of five. If the pigs didn't go back for seconds.

She could see Silas coming down the hallway from the living room, perhaps to check on her, or maybe to go cool Ace's jets on the rough sex coming from the bedroom. Then the gunshot rang out and she saw Silas pause, as did her hand on the door, and the name on her lips as she was about to call to him. She was ready to go. Had a bag of essentials packed and was ready to sail off into the horizon with the treasure of Black Sam Bellamy stowed aboard. Her treasure.

A crashing and smashing noise shook the entire house followed by a screeching. Gina looked to the left and could see the cab of a truck coming to rest, one tire spinning lazily in the sitting room. It was time to go. She stepped hurriedly through the door, pulling it shut behind her, and walked quickly down the backyard to the river.

If Silas followed along, that'd be fine, she could truly use his expertise in creating a new identity. Of course, once that was accomplished, Silas would become expendable. She had no qualms about making him disappear in a much more definitive way after he helped her through her own transformation and disappearance.

Gina walked onto the dock, threw her bag on the deck of the sailboat. She loosened the bow line, walking it back and throwing it on the deck, and was bending to loose the stern line, when the dock creaked and a shadow washed across her. He'd made it after all.

"You want to get this," Gina asked, looking up. It was not Silas.

"In a moment," Dannie said. She held a shotgun aimed at Gina's head. Her one arm was crooked, perhaps a broken bone or a dislocated shoulder.

"Who are you?" Gina asked, standing up. "Not just some antiques dealer on a treasure hunt."

Dannie laughed harshly. "You don't have to die. You can walk up to the house and surrender. It's even possible that your side will win and you can flee. But not with the fire opals."

"*My* fire opals," Gina said. "I deserve them. I earned them. They are mine."

"Life isn't always fair," Dannie said. "You must've learned that by now."

"No. No it isn't." Gina put up her hands. "Fine. Take them. Go."

Dannie laughed. "First, walk this way. Slowly."

Gina took a step forward, and then another. Dannie took a step backward. She had to look down at her feet as she took the next step from dock to land. That is when Gina lunged forward, an explosion and spreading lead whipping past her cheek as her body slammed into Dannie's and they both fell to the ground. Dannie grunted in pain as she landed on her bad shoulder.

Dannie hooked her elbow into her face as Gina reached up and grabbed a handful of the woman's beautiful wavy hair and yanked as hard as she could. A chunk of hair came free in her hand with a clump of scalp attached. Dannie grunted and looped a punch that connected with Gina's nose, bringing tears to her eyes as she slammed her own fist in between Dannie's legs bringing a howl of pain.

The shotgun was lying on the ground next to them, and they both reached for it, their hands colliding and knocking it spinning into the river. Gina's hand encountered a fist-sized rock, and she picked it up and smashed it into the side of Dannie's head. This gave her an opportunity to disentangle her body and rise to her feet. If she could just get to the sailboat, release the bow line, and float out into the river, she'd be safe.

Gina heard her coming as she loosened the line from the cleat, looking up as Dannie slammed into her like a football linebacker on a wide receiver. They rolled over, down the dock, kicking, punching, biting—anything to get the upper hand. Dannie connected with a left hook to Gina's chin, stood up, and went to kick her in the midsection. Gina thrust her foot into Dannie's anchor leg, her other leg swinging forward, and for just a moment, she tottered, and then fell off the end of the dock into the river.

Bloody, bruised, and beaten, Gina crawled down the dock and

finished untying the bow line and rolled onto the sailboat. The river current pushed the boat against the dock, holding it there. The key was in the ignition, the throttle in neutral. As Gina turned the key, there was a splashing noise on the upriver side of the vessel, and then Dannie came over the starboard side like some river monster.

Gina turned her face up as Dannie smashed a rock into her nose, the cartilage and bone disintegrating to a pulpy mess. And then again. And again. Gina felt her teeth splinter to a mouthful of Chiclets and the moon went dark overhead. Gina slipped into unconsciousness, then into death.

*   *   *

Westy leapt onto the porch and put three bullets in the man who'd previously been there. He now lay bloody and broken in the shrubbery off to the side. There'd been gunshots right before Murphy crashed the truck into the house. Westy was fairly certain that the shots had come from the side of the house. He'd seen a glimmer of a flash from the bed of the truck in that direction.

He jumped off the porch and around the corner of the house to find somebody helping another climb out through a window. Westy realized the woman in the window was Baylee, her hands restrained in front of her, and that the other, who swung a pistol at him, was Crystal. He snatched the gun from her hand before it could come to bear.

"Darn, woman," he said. "I take you out boating, and then you try to kill me?" Westy grasped Baylee at the waist and swung her to the ground.

"About time you got here," Crystal said. "I thought I was going to have to save the day all by my lonesome. Is that your truck crashed into the front?"

Westy handed the pistol back to Crystal, leaned his rifle against the wall, pulled his knife from his ankle sheath, and cut Baylee free.

"Damn Irish drivers," he said. "I'm going to go in the front door. Anybody comes in this room, you shoot 'em. That way I won't have to worry about my left side."

"You got an extra gun?" Baylee asked.

Westy pulled his Sig out of the holster and handed it to her.

"Crystal can keep watch here," Baylee said. "I'll come cover your back."

Westy nodded, turned, peeked around the corner, and then did a scuttle run back to the front porch and up the steps. He looked over his shoulder at Baylee, held up one finger, two, and then three, opened the door and went through it in a crouching run.

In front, a man ran past and down a hallway. Westy put a burst of bullets through the wall, knowing they'd pierce the wood and maybe he'd get lucky and hit the fellow, who looked like it might've been Silas.

Behind Westy, there were two pops, very familiar to him as the sound of his Sig Sauer. He saw a man down the front hallway and across in a room stagger back clutching his shoulder, a pistol dangling from his hand. Westy turned and put three slugs in the man's chest.

Westy moved down the hallway, his head and rifle on a swivel, passing the bedroom door to the left, coming to the hallway that ran the length of the house. There was nobody in it. Silas, if it was him, was gone. Westy stepped across to an arched entrance that led into the living room. On the far side was a heavy man with a bushy beard and the signature Buccaneer denim vest. His hands were held high in the air. Westy took three steps and clubbed him in the chin knocking him to the floor, where he lay face down groaning. Baylee stepped into the room behind Westy.

"Keep an eye on him," Westy said. "Anything happens, anything at all, shoot his ass." He turned, exited the room, and went down the hallway.

* * *

Clay would've been better to hide naked with the sex dolls as it turned out. Rifle fire erupted from the front of the house. He figured it was Westy coming in blazing. He reached for the door to come out in support just as it crashed inward, knocking him staggering back. His Glock flew out of his hand across the room.

Silas lurched, fell, and sprawled through the door. Clay regained his balance and kicked the arm holding the rifle. Clay kicked again, jarring Silas' arm, sending the gun skittering across the room. Silas swept Clay's legs from under him with his foot and sent him tumbling to the ground.

They both came to their feet and Silas lunged forward as Clay stepped behind a sex doll with enormous breasts and brown hair. He shoved her forward, the silicone mounds of her chest whacking Silas in the forehead and knocking him to the floor. Clay stepped around her and kicked the man in the side, and then drove his knee into the man's stomach, while punching him in the chin.

Silas knocked Clay off to the side and rolled away from him, toppling another doll with darker skin and large nipples onto Clay, momentarily pinning him there. Silas darted for his rifle as Clay pushed big nipples from him and came to his feet in a lurching stumble through the maze of sex dolls. Silas stumbled and fell over a doll that was bent over at the waist and Clay dove onto his back, slamming his face down into the floor.

Silas rolled, his elbow slamming Clay in the ear, driving him to the floor. They wrestled, each trying to get a choke hold, land a punch, kick, bite, or gouge an eye out. Most of the sex dolls had been knocked down by this time, only two or three women still standing as if watching this melee in mockery.

Silas landed a punch to Clay's genitals, which knocked the breath from him. Silas straddled Clay and punched him in the side of the head, once, twice, three times.

A fog crept into Clay's mind, and he fought to hold it at bay. He reached up and cupped the back of Silas' neck and pulled down as he thrust his own forehead upward. He felt the satisfactory crunching of cartilage as Silas toppled backward off him.

Clay rolled, came to his knees, and they again clinched, both on their knees, as if in some comedic wrestling act. Clay could smell the man's sweat and fear and anger. Silas bit his ear and Clay drove the man's head down to the floor, but only it wasn't the floor, a sex doll lying under him. There was a squelching sound and Silas screamed in pain.

Clay staggered to his feet as Silas raised his head from the sex doll below and looked up at him. Where his right eye had been was now a gaping hole spilling blood forth. He mumbled something and fell onto his back with his hands clutched to his face. Clay looked from him to the sex doll. It was the male, the one called Buck. Clay realized that Silas had impaled his eye on Buck's silicone penis.

The door opened, and Westy stepped in with his rifle leveled. "What the…?" he said.

Clay looked around the room at the carnage of bodies, mostly female, all except for Buck, on his back. And Silas who'd passed out from the pain.

"It seems Silas pricked his eye," he said.

"You okay?" Westy asked.

"Yeah," Clay said. "Baylee?"

"She's okay."

"Everybody accounted for?"

"No sign of Gina Yates as far as I can tell," Westy said. "The homeowner seems to be missing from the party."

"Out the back, maybe," Clay said and led the way down the hall, into the kitchen.

Baylee came from the other direction and joined them. They went out through the rear door as the sailboat engine kicked into life, and the vessel moved from the dock to the middle of the river, the bow turning lazily to face downriver. It was as if there was a single moonbeam through light clouds setting the face of Dannie Cox aglow.

Her face was streaked red, her shirt torn and tattered, her hair askew on top of her head—but she still looked like a Roman Goddess setting off on an adventure.

Westy raised his rifle, drawing a bead.

Clay put his hand up and pushed the barrel down. "Let her go," he said. "Let the fire opals go for a good cause. Seems up to now all they've ever been is a curse."

Epilogue: One month later

Chief Roberts was none too happy with Clay Wolfe. He held him personally responsible for the carnage in and around Port Essex. Annette Ward and her boys. Tobias Yates and wife. The Buccaneer biker that had died. Silas had survived to face trial and prison with only one eye and the publicity (leaked by Clay to Cloutier) that he'd lost the other to the pecker of a sex doll named Buck.

Luckily, the head of the MCU and the Feds were more inclined to be appreciative of all that Clay and Co. had accomplished. Gina's confession to Baylee of killing Annette, the three boys, and Tobias gave them a starting point the case together against her post-mortem.

Thanks to Baylee, those deaths would not be added to the list of unsolved cold cases in the state. Clay also thought that the Lieutenant of the MCU had secretly been grateful that a fairly deadly message had been sent to the one-percenter bike gangs that they were not welcome in the state of Maine.

The CIA were very interested in the assertion that Dannie Cox had been working for the Ukrainian government. The Coast Guard had been deployed within the hour of the police report but had come up empty-handed. That is, until two days later, when the sailboat Dannie had escaped on was found flooded and drifting, ten miles out to sea. There was no body and no opals.

Though part of Clay wondered if it perhaps was the ghost of Black Sam Bellamy who had sunk her ship, conscripted her into the pirate life, and taken the treasure back, it seemed more likely that she'd been picked up by friendlies who she'd contacted and then scuttled her own boat and gone on to receive a hero's welcome in Ukraine. And if that were true, the curse of the fire opals would be lifted, as they'd be used for combating evil rather than making any one man or woman rich.

Murphy's hand had been shattered, and he'd probably never regain full use of it. But, as the Irishman put it, that's why God had given him two hands, and he only needed one to tip a pint or a Jameson.

The only innocent in all of the shenanigans seemed to be Tobias Yates. Everybody else had been hunting the treasure under nefarious purposes. It turned out that he'd been killed by the cake knife with Baylee's prints on it, just another part of Gina's master plan. The MCU believed Baylee's version of how her print came to be on the handle of the murder weapon.

Clay was currently on his way to pick up Baylee and take her out to dinner at the Pelican Perch where, in secret, all their friends were waiting. He thought about the fire opal taken by Westy as proof when they'd first found the treasure in the catacombs in the Winnegance Preserve by the Sibosek River. Clay had gotten a jeweler to set that on a woven gold and silver ring, and it was currently in his pocket. Tonight, at the Pelican Perch, with the whole gang present, he planned on asking Baylee Baker to marry him.

As if in favor of the plan, Frank, who sat in the passenger seat of the Jeep, gave a small yip.

Acknowledgments

If you are reading this, I thank you, for without readers, writers would be obsolete.

I am grateful to my mother, Penelope McAlevey, and father, Charles Cost, who have always been my first readers and critics.

Much appreciation to the various friends and relatives who have also read my work and given helpful advice.

I'd like to offer a big hand to my wife, Deborah Harper Cost, and children, Brittany, Pearson, Miranda, and Ryan, who have always had my back.

I'd like to tip my hat to my editor, Michael Sanders, who has worked with me on fourteen novels now, and always makes my writing the best that it can be.

Thank you to Encircle Publications and the amazing team of Cynthia Bracket-Vincent, Eddie Vincent, and Deirdre Wait for giving me this opportunity to be published. Also, kudos to Deirdre for the fantastic cover art.

Write on.

About the Author

MATT COST (aka Matthew Langdon Cost) is the highly acclaimed, award-winning author of the Mainely Mystery series. The first book, *Mainely Power*, was selected as the Maine Humanities Council Read ME Fiction Book of 2020. This was followed by *Mainely Fear*, *Mainely Money*, *Mainely Angst*, and the newest, *Mainely Wicked*.

I Am Cuba: Fidel Castro and the Cuban Revolution was his first traditionally published novel. His other historical novels are *Love in a Time of Hate* (August 2021), and *At Every Hazard: Joshua Chamberlain and the Civil War* (August 2022). Cost is also the author of the Clay Wolfe / Port Essex Mysteries, *Wolfe Trap*, *Mind Trap*, *Mouse Trap*, and the latest, *Cosmic Trap*, which was published by Encircle in December 2022.

Cost's love of histories and mysteries is combined in the novel, *Velma Gone Awry*, book one in his new series featuring private eye, 8 Ballo, set in 1920's Brooklyn.

Cost was a history major at Trinity College. He owned a mystery bookstore, a video store, and a gym before serving a ten-year sentence as a junior high school teacher. In 2014, he was released and he began writing. And that's what he does: he writes histories and mysteries. Cost now lives in Brunswick, Maine, with his wife, Harper. There are four grown children: Brittany, Pearson, Miranda, and Ryan. A chocolate Lab and a basset hound round out the mix. He now spends his days at the computer, writing.

If you enjoyed this book,
please consider writing your review
and sharing it with other readers.

Many of our Authors are happy to participate in
Book Club and Reader Group discussions.
For more information, contact us at info@encirclepub.com.

Thank you,
Encircle Publications

For news about more exciting new fiction, join us at:

Facebook: www.facebook.com/encirclepub

Instagram: www.instagram.com/encirclepublications

Sign up for the Encircle Publications newsletter:
eepurl.com/cs8taP

Printed in the USA
CPSIA information can be obtained
at www.ICGtesting.com
LVHW040740060324
773411LV00009B/40